Lor‹

Secret ‹‹‹

Louisa Pretty

As the energetic figures pranced and paraded around the dance floor in a whirl of coloured silks and satins, broadcloth and buckskin, perspiration and pomade, his Grace reflected that in spite of all the finery, the basic function of the occasion was almost exactly the same as the livestock market in any town. The aim was to match buyer and seller.

But there lay the rub: how was he to conclude a deal with such an outrageous rider in the contract? And failure was simply not an option.

Also by Louisa Pretty

Lord Hal's Secret Rescuer
Lord Julian's Secret Agent
Lord Wulf's Secret Heir

Sadly, my grandmother died a long time before I was born. I never knew much about her, but even as a child, writing my first 'scribblings', I realised that her name was perfect for the author of historical fiction.

I offer my Georgian romances in her memory.

Lord Dob's Secret Son

1

Caroline Smith, like countless infants, had some difficulty with her own name when she first embarked on the magical journey of learning to talk and, as for many, the early attempt stuck: she was always Callie – even though she was raised in an aristocratic household.

She could never remember exactly when she realised her very odd position in that household; it came as no dramatic revelation since it had never been hidden and it made no difference whatsoever to the young girl who continued to flourish under the wing of the woman whom everyone else addressed as My Lady but whom Callie always called simply Lady.

Callie was always aware that Lady was not her mother. Her real mother, a young housemaid, Rose by name and as pretty as one, had been seduced by the adolescent son of the house: a common enough tale.

What was unusual, however, was that his unmarried older sister took responsibility for his orphaned by-blow. Lady Horatia had been regarded as an oddity well before this: she delved into every volume in the well-stocked library, every book on every subject, even those regarded as un-ladylike – especially those, declared her frustrated mother. But she was no book-worm. She spent every day the Wicklow weather permitted racing around the countryside, her riding habit designed to permit her to sit astride one or other of the horses in whose bloodline and breeding she took a great and personal interest. With her pair of huge wolfhounds always at her side, she took hedges others would never dare, she set her mount to cross swollen torrents, she rode to the farthest edges of the estate, often without any human escort. She came to know many of those who lived and worked on the estate – not really on purpose but simply in the course of events.

One year, her mother arranged to take her to the capital for the Season with the plainly stated intention of marrying her off before tales of her daughter's oddity reached the ears of the London scandal mongers and ruined her chances forever. Lady Horatia, however, made carefully researched visits to young families and contrived to catch the chicken pox she had herself avoided in childhood.

The Dowager did not try again and died, still frustrated, a few years later.

By the time of Callie's birth, therefore, Lady Horatia was well established in her preferred state of spinster-hood and in *de facto* supervision of both house and estate. When the Marquess, her brother, left in search of more exciting lands and climes, Lady Horatia simply carried on running affairs with little Callie as part of them.

Lady Horatia had never wished to be under the thumb of a husband, never wished to be at his sexual beck and call. She felt no yearning for motherhood; but she did, she found, enjoy being the maiden-aunt. She enjoyed seeing that Callie was well-cared for in practical matters by cook and the other women servants; she enjoyed teaching the girl herself, to read and to write and to make free with the books in the library.

As Callie got older, Lady often took the girl with her when she rode around the estate. If Callie asked questions about business matters – the cattle to be sent to market, the linen spun from the flax beds, the corn ground in the estate mill, the fish caught in the fish-ponds, the ploughing to be done for the spring crops, the latest foals in the stables – Lady would answer, show her the accounts and set the girl tests in adding the figures. She would express her pleasure when Callie's answers were correct and simply ignore them if they were wrong – although Callie soon realised that the same questions would most certainly reappear for another attempt.

It was nearly a decade before the Marquess returned, having spent most of his time (and money) at various courts in Europe. In London, he had sought and won the hand of a lady whose fortune proved to be a great deal less than he had been led to believe – certainly nowhere near enough to settle the debts he had racked up. To pay these off, he was compelled to sell all the family's London assets and confess to his new wife that they would have to live on the Wicklow estate.

During his absence, he had rarely thought of the place, nor of his sister, whose management skills he never doubted; of his illegitimate child he had never thought at all.

His new Marchioness, furious at the prospect of a life in exile across the Irish Sea, was incandescent at the discovery of Callie's existence. She exercised what petty power remained to her: Lady Horatia would be provided, under sufferance, with a roof over her head and her keep, but the natural daughter must go and never be spoken of.

2

Lady Horatia explained to a more than little perplexed Callie that she, Lady, had no choice in the matter.

Lady had defied her mother all those years ago; she had lived virtually as she wished since then; she had (as her brother had assumed) run the huge house and lands very successfully, keeping up the wealth of the estate and all its dependents. However, at the end of the day she had no means of her own; she was entirely dependent on her brother for her living. And the Marquess had acquiesced totally with the Marchioness's demands.

Lady tried to make this shattering judgement into a positive step for Callie: the girl would, Lady said, have a better chance of making her own way in the world untainted by her illegitimacy, if she moved right away from where everyone knew her, away from the estate, away from Ireland.

She arranged for Callie to go and live with Margaret and George Smith. She even managed a small gest – Callie would not even need to change her surname! Margaret had once been a friend of Callie's mother. She had left her post as maid to the old Dowager on marrying George and moved to England with him. They would, asserted Lady firmly, gladly take in Callie since they had never had children of their own.

For Callie it was a terrible wrench.

Margaret was a mild soul, but she had a weak chest and often spent time in bed or resting.

George was also good-hearted but suffered from a severe stammer which made it difficult for him to make himself understood and loathe to try. This prevented him from rising above the position of lowly clerk, although he undoubtedly had the acumen for much greater responsibilities. Mills, the steward for whom he worked, benefitted greatly from the situation but never gave George the credit; he also never missed an opportunity for cruel mockery.

In spite of this, George knew he had been lucky to secure the post in the first place and was unlikely to get another, especially one that came with a cottage in the country. He hated to think how Margaret would fare in a town, in air thick with smoke and evil vapours. He had long given up any idea of even looking for anything else.

Yes, George and Margaret were basically kind people, but Callie knew she was expected to pull her weight.

She had a room of her own, beneath the thick straw thatch. She never went hungry. The work she was expected to do about the house and in the garden was demanding but not too hard for a robust ten-year old.

But in the terrible first weeks she felt so lonely she cried herself to sleep each night. Gone were the host of household servants who were always willing to stop their tasks to chat and gossip in their soft brogue. Gone was the library with its laden bookcases so high that the top shelves could only be reached using the heavy wheeled stairs. Gone was the huge globe that could be turned on its axis to reveal all the countries and seas of the world. Gone were the long corridors lined with family portraits darkened by age – the eyes of men and women in strange costumes seeming to follow her however fast she ran past them. Gone were the stables and the dozens of horses, including the little mare that Callie had so often ridden.

Gone was Lady.

There had been many days when Lady was busy and Callie had not seen her, but whenever they were together Callie knew she could say and ask whatever she liked and be taken seriously – as a person in her own right.

To George and Margaret, she was simply a useful extra pair of hands. Perhaps time would change that, but in her misery Callie could not imagine how long that might take.

The first gleam of light in the unrelieved gloom came when Callie met the family in the neighbouring cottage.

It was a fine day and at Margaret's instruction Callie scrubbed and boiled and rinsed, before pegging shirts and shifts out to dry.

As she hung up the last item, she could see a similar operation going on next door, only the laundry there included a great many more garments. The line was full and other clothes were being draped over bushes. A woman waved to Callie then beckoned.

Ignoring the thought that she should go and see what else Margaret wanted doing, Callie took up the invitation.

Inside a cottage almost identical to the Smiths', Callie found a press of bodies of differing ages and sizes. A phrase from a volume in the Wicklow library sprang into her head. *The passion between the sexes has appeared in every age to be so nearly the same that it may always be considered, in algebraic language, as a given quantity.* It had not been the word "passion" which had attracted Callie's attention – that was a part of life she had grown up knowing about; after all it was responsible for the existence of every child born, including herself. No, it had been the word "algebraic" that she had asked Lady to explain. She had been fascinated by the world revealed by the answer and it had been some time before she and Lady discussed the next sentence about *the great law of necessity which prevents population from increasing in any country.*

This family, she now reflected, with the first amusement she had felt since arriving in England, were evidently doing their best to confound Mr Malthus!

She made several head counts before being fairly certain there were seven children including the occupant of the cradle near the hearth, presently bawling lustily in spite of the energetic force being applied to the rockers.

'Lizzie, swing the kettle over the fire,' the woman ordered one child of about five. 'Dickon shift yourself off that stool and offer a seat to our visitor. Excuse me,' she addressed this last remark to Callie, 'while I silence this greedy little beggar.'

She scooped up the baby and its strident cries ceased instantly as she set it to one well-filled, blue-veined breast.

Not that anything like complete quiet ensued, but the woman could at least make herself heard without shouting.

She introduced herself as Mrs Hunt and pointing with her spare hand she named all the children.

Callie was not sure she got them all but did not like to ask for a repeat. 'Caroline Smith,' she said instead, 'but everyone calls me Callie.'

Mrs Hunt looked at her with undisguised curiosity. 'I didn't think the Smiths had any family,' she said.

'Oh, I'm not related to the Smiths; at least not those Smiths,' Callie said. 'There's lots of Smiths around,' she added rather hastily, heading off any further inquiries about her kin. 'What does Mr Hunt do?' she inquired.

Mrs Hunt grinned. 'Barney's a huntsman! In fact,' she added proudly, 'he's kennel huntsman: he looks after his Lordship's hounds.'

As the woman chattered on, Callie learned that his Lordship, Cyrus Roberts, the Earl of Pentridge, came to Pentridge Hall several times a year for the hunting. Most of the rest of the year it was said he spent in the capital at the sizeable Pentridge House; although he also had an impressive Palladian villa in the Richmond countryside.

Whenever he visited Pentridge, he demanded horses and hounds be ready and waiting for himself and his chosen guests. He expected, moreover, to hunt in all weathers regardless of the dangers mud or ice might present to man and beast.

3

Over the years some things did change: Callie's acute misery ebbed to a mostly-forgotten dull ache; she took on without complaint the running of the Smiths' cottage for an increasingly invalid Margaret; outdoors she cultivated both flowers and vegetables; she learned from Dickon how to keep hens and look after the pig who was housed in the sty at the bottom of the garden. From that same personage she learned to wring the necks of birds past laying and to accept the annual cull of the pig. Mr Hunt and Dickon, having dealt with their own animal, did the actual butchering, but Callie learned from Mrs Hunt to hang the flitches of her erstwhile porcine companion in the cottage chimney to smoke and cure; to salt and mince and pot the rest.

It was not that she was particularly squeamish: it was all part of existence, of making the most of the land's bounty so that people could have food on the table – although the parson reminded them in a thunderous voice each autumn that it was to the Earl that they owed the bounty, acknowledging in much quieter tones that God might have had some small part in the matter.

Callie, in fact, enjoyed the ham and pork pies as much as the next person; however, she also appreciated the undoubted intelligence of the animals which provided them. Dickon told her that she was as daft as a pig herself when he found her talking to that year's long, thick, tawny pig while scratching behind its pendulous ears. Callie retorted with a reminder of how *his* pig had managed, despite its short legs, to escape not once but *three times* from its enclosure and feast on the Hunts' vegetables.

And the pigs quite evidently knew exactly what was about to happen when seized for slaughter and screamed their protest in almost human voice.

Callie grew to love Mrs Hunt and her tribe. The eldest three moved out one by one, all to marry other Pentridge tenants and take up positions elsewhere on the estate. Dickon also went, not to marry but to lodge in a tiny room at the large kennels where he worked with his father. However, over the same period there were four new babies, all of whom miraculously survived the perils of infancy making the cottage as crowded as ever.

Mrs Hunt remarked, with a mixture of pride and resignation, that the pups she whelped had pace and stamina to match any of his Lordship's hounds! The Earl, Callie knew from Dickon, demanded that the Pentridge dogs be at least as good as those bred by Mr Hugo Meynell for the Quorn Hunt following the ideas of Mr Bakewell.

Lady had mentioned Mr Bakewell once to Callie – in a distinctly dismissive tone. Lady had taken Callie to see the latest foal in the Wicklow stables and expounded at length on its bloodline. Mr Bakewell had only, in her opinion, discovered what horse-breeders had known for centuries.

Callie smiled to herself at the memory and listened as Mrs Hunt went on to chat amicably of other things, all the while continuing with whatever tasks she was doing and directing her children with theirs.

The talk was always of the everyday, but Callie relished it for what it was. And with it, often, came the chance to learn another everyday skill – how to mend clothes that seemed beyond repair, how to identify herbs and make simples, how to stop milk turning in the hot weather, how to render tallow for lamps and soap.

As well as the Hunts, Callie came to know many of the others who lived on the estate – mainly through the work required by the land and its husbandry. Although the estate was undoubtedly run primarily for the pleasure of the Earl on his periodic visits, there was nothing recreational about the demands made on the tenants and enforced by the steward, Mills, at all seasons. For the sheep and cattle, there were roots to be hoed and pulled and clamped; meadows to be cut for grass hay; tree hay to be gathered into faggots from the pollarded ash and elm; cows to be milked, butter to be churned and cheese to be made. And Callie was expected to do her share; it was mostly about back-breaking labour, but she came to appreciate the wealth of knowledge and skill underlying it all, which made the difference between animals living or dying, crops being successful or ruined. In the midst of the drudgery she sometimes recalled the way it had been on the Wicklow estate and wondered about the differences.

She discovered that Dick, the ancient shepherd, was always willing to talk, to indulge her curiosity – and he, like Lady, had something to say about Mr Bakewell.

'Some folks even call them Bakewell Leicesters,' the man waved his clay pipe in the direction of his woolly charges. 'The old Longwools, in Mr Robert Bakewell's opinion, had good fleeces, with lustre and crimp but were too slow-growing, too big boned to be much use for meat. He reckoned he could breed Leicester sheep that could do both.'

'And do they?' Callie looked at the square animals with their wedge-shaped faces.

A frown creased Dick's weathered features. 'Aye, mebbe, but they need more looking after, 'specially at lambing time.' He looked down at his hands, misshapen by rheumatics, then pointedly at Callie's, small but strong.

In cracking the whip over Pentridge, Mills received the unwavering support of the parson. The clergyman, who owed his living to the Earl, was more than willing to follow his Lordship's dismissal of quaint customs like crowning a May Queen, a Green Man or a King Crispin. Although the major Christian festivals could hardly be similarly banned, in reality permitting the celebration of the Twelve Days of Christmas in the darkest part of winter involved no great loss – even if in some years there were more than twelve before the return to work on Plough Monday; the pancake races of Shrove Tuesday were soon eclipsed by the sombre demands of Lent; rejoicing at the Resurrection of Easter was swiftly buried in the extra work of helping the land to do the same; each long day of Lammastide was taken up with the harvest – with every available pair of hands, young or old, male or female, struggling with abundance in good years or, just as often, attempting to rescue spoiled and meagre crops from sodden fields in the bad ones.

The four quarter days – Lady Day, Midsummer, Michaelmas and Christmas – originally set to coincide with Christian holy-days were, at Pentridge, simply days for conducting business, supervised by Mills with his usual ruthlessness: reluctant in the hiring of extra hands and enthusiastic in pursuing the payment of rents.

For Callie the daily grind changed in character according to the seasons but not in its relentlessness. So much for a better chance of making her own way in the world, she reflected occasionally.

George Smith was more educated than his lowly position suggested, but he owned few books: the Bible, several of Shakespeare's plays and Pope's translation of the Iliad. Callie read Shakespeare's and Pope's works so often she knew them almost by heart; when they began to pall, she resorted to reading the Bible. Its language of nearly two hundred years before was very like that of Shakespeare and she enjoyed its lyricism; she even enjoyed some of the stories, but she found the long lists of names and descendants tedious and many chapters and verses contradictory. She had trouble reconciling the harsh and often blood-thirsty teachings of the Old Testament with those of the New (although the descriptions in the Book of Revelation were almost as threatening as they were fascinating). And she had nobody to talk to about anything she read: Margaret had not the strength nor the interest; George's long hours at the estate office tired him and made his stammer worse.

Callie tried to put down some of her thoughts in the letters she exchanged with Lady, but the post was decidedly erratic. And, in any case, correspondence was a poor substitute for conversation and personal communion.

Her one attempt to engage the parson in discussion was met with a mixture of incredulity and outrage – that she, a girl, could read (he taught only the boys their letters in Sunday School) and, furthermore, dared to think God's will as any more questionable than that of the Earl.

4

The only person who called Darius Roberts, Viscount Kelton, by his baptised name was the man who had chosen it with such deliberateness: his father. What, after all, argued the Earl (except he never argued – he simply decreed) could be more appropriate for his son and heir than to be called after the ancient king of kings.

That son, however, from the time he came to understand its origin and implication detested its pretentiousness and rejected its use. Even his mother addressed him as Kelton in an effort to avoid confrontation with either her domineering husband or stubborn only offspring.

He himself happily adopted the nickname given him by his fellow pupils when he first arrived aged nine at Bromby, the school specially chosen by his father both for its aristocratic patronage and its avowed determination to permit *none* of the disorderly conduct frequently reported in other such establishments. The nickname had not, of course, been intended kindly – Dobbin being the appellation ascribed across the land to draught horses of the lowliest kind. In fairly short time, however, his would-be tormentors had realised that he really did not mind and found other more rewarding subjects to persecute. By the end of the first term Dobbin had become Dob and by the end of the school year hardly anyone recalled why. Occasionally thereafter, some curious newcomer queried the sobriquet only to discover that Dob was a star pupil of the boxing teacher for very good reason – and to drop the matter.

Although what appealed to Dob about pugilism was not really the inflicting of blows but rather the agility of mind and body that could be honed to avoid and deceive the opponent. The parallel with his position *vis à vis* his father could not have been clearer. Similarly, with fencing. And for both, nature connived, furnishing the growing Dob with a lithe and steely body.

He was not as keen on the "games" played on the muddy fields, and outran the brutal collisions of hockey whenever he could.

All in all, however, he enjoyed what he experienced as the freedom of the physical activities – which would have greatly surprised the Earl had he known, even concerned him for that was not his intention in sending his recalcitrant son to an institution with a reputation for its strict regime; not that the intention of the strictness was to punish: rather it was to prevent an excess of juvenile spirits finding outlet in wild behaviour.

Each day started with the boys being roused from their beds at six and sent to run around the boundary of the extensive grounds regardless of rain, fog, ice or snow. In relatively clement weather this was followed by several circuits in the artificial lake. On their return (even after swimming) they were required to perform a thorough wash in cold water before dressing and assembling for a hearty breakfast. Like Juvenal, Mr Jenkerson the headmaster believed in the dictum *mens sana in corpore sano*, and for the bodies of growing boys to be hale it was obvious to him that they needed plenty of both exercise and food. The character of the latter was distinctly more rustic than the school's clientele but deemed by Old Jenkers all the more appropriate for that very reason (although reduced cost was a fact of life never to be ignored). Whatever the rationale, Dob was not the only pupil fed the plain fare to sprout up like a healthy sapling.

Six days a week, from eight to two, the boys were sent to rarely heated classrooms for lessons given by masters untouched by Mr Priestley's calls for Liberal Education. The masters of Bromby were recruited for their Classical credentials and the only liberal thing about any of them was their wielding of the stick.

Dob did well enough to avoid too many beatings, but he could not feel the same enthusiasm for Herodotus, Homer, and Aristotle as he did for boxing; nor for Cicero, Virgil and Ovid as he did for fencing. Nor did he much enjoy grammar, logic, or rhetoric; although arithmetic and geometry held a certain fascination.

After a light luncheon, every afternoon was filled with outdoor physical activities. On days when this really was impossible (a rare occurrence indeed) the pupils were gathered in the room referred to as the Assembly Hall although it had almost certainly originally been designed as a ballroom. It was not spacious: large enough for all the boys to stand for daily prayers and the headmaster's improving homily but definitely cramped for any indoor exercise. It was self-evident that not all the boys could be active at the same time, but it was unthinkable that any should be idle awaiting their turn. Therefore, while some performed extended series of jumps, bends, squats and press-ups, the others were required to be still, holding arms and legs and other parts of the body in positions that soon became excruciating.

Supper was as plain and plentiful as any other meal but more leisurely, if such a word could really be applied. It was eaten in the house where a boy boarded, that is to say with one of the masters and his wife. It was hardly a cosy family atmosphere, nor was it meant to be for the boys were sent to the school in order to wean them from such softness; but it divided the pupils into manageable groups and meant they could all fit around one dining table, where they were required to eat their meal in silence while the master read from whatever edifying book was prescribed for the term.

This in no way reflected any Trappist tendency on the part of the Headmaster – he held no more affection for Papists and their practices than any other loyal Anglican – but it was a very effective way of keeping order.

Nor were the boys allowed to talk once they were in bed and the candles safely extinguished.

Dob had been assigned to board in Bromby Manor itself with Mr and Mrs Jenkerson. When, at some point, the other four pupils with whom he shared one attic bedroom drew his attention to the fact that they were all the sons of a Duke or

Marquess while his father was merely an Earl, Dob suspected that his parent had somehow arranged it so. For him, however, titles and connections mattered little. He had shrugged.

Exactly how much aggrandisement mattered to his father, he learned during the Christmas holiday of what would be his last year at Bromby.

For the first time in Dob's memory, the festive season would not be celebrated at Richmond. This puzzled him considerably, but he had no way of solving the conundrum since the decision was presented as one of his father's unquestionable *fiats*.

5

Even though the winter proved to be kinder than many, it was enough to lay Margaret low and then George caught her feverish cold. Apart from making him feel dreadful it also made his speech thicker than ever. Callie had come to understand him but needed no words to appreciate why George feared what the steward would say or do if George did not turn up to work as usual. She asked exactly what needed to be done on that particular day and discovered it involved totting up and summarising both the monthly and end-of-year figures. Why, she asked, could she not fetch the ledger so George could work in the warm cottage instead of in his usual room which seemed chill and damp whatever the weather or season.

George was dubious. Mills' habitual ill-temper was shorter than usual because of the impending arrival of not only the Earl but, as the whole estate had been roundly informed, particularly important guests. George was convinced Mills would dismiss the idea out of hand and be angered by the very suggestion.

However, he found his legs so shaky he knew he could not even make it to the office and watched with trepidation as Callie set off.

She had been to the estate office on a number of occasions since coming to Pentridge, usually to take the bread and cheese for his lunch that George had forgotten.

As she passed a kennels even busier than usual, she exchanged words with Mr Hunt and Dickon before continuing on to the substantial stable block set a little way from the main house. She nodded to a couple of the lads cleaning out the horse boxes and entered the ground-floor space with its flagged floor where George had his desk. The tiny grate set in the corner contained only dead ash.

A heavy accounts ledger was lying on the desk and she opened it to check it was the right one. George's neat script and immaculate columns were as clear and uniform as any printed book. At the end of all the preceding months were the subtotals and totals and an analysis.

She regarded the pages with interest, relating the entries to the work they represented. The interest faded as she shivered and pulled her thick shawl more tightly around her. She thought she was truly a country girl these days, as hardy as the next, but she was always active while George was required to stand for hours on end, only his hand moving to dip the quill in the inkpot and his fingers, protruding from the woollen gloves Margaret had knitted for him, guiding it across the page.

But the shiver was not just because of the chill: she had been procrastinating; she could not just remove the ledger and take it home: she had to see the steward and ask his permission.

Although she had never been up there, she knew the estate office proper was on the next floor. She could hear no movement on the floorboards above her head, nor any other sound as she went to the foot of the steep stairs and listened hard. She hesitated then took a breath. Holding up the hem of her brown woollen skirt she ascended, the thick soles of her boots counting each bare wooden tread. By the door at the top she paused again. Only silence. With resolution she rapped; there was no response.

She rehearsed yet again what she planned to say and knocked with more force.

There was still no answer, but this time the door, evidently not firmly latched, swung open.

She was met by a wave of warm air, for here a coal fire burned in a deep grate. There was a carpet covering most of the floor and on it stood several pieces of furniture, all gleaming with polish. The room was spacious with light from two windows: the one next to the door gave onto the stable-yard and another, on an internal wall, overlooked a large covered exercise arena. While the Earl was known to care not a whit for the comfort or safety of any man or beast when he wished to hunt, he did ensure that his mounts were kept ready between times in the very best conditions.

Callie realised that Mills had positioned his desk so that he could keep a close eye on everything that happened in this heart of the estate – and on everybody working there.

The desk itself, she mused, might have graced any gentleman's office: its drawers were decorated with fine brass handles and the inlaid green leather on the top was tooled around the edge, matching the padding on the armrests of the chair.

A cupboard occupied one corner while the walls were

almost entirely lined with shelves holding well-ordered ledgers, books and boxes – undoubtedly, she thought bitterly, housed up here to keep them undamaged by the damp downstairs and most, she noted, neatly labelled in George's hand. In the one space evidently left for just that purpose was a large map which she saw immediately was the Pentridge estate. Curiosity made her move a little closer in order to read the shield-shape legend in the top left-hand corner.

A MAP of Pentridge in the County of L … shire, the estate of the Earl of Pentridge, shewing the arrangement and size of each part. Transcribed from the original and amended by C. Proudfoot 1788.

To the side of the map was a table of the woods and fields, each with its area in acres, roods and perches. She saw many names that were familiar – The Orchard, Home Field, Croft Down, Bramble Wood, Fox Covert. Her eye was drawn naturally to the cottages where the Smiths and the Hunts lived.

She considered the whole. It showed every hedge, every path and track, every ditch and stream. The open land was sprinkled with tiny tufts of grass, the woods with small trees. Furthermore, these particular areas had been tinted green – but by a much less precise hand. They were, Callie realised with no surprise, where the Earl and his guests hunted, riding after the foxes and hares flushed out by the dogs.

She gazed at the furthest parts of the thousand-acre estate. She picked out the road beyond its western boundary labelled with the name of the county town which lay some miles in that direction: the road along which she had travelled to Pentridge. Would she ever travel along it again – in the other direction?

Her reverie was abruptly interrupted by a voice behind her.

'And what exactly do you think you're doing here?'

All Callie's well-rehearsed words deserted her.

She floundered on, trying to explain that George was ill but that he could do his usual work if she took it home for him.

'Too ill to get to the office?' inquired Mills sardonically, 'but not too ill to do his work?'

Callie flushed, with confusion and with anger. She answered something about needing to stay where it was warm and could not prevent her eyes moving accusingly towards the glowing coals.

'Getting soft, is he? Not up to it anymore?'

Callie assured him George would be back in his usual place as soon as he was recovered sufficiently.

'And how long is that likely to be?'

Callie could not give a promise that might prove impossible to keep; it might be several days, she conceded.

'Until the start of the Twelve Nights?' asked Mills. 'So that he can extend his holiday by any chance?'

That was not it at all, Callie protested.

Mills eyes narrowed. 'No, he is certainly not going to get away with that.' He frowned at her and was silent for several minutes.

Was he going to insist George come to work on pain of being dismissed? Getting George here was likely to make him worse; standing at this desk downstairs was unimaginable.

Were those the thoughts she could see going on behind the steward's hard eyes?

Finally Mills made an impatient noise. 'I don't have the time to come and see how ill Smith really is; to see if he's ill at all. I have lots of other things to arrange for his Lordship's visit.' He scowled. 'The Earl will certainly wish to see the figures for the estate and Smith is the only one who can produce them in time at this stage. No doubt he has reckoned on that!'

Callie began another protest.

'But if he thinks he can manipulate me, he is wrong; very wrong.'

Callie tried again.

Mills continued regardless. 'I will have to accede to his scheming because I find myself with no choice. But for every day he malingers at home between now and Christmas he will lose three days' wages. And on Plough Monday he will be back at his desk without fail and after that, when I have the time, we'll have a little talk about his future.'

In spite of the fire, Callie shivered.

'Yes, sir,' she managed.

Having found a way of securing the figures he needed and demonstrating his power, Mills' hard mouth lifted in the ghost of a smile. 'Do you think you will be able to carry all the books your father will need?' he inquired. 'Father?' he repeated the word. 'But he's not your father, is he?' He pursed his thin lips. 'I'd wager you don't have one.' He cocked his head to one side. 'I'd bet you are fortunate not to be just one more bastard in the Workhouse.'

Callie clenched her hands within the folds of her skirt.

He looked her up and down with a sudden gleam of curiosity. 'But you've grown up a bit since they took you in, haven't you? And filled out a bit – I imagine.'

Within her thick winter clothes, Callie's flesh crawled.

'You are grateful, aren't you,' he inquired, 'for your good fortune?'

'Yes, sir,' she ground out the words.

'How grateful, I wonder.'

His meaning could not be mistaken; Callie felt sick.

He moved towards her and she was sure he was going to touch her. If he so much as laid a finger on her, she knew she would not be able to suppress her rage.

But he stopped just in front of her. 'Now that's another thing to talk about, I think, after Plough Monday.'

Callie had to swallow down the bile that rose in her throat and his smile showed that he had seen.

'But for now, we have to see that you take only what Smith needs, don't we?'

6

Dob still had no idea why the Earl had insisted they come to Pentridge for Christmas. His Lordship had never before demanded that his son join him there, even for the hunting.

In the school holidays, Dob had made a point of getting himself invited to the home and estate of one of his fellow pupils, the Lord Willoughby Landston, son of the Duke of Branksdown. As well as being Dob's particular friend, Willo just happened to be heir to one of the leading peers of the realm which provided a cast-iron excuse for keeping several counties safely between Dob and his parent. Somewhere at the back of his mind there was a dim memory of just a single previous visit to the Pentridge family seat.

As they left the county town behind, his mother suddenly spoke.

'It's cursed.'

Dob was sure he had misheard. 'Pardon?'

'It's cursed,' she repeated, quite clearly, 'because they took stone from the priory over there to build the Hall.'

Dob looked in amazement at the figure in the opposite corner, swathed in woollen blankets which fell around her feet and captured the warmth from the hot bricks stowed beneath the bench.

'There!' A gloved hand emerged from the cocoon and

pointed.

Dob leaned over to clear a bigger space on the misted glass and peered out.

The road was following a small river and on the far side were the remains of what had probably been a sizeable monastic foundation before the Dissolution ordered by King Henry. Ragged walls that must once have formed the nave were recognisable, the one at the eastern end still holding the lower half of a rose window. Other bits of stonework were much less identifiable, some possibly part of the now invisible plan, others seemingly random. The foundations of more buildings, set at some distance, could be seen poking out of the dead grass – their purpose long gone and only to be guessed at.

As the ruin began to drop behind them, his mother huddled back into her seat – and into silence.

'Curse?' Dob prompted her, his curiosity aroused.

'Pentridge Hall is cursed,' she said eventually. 'The line of anyone who owns it is cursed to fail. The man who first built it had three sons, but they all perished and he had nobody to succeed him. Even though the next owner was not related, the curse followed him and he had only daughters. The place went to the husband of one of them, and their line only lasted for a couple of generations. Your grandfather should never have bought it – as if changing its name could end divine retribution!'

Dob frowned. 'But grandfather had my father and my father has me,' he stated the obvious.

'Your father was born before the wretched place was acquired. And you were sired in Italy and safely delivered in Richmond,' replied his mother.

Dob knew that after their marriage his parents had undertaken a long tour of Europe, returning to England nearly a year later. He had never wished to consider exactly where his existence might have begun since that involved thinking about a relationship between his parents that was simply unthinkable (although he understood the facts well enough).

He had occasionally wondered over the years about the lack of siblings but had avoided broaching the subject for the same reason. 'Why was I the only one?' he blurted out now.

His mother continued to look unseeingly at the passing scene and Dob thought she would not answer.

'You were only two years old,' she said at length. 'You will not remember. Your father insisted we all come to this accursed place even though I was increasing. After all, he insisted, I had carried *you* half way across Europe and suffered no ill consequences. But the instant we entered Pentridge Hall I began to feel unwell and by next day I had lost both the child and any hope of having another.'

His mother was wrong about him not remembering: Dob dug out the dim memory from its dusty corner and recollected waking in the night to distant screams, to his nurse crying so hard that he was petrified and howled with her. However, in the morning a Pentridge servant had taken him out to see some kittens in the stables and he had been happily distracted. He recalled that his mother had not accompanied them back to Richmond – she only arrived sometime later.

The subject of babies came up as an inevitable if erratic topic of conversation among the boys at school and Dob knew therefore (among other related matters) that in many families there were babies born with no breath in them, and babies born too weak to survive.

Two things struck him. How could his mother be so sure it had been the curse at work? And – seeing her in a new light

– small wonder she was such a sad woman.

'And now,' continued his mother, the words pouring out as if some sluice gate had been raised, 'he is inviting the curse to strike again. He could not arrange matters in London, or Richmond, or anywhere else, could he? No, it has to be at Pentridge, to show off the estate and the excellence of its hunting!'

'Matters?' Dob picked out what seemed the crucial word. 'What matters? Why *are* we going to Pentridge?'

The sluice gate dropped shut. His mother stared at him.

'Why?' demanded Dob. 'He never tells me anything,' he complained, 'just issues orders. But why can *you* not tell me?'

'He has commanded me not to.' His mother suddenly looked frightened. 'He would be very angry with me for talking to you about the curse. He allows no mention of it, ever, by anyone.'

And Dob was left no wiser than before – only a great deal more curious and frustrated.

Almost against his will, he looked with interest at the building that came into sight as they crested the top of a low hill and started along the drive across open parkland.

He saw immediately that the stone was certainly similar to what was left of the priory and could easily have been taken from there. Whatever its origins, the light-coloured stone had been used to build a two-storey house, its frontage broken by seven tall mullion windows, the outermost ones of which protruded as small bays. In the centre was a front door of modest size made much more impressive by its frame of carved flat columns supporting a curved pediment.

The roof was of a darker hue, possibly of slate, though Dob could see it was of a rougher texture than that on Bromby Manor. In any case it sat snugly atop the house, pierced at intervals by chimney stacks of the lighter stone. From all of these, Dob noticed, issued plumes of smoke, lifting into the still air – preparations had certainly been made to receive more than just the family.

The drive approached the house from the side so that carriages could draw up on the immaculate gravel before continuing to an unseen stable block. That part of the house (and presumably its matching wing) was also of the disputed stone, but at the rear Dob glimpsed a sizeable extension of red brick before the carriage came to a stop exactly by the front entrance and servants, perfectly primed, shot out. One hurried to hold the horses' heads; one immaculately presented individual opened the carriage door; another placed the step for the passengers.

Dob assisted his mother out of her woollen wraps then alighted, turning to offer his help for her to descend. He thought for a moment that her stiffness might be from the long journey. However, there was no mistaking the reason for her hesitance. She took a deep breath and in a most unaccustomed gesture he found himself squeezing her hand.

She walked towards the door looking neither to right nor left, holding her head high. Dob would previously have put this down to her customary aloofness but now he understood her just a tiny bit better.

He nodded his thanks to the staff in her stead and kept his mother's arm linked in his own as they moved into the hall.

The floor was not of marble like that in the Richmond villa, but the stone flags were even and well-scrubbed. A log fire sent out warmth and cheer from within the large fireplace, its flames reflected in the polished surface of a large sideboard. Tapestries covered large parts of the walls, all depicting hunting scenes. Dob glanced at them and wondered if they had been made just for Pentridge Hall as the countryside behind the classical hunters appeared much more L … shire than ancient Greece or Rome.

Other tapestries hung by the staircase which rose in wide low treads towards a half-landing lit by a long stained-glass window before turning up to the first floor.

A woman came forward, bobbed a curtsey, introduced herself as the housekeeper and offered the Countess a well-rehearsed welcome. Her Ladyship's rooms had been prepared according to his Lordship's instructions and were aired, warmed and ready. Until her Ladyship's personal maid arrived with the baggage coach, a local girl, Ellen Hunt, would help her Ladyship with any immediate needs. His Lordship had ordered tea to be served in the drawing room at four and dinner to be served at six, but if her Ladyship would like any refreshment before then, it would be sent up at once.

Dob's mother, it seemed, had registered only the first part of this speech. 'Which rooms?' The words came out in a low voice.

Dob wondered if the middle-aged woman had been in post fifteen years ago and knew what had happened – and of the supposed curse.

However, the woman answered robustly enough that his Lordship had stipulated that the grandest rooms at the front of the house were to be for the guests who were expected the following day; the Countess and the Viscount would be accommodated in the east wing.

The Earl was, they were informed, in his usual suite in the west wing.

Dob's mother gave a small sigh of relief and allowed the housekeeper to lead the way.

7

Dob too had been appointed a temporary servant, a lad even further from manhood than Dob himself.

At school he was well used to managing for himself, none of Bromby's pupils being allowed personal attendants. And he could most certainly see to his own needs until the staff arrived.

He frowned at the thought – for as well as the Countess's maid there would be a certain Tomkin. The Earl had announced that this individual was to be Dob's valet; Tomkin, it seemed, had served some of the highest-class and best-dressed gentlemen in London and would ensure that Dob was turned out to perfection in the new clothes which had been tailored to Dob's increased measurements.

The personal valet and the trunks of new clothes had added to Dob's mystification about this whole trip to Pentridge.

He also had the distinct suspicion that part of Tomkin's role was to supervise behaviour in the way other young noblemen were monitored by their private tutors.

Dob smiled to himself. Tomkin might have unknown years of experience, but Dob had years of practice avoiding just such supervision!

He became aware that the youth in front of him was regarding him with acute anxiety. Dob might not need his services, but the lad was patently desperate to offer them.

'I'm sorry,' Dob said, collecting himself. 'What did you say your name was?'

'Joseph Hunt, my Lord, but everyone calls me Joey.'

'Hunt?' Dob queried. 'As in Ellen Hunt?'

Joey bobbed his head. 'Yes, my Lord; she's my sister. One of them,' he added artlessly and blushed crimson at his forwardness.

'How many sisters do you have?' asked Dob.

'Six,' came the answer.

Dob's mouth turned down. 'That's rather a lot,' he commented. 'Any brothers, to balance things out a bit?'

'Four, counting little Jack.'

'And why would you *not* count little Jack?' Dob asked solemnly.

'He's only two months old, so he don't do much – 'cept what they all do, boys and girls.' Joey stumbled to a halt; his face redder than ever.

This was a situation totally outside Dob's experience although fellow pupils had described various younger siblings – usually with a shudder.

He nodded however, as if he knew exactly what Joey meant. 'And the older ones, like you and Ellen, do you all work here in the house?' he asked, partly to put the lad at ease and partly out of amused curiosity.

Joey, relieved that he had seemingly not got himself dismissed before he had even started, poured out a potted history of the Hunt family.

'So, your father and your older brother Dickon work in the kennels?' Dob picked out the bit of most interest. He had never had any desire to hunt with his father at Pentridge, but he had joined Willo when staying at Branksdown – where there had been plenty of talk about Meynell's foxhounds.

'Look,' he interrupted Joey's less than fluent description, 'I'd very much like to see the animals and talk to your father. When would be the best time?'

'I could take you now,' came the immediate offer.

And Dob nearly took him up on it – before he realised that he would have to make himself presentable and then present his presentable self to his father. The Earl would, without question, expect to see him for tea at the appointed hour.

Dob sighed and proceeded to give Joey a very brief summary of what he required of his youthful valet.

Amazement was far too mild; *horror* might have been closer. *Dumbstruck* for certain: Dob could not have uttered a single word at that moment.

If his father noticed, he paid no regard and continued to elaborate on why Lady Alicia Tentham was the perfect match. Her lineage was impeccable, the Earl said. She came from a very old family. She was, moreover, the only surviving child, heiress to the ancestral Tentham Hall and lands. Her father's will, executed on his death the year before, appointed a guardian charged with protecting both the estate and Lady Alicia. Baron Stackling, was to use his best endeavours to arrange a suitable marriage for his ward, on which, naturally, her husband would acquire both bride and estate.

Dob finally found his voice and inquired carefully, 'And how old is Lady Alicia?'

A faint frown creased the Earl's forehead. 'Recently turned twenty-seven.'

The arithmetic was simple: a decade Dob's senior! But arithmetic was the least of his concerns.

Before he could even begin a mental list, his father continued, 'Past her prime but not too old to breed.'

A shiver ran down Dob's spine, in spite of the warm room.

'And all the more reason for getting on with things.'

Things? What a prosaic word, thought Dob, to encompass the whole mind-shattering, world-changing idea. No, not an idea – a concrete scheme. He had no doubt his father and the Baron had already engaged in negotiations.

This Christmas assembly was not a tentative introduction, a chance for the individuals most involved to see if they suited: it was meant to see a contract signed and sealed.

Now sweat began to trickle down inside one of his fine new shirts.

He racked his brain for what he knew about nuptial legalities. That was *not* a topic the pupils of Bromby spent much time or energy on and it certainly did not form a subject in the classroom.

There had been some law passed in the middle of the century, he thought. He tried desperately to remember anything about it. Lord Hardwicke! He dredged up the name of the peer associated with the Marriage Act. But what on earth had it been about? His mind searched every corner of his skull with agonising slowness. Finally, it suggested, tentatively, something about having to be twenty-one?

Even as a sense of reprieve began to lift his spirits, he realised that his father would know *all* the details of the Act. His spirits plummeted again.

As if he could read Dob's thoughts, the Earl looked directly at him. 'Your being under twenty-one is no impediment since I will naturally give my consent to the union. And the sooner it is done the better – given her advanced years.'

Dob felt as paralysed as a cornered rabbit. Marry! He was not even out of school! – and with no more experience of women than a few fumbles at Branksdown the previous summer.

'There is no reason why everything should not be settled now and a date set for later in the year – enough time to arrange a suitably impressive wedding.'

Dob gawped. 'What about university?' Up to this point he had imagined nothing other than finishing at Bromby then,

most likely, two or three years at Oxford – before having to
consider the future seriously.

His father shrugged dismissively. 'Jenkerson boasts that a
pupil from Bromby is better educated than most university
students ever manage.' His eyes narrowed and he peered at
Dob. 'Even you, apparently, have achieved satisfactory
results.' He shook his head. 'No,' he said firmly, 'your
attendance at University would offer little more than some
additional connections; this match will be of greatly more
benefit.'

And with that the Earl left.

Dob regarded his mother. 'Did you know about this?' he
whispered. 'And what on earth am I to do?'

Her gaze slid away from his. 'Yes,' she said shortly, in
answer to his first question. 'And how can you do anything
other than what *he* wants?' she responded to his second. 'And
why not?' she put her own. 'You need to make a good match
some time and Lady Alicia might be quite personable.'

Dinner passed in a daze. Dob's still-growing body would not
allow him to refuse the excellent dishes, but his mind seemed
removed to a distant place. He managed a few remarks but
could not for the life of him have recalled what they were.

For all the Earl's assumption that his every *dictum* would
be carried out unopposed, his Lordship had the wit not to
press Dob into conversation and did not deny Dob's request
to retire early.

In his room, Dob's young valet informed him with a grin
that a message had brought the information that the luggage
coach and its occupants had been delayed by a lame animal.

It was now startlingly clear to Dob why Tomkin had been
recruited and likewise why the postponed arrival of his
father's henchman would be but a tiny hindrance to the

inexorable march of Dob's fate. However, he tried not to spoil Joey's evident delight.

The irrepressible lad repeatedly admired the beautifully tailored garments as he assisted Dob to undress. He hung up each item with something approaching reverence and folded the discarded necktie with a completely unnecessary precision since it was destined for immediate washing and starching. A soft cloth wiped away invisible specks of dust from Dob's gleaming evening shoes; extra coals were added to an already glowing fire; candles were replaced.

Finally, Joey stood beside a silent Dob. 'Is there anything else you needs, my Lord?' he enquired.

Dob shook his head.

'Well,' said Joey, evidently disappointed, 'if there's anything at all, I'm to use the little room through there.' He jerked a thumb. 'You only need to call.' He waited hopefully.

Dob managed another small smile at the lad's enthusiasm. 'No, thank you Joey. You go and get your sleep.'

He was certain he would get none himself.

8

He sat in the deep armchair by the hearth trying to order his thoughts. Gradually the fog of disbelief began to clear a little – enough for several semi-coherent questions to emerge.

Who were the Tenthams? His father had said something about them being one of the oldest families in the country. Dob could recall no one at school ever mentioning them. But, of course, if this Alicia was the last of the family she would not, by definition, have any young male relatives.

Was there a Tentham estate?

Or did it have a different name?

Where was it?

Was it very wealthy?

And the question that punctuated all the other ones: why was his father so set on the match?

Was it all about the noble bloodline? He knew vaguely that the Pentridge title which had come to his grandfather was neither old nor venerable, but still an earldom was an earldom. Was that not enough? In any case, a marriage could not bring any higher rank.

So, it had to be about money.

Dob suddenly realised he knew nothing of the extent or origin of the Pentridge wealth – his father never talked about it. But Dob could not believe they were short of funds: he had always had the (albeit unsubstantiated) feeling to the contrary.

There were no answers, no really credible ones anyway.

Dob turned his thoughts to the other obvious question.

Was there any way he could escape?

He was certain his mother would offer no further aid. There were no other relatives to turn to.

Among his fellow-pupils? Even Willo's father, while being a great deal more agreeable than the Earl, would find nothing particularly unusual in such an arranged match.

Run away?

That seemed a much more fruitful line of thought. Dob saw no obstacle to actually leaving. He even considered doing so immediately – before the Lady Alicia and her guardian arrived; not to mention the suspect Tomkin. But a bit more time to plan and prepare would be helpful and his father could hardly keep him imprisoned until he could be hauled to the altar, could he?

But where to?

Abroad was the patent answer to that one and the American States the most likely option, since Britain was currently at war with much of neighbouring Europe.

Dob spent some time recalling the tales he had heard of the erstwhile British colonies on the far side of the Atlantic Ocean and was sure he could survive there, doing something.

The more he thought about it, the more reassured he felt.

By the time the clock on the landing struck midnight, Dob was calm enough to take himself to bed and fall asleep.

That feeling was still with him when he woke. He even managed a few polite words with his father in the breakfast room.

To test how much freedom of movement he might be allowed, he mentioned that he planned to visit the kennels with his young valet.

The Earl nodded, almost in satisfaction. 'Nice hounds,' he said. 'Be good for you to take an interest.'

To hide any sign of his relief, Dob turned to take another slice of ham on to his plate.

'Hunt, the kennelman, has done a decent job with them,' continued the Earl, 'and Mills says the eldest son is coming along well enough. Hunt has a large family, Mills tells me.'

Dob felt the beginnings of disquiet: his father never made idle conversation.

'It's a good thing the estate can employ so many of them, keep a roof over their heads and bread on their plates.'

Dob knew now where this was going. His father's next words proved him correct.

'And a *very* good thing they all understand which side that bread is buttered, eh?'

Dob was slower this time to turn back to the sideboard; he was sure his father had seen, and read, his son's expression – a mix of comprehension and repugnance.

If he, Dob, did anything to cross his father that could be

blamed on any of the Hunts, it would be – with disastrous consequences for the whole family.

Imprisonment, Dob realised bitterly, did not need to be within a locked room or behind iron bars. It did not even require a warder (called Tomkin or anything else). It simply required a threat issued to someone with a moral conscience by someone without.

Any escape definitely required the most careful planning and preparation.

In spite of the gloom hanging heavily over him, Dob found the visit with Joey of considerable interest.

The kennels were set beyond the stable block at some distance from the Hall. As they got closer, Dob realised that there were several substantial brick buildings. They would have cost a sizeable sum to build – not to mention how much was needed to keep them going. For a second time, he wondered about the extent of the Pentridge wealth – and its origin. Did the Pentridge Hall estate generate enough to keep itself and the properties in London and Richmond?

Joey interrupted these thoughts. 'This is for the whelps.' The lad opened a gate into a yard where half a dozen young dogs ran across a clean, paved area, lifting their heads eagerly. Dob followed Joey's example and fondled the soft ears, admiring the variety of black and tan markings on the white coats.

'When they're about a year, they go and join the older dogs,' Joey jerked a finger to the far side of the buildings. 'They has their own yard over there.' A bell rang from that direction. 'They'll all gather there now.'

Before Joey could explain further, a middle-aged man appeared. Dob needed no introduction to know that Barnabas Hunt was Joey's father. He returned the respectful greeting and accepted the offer of a personal tour.

This started with the larder where a couple of large and bloody, and malodorous, carcasses were hanging.

'Hounds is fussy,' Hunt said. 'They like their meat good and flavoursome,' he explained. 'We don't cook it of course, so as they keep their taste for raw flesh.'

That was eminently logical, thought Dob, even if the fact that this flesh was obviously horsemeat was less so. He was happy when the thick door was closed on the stench and Hunt led the way into the next building which turned out to be the kitchen. The meat might be served raw, but the oatmeal with which it was mixed was cooked in large pans on a spotless stove. The young man stirring it turned out, predictably, to be Dickon, Joey's elder brother.

The largest building, in the centre of the collection, was what Hunt called the dinner hall. On the neatly swept floor were set four feeding troughs into which Dickon ladled exact amounts of food.

Dob became aware of several hounds watching from an open door.

'Ponto! Jowler! Music! Trinket!' Hunt called out and four dogs came in; no longer soft and playful, these were full-grown hounds, tall, with lean, muscled bodies clad in rough fur. Each took a separate trough and proceeded to lick it clean. When Hunt cracked the whip he was carrying, the four dogs, without hesitation, left the way they had come.

Dickon refilled the troughs and Hunt called out four more names.

And so the whole pack was fed in disciplined order.

Dob was fascinated by the whole thing and appreciated the skill and hard work that must have gone into its achievement. He could not, however, in the light of his present predicament, help feeling his father imposed very much the same kind of regime on people.

The final surprise was two small circular huts with domed roofs. Peering inside one, Dob found the floor was several feet below ground level. Vertical brick walls enclosed a space roughly fifteen feet across and supported a shelf some fifteen inches wide. In the centre of the floor was a hole in which Dob could see the ashes of a fire.

'These are drying rooms,' Hunt explained. 'The dogs are shut in here after they've been washed and groomed. We can't have them catching cold.'

Dob was certain the Earl had no such concern for the welfare of his human servants.

During the time they had been at the kennels, the wind had got up and dark clouds were massing on the horizon.

Dob looked at them in desperate hope. Might there be snow?

9

Callie looked at the ominous sky and hoped Mills would agree to her taking more work home, for, if anything, George was worse.

Callie had brought the first lot of books back to the estate office with considerable trepidation. Not that the task was incomplete in any way, but she knew Mills would peruse it minutely and would find fault if he could. And she feared he would not wait until Plough Monday to carry out any of his implied threats.

The steward had indeed inspected the ledgers carefully, run his finger down the figures, checked every line of the yearly summary.

Callie had tried to keep her anxiety from showing.

'His hand looks firm for someone supposed to be too ill

to leave his house.'

Of course, it wasn't George's hand at all: the poor man could barely lift the quill let alone use it. Callie had hardly dared to breathe.

Mills had finally nodded, almost in disappointment. 'It all seems in order.'

It had not entered his head that it could possibly be Callie's work.

This time, she had to wait for some while in the unheated downstairs room before he arrived, evidently even more pressed. He scarcely looked at the books she had brought, before thrusting a larger pile at her with curt orders about how many copies he required of what.

She desperately hoped she could remember them all.

He turned on his heel and left before she had a chance to ask about more ink and paper.

Well, she reasoned, she would simply have to take the necessary supplies, otherwise it would be impossible to carry out his instructions.

The ingredients for the ink were in George's desk, but she guessed that paper would be kept dry in Mills' office. She peered into the yard to make sure the steward had really gone then slipped up the stairs. The door was unlatched as before, but the cupboard was locked and there was no sign of a key. Might the man keep some paper in one of the desk drawers? Did she dare look?

She glanced out of both windows, the one onto the yard and the one onto the indoor arena, but there was no sign of him.

She dreaded to think what the steward would do if he found her not only in his office but searching his desk.

On the other hand, she feared what he would do if George (and she) were not able to do the latest assignment.

She seized the brass handle of the shallow central drawer. It was immediately clear it contained no spare paper and she was about to close it again when she noticed an article torn from a broadsheet. It was an account of the latest outrage committed on the king's highway. Footpads had, in broad daylight, waylaid a private coach and slaughtered all those aboard, including a Baron Richleigh (whoever he might be). The newspaper suggested that the fine nature of the coach and the Richleigh coat of arms on its lacquered panels had attracted the attack.

She closed the drawer firmly and opened another. The third one held paper. She counted out a few sheets and hoped against hope that the steward would not notice their absence.

As she hurried past the kennels someone came around the corner, talking over his shoulder. There was no way Callie could avoid the collision. One thought screamed through her head: the total disaster of the ledgers getting damaged!

Against all her instincts to break her fall she kept her hands firmly clamped on her load.

She staggered wildly, felt herself toppling.

Suddenly there were arms around her, but still she was certain they were all going to end up on the ground. She gripped the ledgers more tightly and waited for the painful landing that seemed inevitable.

It is astonishing, in time of peril, with what detachment and in what detail the human mind can analyse and record the events of mere moments.

Callie was perfectly aware that the person holding her was a stranger; a man; taller than her; not broad or barrel-chested like a farmer but strong; and with a remarkable sense of balance. It was, ridiculously, almost like being led in a dance.

There was an instant when she thought he would succeed in righting both of them.

Then she felt him lose his footing.

Then the inevitable sensation of falling.

But even so, he somehow turned so that it was he who hit the ground first with Callie (and her burden) on top.

The long moment of silence was broken by Joey's anguished voice.

The arms around Callie released her, but scrambling to her feet was made tricky by her thick winter skirt which had wrapped itself around her legs – and by the heavy books she still held.

Later she was a little ashamed to recall that her first concern had been the books. She sighed with profound relief when she discovered them all unharmed and the spare paper still safely tucked inside the largest ledger. Even the packet of ink powder had escaped with only a couple of extra creases.

Only then did she look down at the man rising to his feet.

And register Joey's words.

'Are you all right, my Lord?' Joey Hunt repeated them anxiously.

She gaped at the figure unfolding its gangly length.

Lord? Comprehension struck. This must be Viscount Kelton. Joey had been beside himself with excitement over being appointed his Lordship's valet – if only for twenty-four hours.

She hastily dropped an awkward curtsey.

The young man grimaced a little as he inspected one elegantly tailored leg.

'I'm so sorry, my Lord,' she said.

A fresh face lifted. 'Why should you be?'

Callie stared at the unexpected response.

'It was I who was not looking where I was going,'

continued his Lordship ruefully, his fingers continuing their exploration.

'Are you hurt, my Lord?' demanded Joey.

Callie was in for another surprise as the Viscount laughed. 'Possibly a bruise or two which will fade soon enough, but these breeches,' he said with astonishing cheerfulness, 'will never be the same.'

Callie looked at the garment more closely and saw that he was right: the dark superfine was ripped, revealing a length of lean thigh.

She had seen at least as much often enough, "accidentally" exposed by hopeful swains during hay harvest (and other occasions) but hastily averted her eyes in case *he* was embarrassed.

He did not, however, seem to be. 'Are *you* all right?' he asked, giving up the vain task of holding the ragged edges of cloth together.

Callie hastily assured him that she was quite uninjured.

He nodded his silver-blond, hatless, head towards the books. 'And your precious burden too?' he inquired with a smile.

Then Callie *was* embarrassed: he had noticed. She could think of no suitable reply.

It was Joey who filled the pause. 'Is that more books for Mr Smith? Is he still poorly then?'

Callie managed a nod, in answer to both his questions.

'Valuable books, are they?' The Viscount's clear blue eyes glinted with amusement.

Again, it was Joey who replied, 'Old Mills'll create merry hell if they gets damaged.' Callie glared at him as he added, 'Doesn't need any excuse.'

'Mills, as I recall, is the steward here is he not?'

Callie and Joey nodded; both now equally wary.

'So what books are they?' The Viscount's tone was curious rather than threatening, Callie thought.

She explained the situation in words as few and neutral as possible. Only she and George knew about the price Mills had set on the arrangement – and nobody but she knew about the unspoken threat against herself.

'But Mills often creates "merry hell" does he?' The Viscount had evidently spotted her ploy.

Joey started to nod his head vigorously but stopped as Callie caught his eye in warning.

The Viscount did not press the point but instead stared at the books before lifting his blue gaze to her. 'Those books show how well the estate is doing?' he queried.

She let herself be distracted for a fatal moment. 'We – Mr Smith that is,' she amended hastily, 'just did the annual summaries for Mills to present to the Earl.'

Those blue eyes narrowed. 'Did you – he – now?'

Callie was silent.

'And would you – he – say the estate was doing well? Is it, in vulgar language,' his lip lifted sardonically, 'a profitable business?'

Callie nodded cautiously.

'How profitable?'

Callie drew a breath and quoted the relevant figures.

He listened closely and asked a couple of sharp questions. She answered them.

He frowned and was still for so long, Joey began to hop from one impatient foot to the other.

'So,' the Viscount mused softly, 'in sum, it pays its way but makes no fortune. So, perhaps it *is* about wealth.'

What was? Callie wondered.

The Viscount seemed to become aware of his surroundings. 'Well, I thank you very much for that most useful information – Miss Smith is it?' She nodded.

He took up his lost hat then looked from her to Joey and back again. 'I believe we would do well to keep this conversation between ourselves, don't you? I see no benefit in either Mr Mills or the Earl learning of it.'

Callie wondered once more but agreed with alacrity.

'Joey?' the Viscount turned.

Joey Hunt, overcome at this show of trust in him, was lost for words, although he managed a vigorous nod.

10

Dob was sorry to lose the services of the passionately devoted Joey.

The clouds had not after all produced snow, not even much rain, and the procession of coaches carrying Baron and Baroness Stackling, Lady Alicia Tentham, various servants and huge amounts of luggage had arrived without further delay.

Dob found his worst suspicions about Tomkin confirmed. The man was in his fifties (probably), of unreadable expression and quite immovable in his "suggestions" about what Dob should wear and how Dob should comport himself.

Dob initially resisted but then thought better of it. He could hardly suddenly become as meek and obedient as the proverbial lamb, but in the circumstances it would not, he realised with clenched teeth, help with anything to alienate the fellow completely.

Dinner was, naturally, a fine affair with the Earl intent on making the maximum impression. Equally naturally Dob found the whole occasion acutely uncomfortable.

Tomkin had decked him out in yet another new suit of clothes. The dark evening wear contrasted starkly with Dob's carefully dressed fair hair. The immaculately laundered and fastidiously arranged neckcloth disguised the slenderness of his neck. The padding in the shoulders of the jacket added a breadth its wearer had still to achieve. In a word, Dob had been deliberately (and skilfully, he grudgingly admitted) made to appear several years older than he was.

At the same time, it was almost impossible to disguise the freshness of his face and the fact that shaving it was scarcely necessary.

On the other hand, the Lady Alicia looked every inch a mature woman. She was, Dob discovered on being introduced, almost as tall as he, her statuesque figure set off by an evening dress which draped her body to perfection, its rich green picking out the flecks of colour in her eyes and somehow enhancing the deep mahogany of her hair. The pile of artfully arranged curls and coils gleamed in the steady light of the beeswax candles. Her creamy complexion appeared unpowdered, her red lips free of carmine – although Dob knew he was hopelessly ignorant about such artifices.

Her face, with an expression singularly neither hostile nor friendly, was framed by gems in her neat ears. Around her throat was a matching necklace of stones that Dob guessed were of the finest quality, judging from their inner fire.

He was not surprised to find himself seated at the dining table with the Lady Alicia on one side and the Baroness on other. He managed to exchange polite, and totally meaningless, talk with both for the duration of the lengthy meal.

From the start he was aware of the close scrutiny of the Baron opposite; it was only as the dessert was served that Dob registered that the scrutiny was directed at Lady Alicia.

He knew perfectly well why *his* every move and word was being watched. Was Lady Alicia under similar coercion? Was the match as objectionable to her as it was to him?

Of course, it must be. He kicked himself mentally. What fully-grown woman would want to be hitched to a boy not yet out of school?

Perhaps, he suddenly thought, they could collaborate somehow. She was over twenty-one, so needed no parental consent to marry, but presumably she could also *refuse* to marry, couldn't she?

Or was she as powerless as Dob to resist the pressures on her? He felt the stirrings of hope fade.

Nevertheless, he would try and find an opportunity to talk to her about their mutual problem.

None arose. None was permitted to arise.

The Earl, evidently with the full cooperation of the Baron, orchestrated every occasion indoors or out. Never once did Lady Alicia appear without the Baroness close at her side.

And so, the time passed in artificially cheerful preparations for Christmas: a morning spent gathering red-berried holly; a musical evening at which Dob and Lady Alicia managed to sing a few duets in tune if seriously lacking in feeling; decorous games before a roaring fire in the sitting room.

Then came Christmas Eve with carefully selected tenants allowed through the front door to sing equally carefully vetted carols in the flagged hall. At the midnight service, the common folk were relegated to the gloom at the back of the church while those from the Hall took their place in the richly carved pews at the front.

On Christmas Morning itself, the tenants were likewise

herded out of the way.

Back at the Hall, gifts were exchanged. Dob had apparently had a beautiful string of pearls specially commissioned for Lady Alicia; she had likewise ordered a cravat pin set with a sapphire that matched the colour of his eyes. The surprise was genuine enough, he reflected sourly; the exclamations of delight and appreciation definitely forced.

The magnificent meal lasted from mid-afternoon well into the evening – with goose and turkey and venison, duck and capon, frumenty and lum pottage, mince pies and cheeses; all served with an unending assortment of wines (nobody would guess there was a war going on, reflected Dob).

Next came Boxing Day – with the tardy dawn promising exactly the right weather for a hunt which evidently the Baron was looking forward to as much as the Earl.

Custom dictated that the ladies would take Boxes around the estate, although an unguarded flash of Lady Alicia's eyes made Dob wonder if she would not have preferred to ride.

Which tenants would they visit? he mused. And knew the answer immediately: those recommended by the Earl's steward. He guessed the Smiths would not be on Mills' list. He wondered, in passing, if Mr Smith was improved.

And for the first time he was struck by Miss Smith's competence in book-keeping. He had been so busy at the time pondering the figures she had quoted that he had missed that enigma. She must have learned from her father, he assumed – but that was unusual, singularly unusual.

He tried to recall what she looked like but had little more than an image of a thickly-wrapped personage, shawl tied tightly, clinging to those books as if for dear life.

He was rudely brought back to the present by his father's words.

'Otherwise Bromby provides a decent education,' the Earl was saying to the Baron. 'But,' he turned to Dob, 'the Duke of Branksdown has a fine stud; no doubt you and that son of his have ridden some of them to hounds.'

Dob and Willo *had* gone hunting, but their riding had just as often taken them to race meetings or boxing mills; neither of which, naturally, Dob had mentioned to his father. He nodded cautiously.

'So, you will not get left behind today.' It was clear that the Earl would regard that as a personal disgrace.

Dob felt a surge of pure rebellion. 'I think I can promise you,' he said as evenly as he could, 'that I shall reach the kill first.'

11

Callie mixed more ink and started on the latest papers that Mills had demanded. She had not consulted George: the work seemed straight forward and both George and Margaret had been exhausted by the events of the day before.

They had not been well enough to attend either of the Christmas services but had insisted on getting up and dressing suitably for the meal Callie had prepared. However, even sitting at table, trying to do some justice to the roast capon and vegetables, forcing down a few spoonsful of plum pudding, had been a huge effort and they had retired soon after the festive wax candles had been lit against the early dusk.

As she had cleared away the sorry remains, Callie could hear them coughing in concert in the room above. In spite of the syrup sent over by Mrs Hunt, a concoction of honey infused with herbs including marsh-mallow and thyme, Margaret's weak chest was weaker than ever and her spirits lowered by George's fevered hacking.

Callie tried not to think what would happen if George was no better by Plough Monday.

She ignored the distant sound of the hunting horn and concentrated on her work, dipping the quill carefully, forming her letters as like George's as she could manage, waving each finished page gently to dry the ink since she had no sand.

She took up hot drinks to George and Margaret; she dosed each with Mrs Hunt's simple; she took up bowls of steaming broth – then retrieved them, untouched. She refilled the stone bottles that warmed their feet under the bedclothes and lamented that the bedroom had no fireplace. She dealt with the chamber pots.

As the short day drew to a close, she lit an everyday tallow lamp and, in its poor, malodorous light, she sharpened a new quill and set about finishing her task.

12

Dob nodded to the stable boy – the horse would do as well as any other. There was something of much greater importance for Dob to see to and he dared not involve Joey.

He walked as casually as possible out of the stable yard. A short distance away he could see the dogs being brought from the kennels to the assembly point. The animals were evidently well aware of what was happening and were excited about the day's hunting, but Dob could make out Barney Hunt, Dickon and the whippers-in keeping them all perfectly under control, obedient to every command.

Dob strolled along, looking out at the countryside and at the ground, assessing conditions. He hoped anyone seeing him would assume he was inspecting the going for the horses. He also very much hoped nobody would wonder at his stooping briefly by a thick bush before turning back to the stables.

As horses and hounds set off, Dob made an apologetic sign to his father and pulled his mount to the side.

The Earl scowled his annoyance but could only, at that point, make an irascible gesture as he and the Baron headed the cavalcade out across the park towards the open countryside.

Dob halted by the thick bush, located the hob-nailed boots he had put there and swiftly exchanged them with the tall riding boots that Tomkin had polished to a perfect gloss.

Within a few minutes he had nearly caught up with his father, staying just far enough away for the new footwear to remain unnoticed.

Cast in the coverts, the dogs fanned out and put their noses to quartering the ground. Every hound knew its task: at speed but with complete concentration it ran to and fro, following a possible lead but then almost as quickly abandoning it as it was identified.

Then one dog gave voice and drew others.

More animals picked up the scent, more heads lifted and issued a deep-throated confirmation.

Then Barney Hunt sounded the horn, its doubling informing hounds and huntsmen alike that the quarry had been located. Both responded, the pack moving with increasingly deadly purpose, the horsemen following.

The dogs wove through dense scrub, over the open ground, between trees, as their target tried to evade pursuit.

Those on horse-back sometimes had to divert – to find a place where they could jump a gulley or avoid low, black branches.

Dob made no attempt to stay with them. He stood in his

stirrups one last time to make sure of the lay of the land, then dismounted and flung the reins at a startled follower and took to his heels.

It was so much like running at school that he almost laughed, except that he needed all his breath to keep up with the dogs. His nailed boots gripped wet ground, shrivelled grass, old leaves, dead vegetation; sometimes they slipped on mud or loose stones; however, quick footwork enabled him to recover his balance and continue the race.

He was soon at the front of the whippers-in, not far behind the dogs as they slowed sometimes, momentarily thrown off the scent by a sudden sideways dive of their quarry.

Then the hunting horn sounded for a view as reynard broke cover and raced off once more. Now the leading hounds could see the fox; they lifted their heads; their muscles rippled as they directed all their power into running.

The followers fell behind but were, a glance showed Dob, still ahead of the horsemen.

Occasionally on a hunt, a fox escaped, cleverer or more likely just luckier, but this one would not. Dob saw the dogs overtake it; saw the melee form and heard the hounds' cries turn to red-blooded triumph.

Then those on foot caught up, Dob making sure he was the very first. Pausing only for the horn to order the dogs back, he waded through the packed bodies and picked up the limp body of the fox, the gore spattered from its severed throat still warm.

He held it aloft as the Earl arrived, inevitably at the head of the horsemen.

'As I promised,' Dob managed to control his heaving chest but could not quite keep the jubilation out of his voice, 'I was first to the kill.'

His father glared at him; his mouth lifted in a snarl, but the words he would undoubtedly have liked to utter – to hurl at his son – remained unspoken as the Baron arrived and drew his steaming mount to a halt.

Dob made an elaborate bow. 'Perhaps, my Lord Stackling,' he said, deliberately ignoring his parent, 'you would honour us by taking the brush, the pads and the mask as a gift?' He gulped in a much-needed breath before adding, 'As a souvenir of your august visit to Pentridge.' He met the Baron's leery stare with his own wide, blue-eyed gaze which he had long ago learned to turn on mistrustful school masters.

13

Over the following days there were other hunts, but Dob was given no further opportunity to foil his father: he was forced to stay mounted.

Each time they returned triumphant to the Hall, he submitted to Tomkin's ministrations then, washed and changed, made completely unexceptionable conversation with the ladies.

He tried numerous times, unsuccessfully, to catch Lady Alicia's eye as he handed her a porcelain tea cup or turned her music at the fortepiano. How much, Dob wondered in passing, had it cost his father to purchase this instrument and bring it to the rural depths of L … shire? It was presumably intended to show off the Pentridges' refinement and wealth. Dob knew for certain that the Earl had little of the first – the second was a conundrum which he still felt *had* to be the reason for this infernal match.

Otherwise what *was* the point?

The guests were due to depart after Epiphany – not that there would be, at Pentridge Hall, anything like the rustic tomfoolery that still survived in some places to mark Twelfth Night. Dob had never experienced those revels but had heard of them; and could not imagine his father surrendering his position and authority for one moment, never mind a whole day, to servants and minions.

For the last evening of the visit, there would be yet one more fine dinner served by the staff to their betters as was the rightly ordained order of things.

But on the last morning there would be no hunt. That in itself alerted Dob to the seriousness of the meeting to which he was summoned instead. The subject he could guess only too well and this was confirmed when he found his parents waiting for him in the sitting-room with Baron Stackling, the Baroness and the Lady Alicia.

With sinking heart, he greeted his mother and the Baroness before bowing over the soft hand of Lady Alicia. As he raised his head, he thought he glimpsed the tiniest lift of an elegant eyebrow: it was only a slight movement and was gone in a moment. If he had not imagined it, thought Dob, what was he supposed to infer from it?

'Now, Darius, old chap,' his father was all smiles and bonhomie. Dob squirmed at both the name and the pretence. 'The Baron and I have been discussing the few details of the match that need to be settled immediately – namely the announcement of the happy event to the *monde*. There will, of course, be several months to make the actual wedding arrangements.'

Never any question at all of the union itself.

'We see no reason not to issue the notice now, to be followed by handwritten cards to everyone of note.' The Earl looked at the Baron who nodded his head in confirmation.

There followed a heavy silence, broken only by the settling of logs in the grate. It was as if his father had announced a death in the family, thought Dob.

Unexpectedly, it was his mother who spoke first. 'No.'

Dob had never heard her contradict the Earl before and now she did not speak timidly. 'No,' she repeated firmly. 'This should never have been done here.' Her husband's smile had faded and his brows drew into a frown, but she took a breath and continued, 'Their issue will be cursed.' She did not wait for the angry denial that she knew was coming. 'Do you want to risk that?' she demanded.

The Earl glared at her.

The Baron looked incredulous and annoyed.

The Baroness looked intrigued.

Lady Alicia looked surprised but then almost (was Dob imagining things again?), almost pleased.

The Earl made a blustering speech trying to excuse his wife's outburst and explain why she might have such a nonsensical notion – pointing at Dob as proof of the ridiculousness of the superstition.

And glared even more ferociously as his wife dissolved into tears and began to sob out some of what she had told Dob.

The Earl hastily suggested she needed to withdraw and compose herself.

Seemingly with the same idea the Baroness reached for the Countess's hand, urged her to her feet and accompanied her from the room.

Only as the door closed behind them, did the Earl appear to realise that the Baroness's purpose might be more than silent sympathy. As he scowled at the gilded panels, the Lady Alicia put in rather quickly, 'This is all rather distressing.' She put a hand to what Dob thought was a singularly undistressed brow – although she did manage to produce a fairly convincing crease of concern almost immediately and a small sigh. 'Dear Baron Stackling,' she addressed her guardian, 'I do believe I feel quite faint and must beg to be excused.'

It was hard, thought Dob, to decide who looked the more angry, the more thwarted, the more impotent – the Earl or the Baron.

He turned hastily in case black humour overcame him and took up the Lady Alicia's limp hand. For the first time their eyes met and Dob had not imagined anything.

She murmured her thanks.

He responded with the politest of commiserations and inquired if he should call her maid to accompany her to her room.

She wondered, softly, if he might lend her his arm.

'I will assist you,' the Baron's voice abruptly frustrated them. 'Then I must go and see to my wife.'

'As I must to mine,' added the Earl grimly. 'We will *all* meet again after luncheon,' he declared in a voice that brooked no argument, 'when the ladies have recovered themselves.'

Dob had no way of knowing, of course, what had been said – what his mother had had the time to say to the Baroness; what the Baroness had said to her husband; what the Earl had said to his wife; what anyone might have said to the Lady Alicia.

His mother looked wan but at the same time somehow unrepentant; Dob's kiss of greeting was more than perfunctory as she offered him her pale cheek.

The Baron looked just a little less relentless, the Baroness a little less totally compliant. The Lady Alicia kept her eyes lowered and Dob drew his own wishful conclusions from that: she had something to conceal – could it be hope?

'I believe,' said the Earl, without prevarication, 'that we may now conclude the business we started this morning.' That did not sound so hopeful. 'The agreement reached between myself and the Baron remains unchanged.' Definitely not hopeful. 'The match between my son, the Viscount Kelton, and the Baron's ward, Lady Alicia Tentham, is eminently and unquestionably advantageous to all parties.' Not unquestionably and not all parties, fumed Dob in silence. 'And will be legalised, as planned.'

So, *had* anything changed?

'However.' Dob hated himself for hanging so hard onto every word and his father for making him. 'However, it appears that it would be beneficial to proceed with matters from London.'

Beneficial? Before Dob could ponder further on that particular word, his father continued, 'The postponement will allow the Viscount time to gain the polish that Bromby has sadly not provided, while the Lady Alicia will have the chance to participate in the social round that her father's long illness and death prevented. It will be an excellent opportunity to fully advertise the match to the *beau monde*.'

Dob grasped two essentials: his father was making a virtue out of the necessity of delaying matters (his mother had, it seemed, actually prevailed); and he, Dob, was going to be "polished up" in London. Exactly how his father proposed to ensure this polishing process was not clear, although Dob suspected several Tomkins would be involved, but the main point was that he (and the lady Alicia) had been granted a breathing space – of a kind.

14

The reckoning with Mills on Plough Monday never came. But its threat grew infinitely worse, for in the early hours George Smith's congested lungs took a last creaking breath.

As Mr Hunt and Dickon gathered him up for Mrs Hunt to lay out in the sitting room, Margaret's anguished eyes followed them then closed. Callie grasped the thin hand and willed into it some of her own strength and vitality, but she knew in her heart what was coming.

Margaret Smith never opened her eyes again. Her last reason for hanging onto a frail existence had gone. By evening her spirit had followed that of her husband and her body was laid out beside him.

A double grave was prepared in the churchyard.

Mills was furious at the inconvenience of losing the clerk; at the bother of having to find another. Following the Earl's departure, the steward had been looking forward to a quieter life – and now this! He wanted to forbid every tenant from taking time off work to attend the funeral, but the parson persuaded him against that, fearing a revolt by those all too aware that it was only a matter of time (perhaps a short time) before they would be in the Smiths' position and in need themselves of a proper Christian burial.

Mills made certain that Callie Smith knew she would be required to vacate the cottage immediately, although, he had added, he *might* be able to offer her accommodation elsewhere – on certain conditions. In any case, he expected her in the estate office the following morning to account for every single one of the ledgers she had carried away for George to work on.

Callie endeavoured, nevertheless, in the tomb-like cold of the church, to keep her mind on George and Margaret, remembering their kindness and blotting out the dullness, and keeping for later any thought of what she was to do now.

She dodged all such enquiries as they inevitably came up during the wake and even waved aside the question when put by Mrs Hunt after all was finished.

'You know you will always have a bed with us,' the woman said, 'or part of a bed,' she amended with a rueful concession to reality.

Callie did not doubt it and gave her a hard hug for the offer and for all she had already done. But Callie knew there was no space with the Hunts and that they could not afford to keep her even if there had been.

She reflected bitterly that she could well fill George's position of clerk, but Mills would never consider it – there was clearly only one "position" he had in mind for her.

As she lay down for her final night in the Smiths' cottage, she considered her options – they were very few. She had a very small amount of money, saved from what Lady had given her; it would not keep her for long, but it might take her somewhere. But where? There was no question of returning to Ireland, however much she and Lady might wish it.

She was coming up for eighteen (although she knew she looked older): a woman, a single woman. How could a single woman survive?

Number one (the obvious answer): find herself a husband. But she knew of no man, unwed or widowed, that she could imagine sharing her life (and her body) with.

Number two (following on from that thought): selling herself outside marriage, as Mills had unsubtly suggested. She dismissed that with a shudder – it would be a very last resort (as it surely was for the women forced to it).

Number three: find employment. Most employment (like

being a clerk!) was not open to women. What employment was? Cooking, cleaning, washing, sewing for anyone who had the means to pay for it. Well, Callie could turn her hand to all those. And the most likely employer? In the country that would be one of the big houses; in the town a merchant, a trader, a banker. Which big house or which town?

London! The name screamed at her. A huge city, they said, full of people of every sort, full of every occupation and business, full of every opportunity – and vice.

15

It was well-before the late mid-winter dawn when she left the cottage, dressed in every garment she could reasonably don and struggling mightily with the estate ledgers and the small bundle that contained her few possessions.

Fortunately, there was enough starlight for her to follow the familiar path. A lamp or two burned in the stables, evidence of the stable lads already at work. The estate office remained dark and Callie hurried to deliver the books – the last thing she wanted was to meet Mills. She groped her way into the small downstairs room and placed the ledgers on what had been George's desk.

As she closed the door quietly, she made sure none of the lads was around, hoisted the bundle over her shoulder and walked across the cobbled yard, out through the great iron gates for the last time.

By the time a pale sun had lifted itself above the horizon behind her, she was walking briskly along the road towards the county town.

At one point she heard the sound of a horse coming up and just had time to duck behind some bushes, bare of leaves but dense enough to hide her. She had done nothing against the law and surely the steward would have much more important matters to see to than chase after her; but at the same time, she knew the man would not like being crossed.

However, it was not Mills and she continued on her way, growing ever easier as she neared the town and mixed with the other swathed figures going about their chilly business.

She could not recall the way to the posting inn where the coach had delivered her as a child, but a few enquiries soon led her to the vaguely remembered enclosed yard where there was a promising amount of activity.

'It seems like the whole world wants to travel, now Twelfth Night is past,' commented the man in the booking office. 'Travelling alone, are you?' he inquired.

Callie nodded.

'And you want to go right into London? As far as the Bull and Mouth?'

Callie presumed she did, but she must have looked unsure because the clerk added, 'It's in St Martin le Grand, near Smithfield Market.'

None of which helped Callie; she just needed to get to London. 'Do you have a seat inside the coach?' she repeated her original question.

An ink-stained digit ran down the names on the page in front of him. 'Just the one left,' he said.

Callie asked the price. He pointed to the bill displayed on the wall next to him and she swallowed hard: it would take one of her precious sovereigns and nearly three-quarters of another – not to mention the cost of staying one night en route, the rates for which were helpfully appended.

'There's nobody booked outside,' suggested the clerk.

Callie ran her eye over the price of an outside seat which would cost only half as much, then, imagining what that would be like at this season, abandoned the idea.

The clerk entered her name in the book and wrote out a ticket. 'The coach leaves on the hour,' he said as he passed it to her. 'Sharp. The driver can't wait for stragglers – he needs to make the most of the daylight.'

The six passengers were packed so tightly that not even the fierce jolts on the un-tolled stretches of road dislodged them.

On Callie's right, in the corner seat, was a man who announced that he was a regular traveller; procuring goods for the Admiralty, he added with a distinct note of self-importance. He had a pocket-watch of which he was conspicuously proud: whenever they reached a stop, he dug out the piece and announced both the hour and how much this varied from the printed schedule. Otherwise he had little chance either of saying anything or of being heard.

This was the natural consequence of the extreme garrulousness of Callie's other neighbour. She was not only over-talkative but also over-size, taking up her own allotted fifteen inches of the hard, wooden bench and half of Callie's as well.

'We'll all keep a bit warmer this way,' declared the woman blithely. 'Now young lady,' she continued, 'since we are the only women aboard, we must get acquainted. I,' she announced, 'am Widow Fletcher, my dear husband being deceased these ten years. And what may I call you?' she inquired.

After giving her name, Callie was not required to contribute anything further which suited her. She put in the odd nod and made the occasional noncommittal sound as Widow Fletcher kept up an unceasing narrative. Starting with the daughter whom she had been visiting, she then proceeded to describe her other four children and *their* children. These were such interesting people that the tale was still not finished when the coach drew into Baldock's largest inn and the weary passengers levered themselves out to seek food, drink and a bed for the night.

It was, Callie realised, almost inevitable that she should find herself sharing both room and bed with the widow. She could only hope that the woman did not talk in her sleep!

In the event, Callie fell into an exhausted slumber almost the instant her head touched the more or less clean bolster. It had been a very long day.

She was woken early the next morning by a thunderous knock on the bedroom door. She hurried down to where a frugal breakfast was laid out. As she hungrily devoured the bread and cheese, she perused a newspaper that had been discarded.

On the front page, there were headlines about the latest developments in the war with revolutionary France.

Of far greater personal interest to Callie, were the notices advertising various products and services. The one that caught her eye proclaimed the superiority of a particular employment agency: gentle women of impeccable credentials, it declared, were placed in the most-select positions, such as that of lady-companion to an invalid Lady, currently required by the Duke of U … in the county of G … shire.

Currently? How current?

There was a loud shout from the landlord that the coach for London was about to depart.

Callie hastily looked for the date on the top of the broadsheet – it had been printed just before Christmas.

As the warning call was repeated, she tore out the post and stuffed it into her pocket.

The second day they travelled exclusively on turnpikes: well-maintained and well-used.

As they drew closer to the capital, the traffic thickened and the driver had constantly to slow or swerve to avoid all manner of wagons, carts and carriages.

It was well after dusk when they reached the final stop. Callie peered up at the lamplit galleries overlooking the courtyard of the Bull and Mouth; there were three storeys, with the roof and sky lost somewhere above them in the darkness.

She brought her attention smartly back to ground level as another coach arrived.

'There are coaches coming and going to all parts of the realm,' the naval procurement man displayed his familiarity with travelling. 'Wales, the Midland counties and even up to Scotland.'

Callie did not, at that moment, wish to consider any of them.

'Are you staying here for the night?' he enquired.

'Of course not,' interrupted Widow Fletcher. 'Haven't I said that I live quite nearby, with my daughter? Miss Smith must come and stay with us.'

Certainly, the widow had said something of the sort – probably several times over – but Callie had not been sure either that the widow meant it seriously or that she, Callie, wanted to prolong the acquaintance for any longer than was necessary.

However, it would undoubtedly be cheaper than the inn and a familiar face (even one with a big mouth!) was an attractive idea.

And perhaps tomorrow she could seek the direction of the employment agency.

16

Callie discovered thankfully that Widow Fletcher's daughter, Ruth Giblin, had learned the knack of either stopping her mother's flow of words or diverting it – most often towards the children, who allowed it to shed off them as water from a duck's back.

Callie was supposed, of course, to already know all about the children, both names and boundless talents, but she had to admit to Ruth that she had not quite taken in *everything* the widow had said during the long hours of the journey.

Ruth laughed. 'Mother could talk a horse's hind leg off, couldn't she?' And identified the two girls and a boy, little more than a baby. 'Our eldest, Peter, works with his father at a butcher's near Smithfield market. He's been helping with the deliveries since he was a lad and knows all the streets and houses up west.'

Which turned out to be an asset of unimagined importance.

Even with Peter keeping a proprietorial (if grubby) hand on her arm, Callie nearly lost her footing on several occasions as she was almost overwhelmed by the narrowness of the streets, the gloom cast by overhanging buildings, the foulness of the pavements and roads, the press of people.

Her only previous experience of a city was passing through Dublin as an anxious ten-year old, on which occasion she had noticed very little, being much more concerned with the unknown future awaiting her.

And she suspected now that Dublin was a small town compared with London. The capital's sheer size and busy-ness assaulted her every sense.

Peter seemed to guess at some of her thoughts. 'It gets

more open where the nobs live – grand houses, broad streets, parks and such.'

'And that's where the employment agency is?' she asked; that being where she had asked Peter to take her.

He shook his head, his spiky hair showing around the edge of his battered woollen hat. 'Not likely: too expensive! But it's in an area a sight more *genteel* than where we lives.' He grinned at her, not bothered by the comparison and pleased with the word.

'Lady used to say that *genteel* people were, in her experience, often the worst-mannered.' Callie enjoyed the memory.

'Lady? Lady who?'

'The Lady who I used to live with,' she answered. Or should that be "with whom I used to live"? Or would Lady have found that too affected? Probably!

She smiled to herself.

'There's plenty of Lords and Ladies in Grosvenor Square, Berkeley Square, St James's Square, Hanover Street.' He counted off some of them on his fingers.

'Most of them will have gone into the country for Christmas, won't they?' Like the Pentridges.

Peter scowled. 'Slows down trade,' was his complaint. 'But they'll trickle back for the Season.'

Callie knew very little about the Season. Lady had made few comments about it, and those scathing, but Callie understood its primary purpose: forming and maintaining the essential links between aristocratic families and fortunes and estates.

'Who?' she demanded as Peter mentioned one nobleman who had *not* left. Could it be? The advertisement had only referred to the Duke of U... How many such Dukes were there? Lady had spoken from time to time about acquaintances of hers and also about people related to both of them, but she had not provided a comprehensive map of the British nobility.

'Uppworth,' Peter repeated the name. 'Ordered some best topside just the other day. They're decent there,' he nodded in approval. 'Treats you civil-like and always gives you a bite and a sup for your trouble.'

'Why did they stay for Christmas?' put in Callie, seeking other clues.

'Very difficult for the Duke and his family to travel about,' Peter said, 'and he wants to be here, making preparations to launch Lady Sophie.'

'Why is it difficult?' Callie pressed.

'The Duke's sister-by-marriage, Lady Olivia, is an invalid,' Peter confirmed Callie's suspicion. His next statement, though, surprised her. 'And the Duke himself has been in one of those wheeled-chairs ever since the carriage accident that killed his wife.'

What great misfortune.

'They are both constantly seeking out yet another *eminent* Marylebone physician who claims he can help – for a price.' Peter evidently drank in the household gossip as well as its ale.

'Do you know if Lady Olivia has a paid companion?' Callie tried to suppress the unreasonable tremor of excitement at this turn of events.

Peter looked at her. 'Recruited through that employment agency?' he said shrewdly.

Callie dug out the crumpled piece of newsprint and read out the post.

'Sounds like her Ladyship,' Peter commented. 'As it happens,' he grinned, 'Cook did remark that so far nobody has been found to the Lady Olivia's liking.' He peered at her.

'We could walk past that way.'

Why not? thought Callie – even though she had yet to cross the very large hurdle of getting herself accepted by the agency as a "gentle woman of impeccable credentials". She had done her best (with Ruth's help) to remove as many creases as possible from her Sunday dress, but her boots were nothing more or less than country footwear and no amount of cleaning and polishing could disguise the fact. And her bonnet, covering her strictly pinned braid, was equally obviously rustic. One look at her stained and chilblained fingers would give away her lack of gentility. And as to credentials …

Her spirits fell still further as Peter led the way into the sizeable expanse of Grosvenor Square. In the centre, protected by a fence of wrought-iron railings was an oval park. At this time of year, the shrubs and the quartered garden beds were bare, but in the warmer months it would make a pleasant place to sit, thought Callie – a haven in the midst of a well-swept pavement that was broad enough to carry a large amount of traffic without hindrance; although at present there were few vehicles or pedestrians.

The houses making up the sides of the Square were mostly of an individual design, with only the odd pair or trio matching. However, despite this and the evidence of ongoing alterations and enhancements, they made a pleasing whole, Callie thought.

One mansion, set in the middle of one side, stood out from its neighbours with six stone pillars framing the five bays of the first and second storeys. On the ground floor an imposing front door stood at the top of a few shallow stairs. Peter drew her attention to the large brass knocker.

'Shows the family's in residence,' he informed her. 'There's a basement below street level and an attic of course.

The kitchen and such are at the rear and a sizeable mews.'

A house fit for a Duke of the realm. Callie felt even more drab and depressed.

'Come on,' Peter's friendly hand guided her towards the corner of the Square, around into the alley that served the rear of the mansions. He grinned at her. 'Got no delivery to make today, but maybe Cook'll find something warm for us.' He shivered theatrically, though in truth it was not that cold.

The appearance of Peter and Callie at the kitchen door was met with a remarkable enthusiasm. Peter smiled a little uncertainly: he had been hopeful but not expectant. He raised a puzzled eyebrow at Callie as they were ushered into Cook's own sitting room.

That worthy brought with her a sweet-smelling cloud of baking as she bustled in after them.

She nodded her head in brief greeting to Peter then regarded Callie, looking her up and down appraisingly. 'You look healthy and strong enough,' she commented. 'Are you?' she demanded.

Healthy and strong enough for what? Callie's brain had not worked out the conundrum. She was evidently being inspected for work of some kind, but it couldn't be for the post of companion, could it?

'I am in perfect health, thank you,' she replied neutrally.

'And not afraid of a bit of hard work?'

The past years had held little else, Callie thought ruefully. 'No,' she said.

'Good,' the grey head bobbed in approval. 'And you can start straight away? The housekeeper, Mrs Ballance, will have to approve of course – it's her day off today – but I think we can take that for granted, provided your work is satisfactory.'

Callie had gathered by then that she was definitely being

offered employment. She wondered exactly what the post was and the pay and conditions.

'How fortunate,' Cook beamed at Peter, 'that you heard we were looking for extra staff. His Grace intends to spare no effort in launching Lady Sophie.'

'Pleased to be of help,' Peter accepted the unmerited credit without hesitation. 'To such a kind person as yourself,' he added with just the right weight on the word "kind".

Cook clucked her tongue at him. 'Go along with you, Peter Giblin,' she pretended the smallest outrage at his cheekiness. 'I'll see you get a pastry to take with you, hot from the oven.'

'Do you really want to work as a maid-of-all-work?' Peter asked Callie.

'A bird in the hand is worth two in the bush,' she replied, reassuring herself as much as him.

'Then I'll bring your things over later,' he said. 'And I'll be back with deliveries often enough. Just let me know if you wants to leave. Mother'll be happy to see you back anytime.'

Callie had a sudden thought. She needed to send a note to Lady about the much-changed circumstances.

No problem, he declared.

She thanked him heartily for his help – and that of all the family.

'Even Grandam Fletcher?' he asked with a grin.

17

Callie was provided with an apron of sturdy linen and cap of the same fabric and spent the next hours in the scullery, tackling a seemingly never-ending pile of pots and pans.

Finally, a visit the privy could be delayed no longer. She

asked another of the maids, Maisie, where to find it and wondered at the grin that accompanied the offer to show her.

It was, as expected, in an outhouse behind the kitchen. However, there all expectations ceased. The first thing Callie noticed was the lack of the usual noisome odours; the second was the contraption standing on the scrubbed brick floor.

Maisie laughed. 'It's one of Mr Bramah's water closets,' she said. 'The first to be installed anywhere in Grosvenor Square, according to Mrs Ballance. Here,' she gathered the hem of her skirt, 'I'll show you how to use it.'

Squatting over the bowl was nothing out of the ordinary; what came afterwards definitely was. 'See this handle.' Maisie pointed. 'When you pull it up, like this,' she demonstrated, 'it lifts a flap at the bottom of the bowl and lets *out* all the doings. And at the same time, it pulls a wire which lets *in* water to flush it clean.'

Callie stared. She saw now the reservoir fixed near the ceiling which obviously supplied the water. And what about the soil? Where did that go after it was conveniently washed away? Did it go into a tank to be collected by the nightmen?

'No need for that smelly business,' replied Maisie. 'There's pipes under the streets. Some bring in clean water from the Chelsea Waterworks and others take waste water down to the river.'

Callie pondered that: much nicer for it to be *under* the streets than *above* – littering the roadway, clogging the gutter and stinking – as was the usual case.

Would *every* house in London have a water closet one day? she wondered. How many houses were there in London? How many people, all doing what every human being had to do? (Probably getting on for a million, she discovered later; a number so huge she simply could not imagine it.)

'Here!' Maisie's voice broke into Callie's thoughts. 'You'd better use that thing sharpish We need to get back to work.'

Sometime later, Peter reappeared with her small bundle.

There were still pots and pans to scour and her hands were deeply wrinkled – but at least all the ink stains had gone! Callie assured him she was doing fine, thanked him for bringing her things and bid him a hasty farewell.

At the end of the long working day there was a generous meal for all the staff. By then, however, Callie was so tired she hardly took in any of the names (still less the conversation) and was already more than half asleep as she followed Maisie up the back stairs to the attic.

The room they were to share had two narrow beds, a wash-stand and a chest of drawers on a floor of tightly-fitting pine boards. In the light of the candle that Maisie stood in its dish, Callie could also see that none of the walls had windows, although in the sloping ceiling there was a skylight revealing a black rectangle, lightly dusted with stars.

Very similar to the accommodation on the top floor of the Wicklow mansion, Callie thought; except that this room was not icy. She stared around in bleary puzzlement and registered that there was a small hearth containing live embers.

Ever since the Lady Olivia had come to run the household, there had been fires in *all* the servants' rooms in winter, Maisie informed Callie grandly, fed with the very best coal; only a few lumps, she admitted, but those burned as well as a whole basket of wood.

Callie struggled into her night-shift and reached under the bed – it was the usual chamber pot up here. There had been talk of installing other water closets in the House, Maisie said, but it hadn't happened. All the jordans were carried to the one in the backyard.

The skylight was still dark when Callie was roused from a deep slumber. 'What time is it?' she asked Maisie sleepily.

'Getting-up time!' came the response in exact mimicry of Cook's voice.

Downstairs, the clock in the kitchen informed Callie that it was half-past five. Mrs Ballance (back in residence and evidently prepared to try out Callie for at least one more day, even with no reference other than that of Peter Giblin!) informed her what she was expected to do in the two hours before breakfast was served in the kitchen. After that, there would be another two hours before any of the Family was likely to appear.

By then, Mrs Ballance said sternly, *everything had to be finished* so that there remained no trace of housework – or houseworker.

Callie cleared out grates, hauled away ashes and brought in new coals; she washed hearthstones and carefully reset fires.

In the light of the candle Mrs Ballance had issued there was a tantalising glimpse of a small bit of each room, but for the most part ceilings and corners were lost in darkness.

Callie was curious to see the style and décor in its entirety. She was surprised by how keen she was – to move among fine furniture, to gaze at elegant mouldings and well-executed paintings, to lap up the colours and textures of skilfully worked stone and fabric and wood. In her childhood these things had formed the ambience of everyday life.

During all the time at Pentridge she had never set foot inside the Hall, never even had the chance to peer through one of the tall mullion windows. She had lived out the years in the Smiths' cottage and the almost identical one occupied by the Hunts. She was well aware many people had much less: the really unfortunate not even a roof over their heads or a crust of bread in their bellies. Still, she had once known something different and she had not realised until now how much she had missed it.

As daylight finally broke, she stood in the main hall and stared at what was revealed.

Behind the plain front door that she had seen from the Square, was the entrance hall, its floor chequered in black and white marble. In spite of the deep apple-green distemper, the space was not dark: light came in from windows on the first and second floors and picked out the white of the intricate medallions and mouldings on the walls, of the underside of the shallow treads that floated upwards.

On the landings of the two upper floors, white marble pillars guarded galleries and provided an echo of those external columns. All the way up the stairs and between the pillars was wrought ironwork so fine it could have been filigree, its repeating motifs of exotic foliage cupping either a stylised spiky flower or perhaps – Callie chewed her lip – a pineapple? She had seen pictures of a pineapple, but Lady had never demanded a real one from the Wicklow orangery, though perhaps the Marchioness had since ordered one to provide the centrepiece for the enormous, gleaming dining table set with heavy silverware, sparkling crystal glass and wafer-thin Chinese porcelain to impress important guests …

Callie brought her attention back to Uppworth House. The distant striking of a long-case clock reminded her it was time she retreated, but she could not resist a peep into the dining room first.

The table there was of some deep-red wood, buffed to a rich gloss, but Callie's eye went to the fireplace which she could now see in all its glory. The surround was inlaid with marble of manifold jewel-like colours: green leaves cradled terra-cotta flowers, within diamond-shaped frames of black, mottled brown and ochre. Other flowers of more delicate hue were held in contrasting rondels. Along its top edge, gold-leaf picked out stone beading and unknown vegetation, exactly as it did along the cornice.

She drew a deep breath and hurried for a quick look at the sitting room.

The fire there lent a mellow tone to its frame of sculpted white marble; to either side, two statuettes in the scant drapes of antiquity supported the mantel.

The silky pile of the carpet, with its roses, daffodils, crown imperials, morning glories and tulips perfectly complemented the plasterwork of the ceiling. The upholstery on the elegant chairs and sofas exactly matched the main colours.

Her eyes swept around the rest of the furniture and paused at a side table holding a small hand-bell and a book. A couple of steps brought her close enough to read the title.

She was afraid her work-roughened fingers might damage the paper, but still she could not prevent herself from turning to the first page:

TWELFTH-NIGHT:
OR,
WHAT YOU WILL.
By Mr. William Shakespear.

LONDON:
Printed for J. Tonson, and the rest of the PRO-
PRIETORS: and fold by the Booksellers of
London and Westminster.
MDCCXXXIV

Nor to the second page:

DRAMATIS PERSONAE

ORSINO, Duke of Illyria

She softly read out the list of familiar names. '*Olivia, a lady of great beauty and fortune*   '

'But she was foolish to abjure the sight and company of men,' said a voice behind her.

Callie swung around and nearly dropped the precious volume.

'For even a single day,' continued the woman in the doorway leaning heavily on a stick, 'never mind seven years – when what's to come is so unsure!'

Callie knew she was facing the disaster of dismissal. However, the horse of abject apologies which formed in her mind refused the jump of utterance – after all, what was she really guilty of?

She took a breath and what came out, for better or for worse, was:

'What is love, 'tis not hereafter,
Present mirth, hath present laughter:
          What's to come, is still unsure.
In delay there lies no plenty,
Then come kiss me sweet and twenty:
          Youth's a stuff will not endure.'

'I will not make any comment on the kissing,' the woman remarked ruefully, 'but I will swear to the truth that youth does not endure.' She grimaced. 'For that is exactly why I am standing here with my legs refusing to obey me. Come, child!' she said. 'See if you can persuade them or I shall be stuck here all day.'

Motion once started seemed equally unruly: all of a sudden, the forward-leaning body was virtually running on tiptoe.

Callie realised immediately the catastrophe posed by the edge of that beautiful carpet and with no thought for propriety, she grasped Lady Olivia firmly by both arms and moved backwards before her, supporting her until she could be lowered into the wingback chair by the fire.

Just as this was achieved, a young woman rushed in. 'Aunt Olivia, what were you thinking? Walking around by yourself!'

Was this the Lady Sophie?

'If only I could,' came the plaintive comment from the armchair.

'Have you hurt yourself?' The loosely-tied hair was testimony to a hasty interruption to the morning's toilette. Lady Sophie noticed Callie for the first time. 'Oh!' she exclaimed. 'Who is this?'

'I have no idea,' said Lady Olivia, 'but it was fortunate she was here to lend me a hand, two hands in fact.' She looked up at Callie. 'I assume you are new, since you are apparently ignorant of Mrs Ballance's usual rules?'

'Mrs Ballance gave me clear instructions,' Callie quietly exonerated the housekeeper of any blame.

Lady Olivia's keen eyes narrowed. 'Then your disobedience was deliberate?'

Put that way, there was only one answer, but Callie could not bring herself to give it. She continued to stand there, her ruined hands folded in front of her in an unconscious and vain attempt to ward off fate's next decision on her behalf.

To her surprise Sophie laughed. 'Coming from you, Aunt, that is rich! You know, perfectly well, what Uncle Uppworth told you.'

Evidently, Lady Sophie was neither the daughter of the Lady Olivia nor the Duke.

Lady Olivia hmphed. 'And why he wants to hire a companion to make sure I obey! And,' she added, 'why I would have none of the over-corseted females that agency recommended for the post.'

'Now, Aunt,' Sophie chided, 'you know his Grace only wants what is best for you.'

Lady Olivia looked as if she was about to dispute this but sighed instead. 'I know, my dear. He has always been most kind, treating us both as members of the family. I was so glad I could run the house for him after my dear sister the Duchess died, but now I fear this damned palsy has made me more hindrance than help.'

Sophie knelt by the chair and took a shaking hand in her own. 'Aunt,' she said, 'you *know* you could never be that.' A small dimple showed. 'Even at your most cantankerous!'

'But I will *not* become a care case!' Lady Olivia declared. 'Any more than Uppworth allows himself to be. Telling me that I must not take a step *anywhere* on my own – indeed!' Lady Olivia's humph this time was decidedly more of a harrumph.

In spite of her precarious situation, Callie had listened intently to this exchange. There was something about Lady Olivia's spirit of independence that reminded her of her own Lady.

She put her hand in her pocket and dug out the piece of newsprint, now even more crumpled, and offered it to Lady Olivia.

'Ah,' said her Ladyship, glancing at it then peering at Callie. She turned her head. 'Sophie, I believe I would like to have a serious and private conversation with this young woman. You may go and complete your toilette.'

Sophie hesitated, a mixture of wonder and concern clear to see.

'I promise, this once,' said her aunt with a wry smile, 'not to move without assistance. See,' she pointed to the hand-bell, 'I do not even need to leave my chair to summon it.'

As the door closed behind Sophie, there commenced possibly the most important conversation in Callie's life.

18

'Let me see if I have understood,' said Lady Olivia. 'You say, Miss Smith, that you are the natural daughter of a Marquess and were raised for the first years of your life by the Marquess's sister, but you will not name them because the Marchioness has forbidden the connection to continue, indeed wishes to suppress all acknowledgment of your existence and might punish Lady, as you call her, if it were to become public. You do realise that makes your story very difficult to believe?'

'I realise that,' replied Callie. 'But I cannot risk Lady's livelihood.'

'Even at the risk of your own? No? Nor will you name the estate on which you have lived since!'

'I explained,' repeated Callie, 'that my foster parents there are both dead and I only ever saw the Family from a distance: they could have nothing to say about me. The one person likely to respond to any inquiry would be the estate steward and I fear he would provide an untrue and malevolent testimony.'

'You are asking any employer to take a very great deal on trust,' her Ladyship commented. 'Did you really imagine the agency would accept you without "impeccable credentials"?' she nodded at the advertisement.

'Such as all those "over-corseted females" had?' Callie responded.

'That does not answer my question, but it does make a very pertinent, or *im*pertinent, point!' Lady Olivia's lips curved slightly. 'List all the credentials you claim for yourself that you believe would make you my ideal companion.'

Callie lifted her fingers to count. She looked at their state then stuck them out defiantly. 'I am used to hard work. I am strong of body.'

'And have the blind audacity of the young,' murmured her Ladyship.

'I tended my ailing foster-mother for years. I cared for both my foster-parents in their last days. I am used to seeing to all the needs of the sick or frail, even the most basic ones. At the same time, I can also read and write and factor well. I am very familiar with the Bible, several of Shakespeare's plays and Pope's Iliad, and I would love to discuss any or all of them. But,' she said firmly, 'what I would love as much is to become familiar with other works – anything and everything that I have so far had no chance to discover.'

When Lady Olivia did finally lift the little bell and ring it, it was not to summon assistance but to ask for refreshment to be brought.

Maisie looked at Callie with astonishment, had to ask her Ladyship to repeat herself, made an awkward bob and a swift exit.

Before they had finished the tea and cakes, Sophie reappeared, looking at her aunt with great curiosity.

'I have made my decision,' said Lady Olivia without prevarication. 'I believe my preferred companion has presented herself.'

Sophie looked at Callie and back again.

'Yes, I know she does not look at all the part,' said her Ladyship drily, 'but I believe we shall suit very well. However,' she paused, 'we also need to convince His Grace.

And to do that, dear Sophie, I think you may offer invaluable help.'

She explained what she had in mind. 'I shall sit here – with the little bell close to hand – until you return.'

The Duke of Uppworth was probably only in his forties, thought Callie, looking at the man in the wheeled-chair, although the lines etched on his face made him seem older.

In just over an hour Sophie (and her personal maid) had achieved little short of a miracle: Callie's hands would take weeks to be anywhere near soft and ladylike, but they were as clean and trim as was possible; her dark hair shone with brushing and was neatly dressed; the "old" dress of Sophie's far outshone Callie's Sunday best even though it had had to be hastily taken in at the seams; like-wise an out-dated pair of walking shoes were infinitely more elegant than Callie's country boots.

But would it all be enough to convince his Grace?

Callie took a deep breath, lifted her skirts a fraction and made her best curtsey (as she had practised for Lady, years before).

19

While Pentridge House stood on the south side of St James's Square, it actually faced on to the busy thoroughfare of Pall Mall and could not claim the fashionable address of those grand houses on the east, north and west sides of the Square. Likewise, the Earl of Pentridge and his family could claim no right of access to the exclusive central garden.

Ironically, the Baron (lower in the order of nobility), his wife and his ward could, since the Lord Stackling had taken a lease on a house in the Square itself.

Although matters of rank were central to the Earl's very

life-purpose, this social and geographical situation did not for the time being bother him overmuch, as it was merely a small detail in a far greater design. What concerned him considerably more was the postponement in making the contract between his son and the Lady Alicia Tentham. It was some weeks before he could feel sure that in the familiar surroundings of the Richmond villa his wife's hysteria had subsided to a point where she would cause no more mischief.

Meanwhile he concentrated on ensuring that his son knew exactly what was expected of him – and conformed to it. If business necessitated the Earl's absence from Pentridge House, a carefully recruited team, commanded by the unbending Tomkin, "served" the Viscount at all times: in his bedchamber, in his dressing room; at breakfast, luncheon and dinner; to the tailor, the hatmaker, the bootmaker; to the dancing master, the fencing master, the boxing master. Dob was escorted to all social functions – afternoon tea parties, evening concerts, plays and masques, where the Baron and Baroness included him in their equally unfailing diligence.

Although the formal announcement had not been made, it was evident to Dob that the *ton* were expected to notice that he and the Lady Alicia invariably attended the same event.

It was equally clear to him that the pair would be permitted scant opportunity for any private converse. Dob tried hard not to show his frustration as he exchanged meaningless phrases with the gathered throng of titled personages, with the Baron, with the Baroness, with the Lady Alicia herself.

She comported herself with such bland hauteur that he began to think he had misjudged her, but as he led her out for a reel, she murmured, 'It won't do, will it?'.

He just managed to control his features and as he placed

her in the line opposite him, he replied in kind, 'Not for either of us, I believe.'

For some time, the pattern of the dance kept them separate then it was their turn to promenade down the centre.

'I'm sure you will make a perfectly nice man one day,' the Lady Alicia stated frankly.

Dob could not prevent a smile at the back-handed compliment but turned it into encouragement of the mousy lady who was his contrary corner. As he swung his own partner, she continued, 'But my heart already lies elsewhere.'

What, wondered Dob, leading her outside the set, did heart have to do with anything?

As he took both her hands for the ballance, he queried softly. 'But the match is unacceptable to your guardian?'

'Out of the question,' she said, following his lead in the pousette.

As the chain ended the dance, Dob escorted her to the chair awaiting her next to the Baroness. 'Then how are we to proceed?' he queried softly.

'Don't let them suspect anything!' For once her voice held real passion, albeit suppressed almost to the inaudible.

And there was nothing to do except practise that until the next occasion arose for a few more equally inadequate exchanges.

20

'How old are you really?' Lady Olivia's question took Callie by surprise. 'I think that you have not been untruthful so far,' said her Ladyship, 'although you have managed at times to divert me or provide less than the whole truth! I hope my trust in you is not about to be broken?' she said severely.

'No, my Lady,' said Callie uncomfortably. She had come to like the woman, as well as the position of companion. 'I am in my eighteenth year,' she said reluctantly.

'Seventeen then,' Lady Olivia said shrewdly. She put her head slightly on one side and looked at Callie critically. 'That outfit makes you look like an old maid. If that is the best the dressmaker could produce, I think we must take our custom elsewhere.'

The dressmaker had come to Uppworth House at Lady Olivia's behest. Expecting a prestigious commission from such a titled personage, she had been decidedly put out to find she was expected to dress a mere domestic. With poor grace she had taken Callie's measurements then set one of her seamstresses to produce what she deemed a suitable garment: plain in style and of an indeterminate grey twill.

'It fits me,' Callie pleaded in its favour. 'And the woollen cloth is of good quality.'

'I find it depressing,' judged her Ladyship. 'I shall accompany you to a different dressmaker and ensure she dresses you in a manner that I can find cheerful.

'And don't presume to tell me that such an outing would be too much for me,' she warned.

Callie repressed the protest that had been on her lips.

'And in the meantime, you must have one of my Indian shawls to cover at least some of it.'

The expedition to the dressmaker off Oxford Street was rated a success by her Ladyship. By then Lady Olivia had decided that Callie needed more than a dress or two to wear in the house: she would need others suitable for when she accompanied her Ladyship to the increasing number of functions that the Season would generate.

'For I *will* see my niece properly presented and settled,'

she said fiercely, 'before the palsy prevents me.'

Callie knew better than to protest against the undeniable.

The Duke, however, was annoyed that his sister-in-law had tired herself so much with the outing and was positively furious when she calmly announced her future plans – to chaperone Sophie *in person*. 'After all,' Lady Olivia met his Grace's wrathful stare, 'was that not exactly the point of finding me a companion: to help me do things which are becoming increasingly difficult? And I am convinced Miss Smith can do exactly that.'

The ducal glare swung towards Callie. For a moment she wondered if he would end the employment he had so recently endorsed – for he had that power: he was the one holding the purse strings; in that respect Lady Olivia was as much in thrall as Lady. Callie's fears for her own position were superseded by anger at the injustice done to women simply because of their sex. She had read the account of Adam and Eve in the Bible many times and debated it in her head (having nobody else with whom to discuss it). God had created humankind, male *and* female, in His own image – why, Callie wondered, had He included curiosity and the power of choice if He never wanted humans to exercise either? If it was to test their "free-will" (a word the parson at Pentridge used interchangeably in his sermons with human depravity and sin) then the serpent was a necessary part of the exercise – so why then blame it? And when both Eve and Adam had been equally disobedient and given their respective punishments, why should Adam have rule over Eve (and by implication every man over every woman forever after)?

'And I might point out, your Grace, that you have a similar attitude to *your* challenges,' said Lady Olivia.

The Duke of Uppworth opened his mouth with, Callie suspected, a retort or denial on his lips; then shut it again.

The two of them continued to glower at each other before they hmphed at almost exactly the same instant – and laughed.

'Humour, even black humour,' said the Duke, still smiling wryly at his sister-by-law, 'is the most underestimated physic of all, is it not? When there is nothing left to laugh at, all is most surely lost.'

Presumably humour was also given by God, reflected Callie, but she could recall little of it in the Bible. There was wit, irony and mockery aplenty among the strict commands and violence of the Old Testament; and in the New Testament there was compassion and kindness (until one got to the book of Revelation, of course) but nothing she could think of as comedy. Mind you, her thoughts wandered, Shakespeare's comedies were not all fun and laughter – the Bard used humour to highlight the serious and the downright tragic…

'I must seek your aid, it seems, Miss Smith.'

Callie started.

'To try and moderate my Lady's ambitions.'

Callie looked from him to Lady Olivia and back again.

'Come! Has the cat got your tongue?'

'Miss Smith,' said Lady Olivia dryly, 'is trying to find some way of answering you that does not involve dissembling – she is not very good at that, thank goodness!'

The Duke peered at Callie. 'Is that so?' he said. 'And what answer do you not want to give?'

Callie stood tongue-tied: how could she reply? How could she not, when they were both waiting for her to speak?

'I am very content, your Grace, to serve as the Lady Olivia's companion. It is my sincere hope to continue to do so.'

'But in a way that would not concur with *my* wishes?'

Callie was silent again.

'And would, you fear, lead me to dismiss you,' the Duke finished for her.

Callie nodded. It was, after all, exactly so.

The Duke of Uppworth frowned then sighed. 'As a consequence of my birth and the law of the land it is I with the title and control of the Uppworth monies, but I will never see anyone I regard as an intrinsic part of my family either go short of funds or have to meet any conditions in order to receive them.

'You, Miss Smith, are quite safe in your employment as long as the Lady Olivia wills it.'

Callie let out an involuntary breath.

'I would, however, like to hear why you think your service to her might conflict with my bidding?'

Callie wanted to help Lady Olivia live as *she* wished. She tried to explain this to his Grace but feared she had put it badly.

She knew she had limited experience of the world, but she was not completely naïve: it would be a perpetual balancing act between caution and determination, between concession to the illness and defiance of its limitations.

21

Callie grew well-content in her position of companion to Lady Olivia – that is to say, she liked the woman increasingly and was glad to be able to help in all the ways that seemed needed. There was physical assistance, certainly, with all the bodily tasks that had become difficult (including use of the commode, although Callie was not required to actually take the earthenware pot to the water closet). There were often calls at night when regular and restful sleep was elusive. In the day she aided her Ladyship and Sophie to make preparations for Sophie's come-out (putting into effect Lady Olivia's declared intention). This necessitated numerous visits to dressmakers, milliners, haberdashers, glovemakers, shoemakers and hosiers, each expedition a challenge in organisation, improvisation, exertion, frustration and – sometimes – hilarity. Callie liked to think she was getting better at it with practice, as she understood more of the horrible aspects of the illness and could anticipate things without Lady Olivia having to ask, sometimes averting potential disaster.

As well as outings there were the regular visits to Uppworth House of a music tutor and a dancing master, the one to further Sophie's skill on the pianoforte, the other her poise and elegance in the many variations required for the dances currently *à la mode*. Lady Olivia and Callie would sit in on the lessons, as appreciative listeners and spectators. Lady Olivia had been an accomplished pianist herself until the palsy had denied her. She was not, however, as Callie had learned early on, a woman who wasted time being sorry for herself (although she sometimes gave in to frustration and outright anger at her limitations). Lady Oliva could enjoy her niece's playing entirely selflessly and could likewise make criticisms or suggestions that were devoid of bitterness or envy. All in all, she said to Callie (in front of Sophie), her niece performed very nicely.

Callie was not qualified to judge one way or the other but marvelled at both the sweet sound of the music and the ease with which Sophie's two graceful hands and white fingers flew across the keys to produce it.

Callie also had no personal experience of the formal dances, but she viewed the moves and patterns with interest, comparing them with the country dances she did know; and was delighted on the occasions when Lady Olivia prompted her to join the lesson, partnering Sophie or being used by the master to demonstrate a particular stance or step. Callie knew she had a good sense of rhythm and was pleased when the master complimented her lightness of foot.

In between all these excursions and activities, there were hours when Callie simply kept the Lady Olivia company. During the day or when sleep evaded her ladyship at night, Callie would read out loud – it might be a requested book or play or journal, or sometimes Callie was told to go to the library and "find something".

Callie had been, as she had said, used to tending Margaret Smith, but in truth that had rarely been at night and she, Callie, had a perfectly normal young woman's habit of deep sleep. She did, at least in the beginning, find it difficult to rouse herself from her bed in the dressing-room adjoining her Ladyship's chamber but found it easier as she became attuned to the sounds that meant she was needed, and also as she appreciated the "compensation" that often went with the call: being able to read the next chapters or acts of whatever work was in hand.

Most days there would be a letter or two to be opened then passed to her ladyship to read. Callie would pen replies to Lady Olivia's dictation and see them despatched. Each morning her Ladyship met with the housekeeper, Mrs Ballance, to discuss supplies, menus and other household matters. Callie made notes as required and totted up the bills and expenses at the end of each week.

Not surprisingly, Mrs Ballance was (as were all the staff who had seen Callie taken on as a lowly housemaid) initially deeply suspicious of Callie's sudden elevation to her Ladyship's right-hand but as Callie persisted in being her usual self, with no airs and graces, no taking of liberties, the shock and reservation subsided, particularly as they all saw how much a woman who had their respect and affection benefitted from the help Callie provided.

The counterpart to all this satisfaction, in being useful, in becoming an integral part of a warm (literally and figuratively) household, of at least looking through doors she had thought forever closed to her into a world of cultured living, wide interests, sophisticated events and, above all, literature, was increasing sadness at the nature and progress of her Ladyship's illness.

It could have just one end – the question only how quickly that might come and via what tortured route.

As Callie had gathered from Peter, Lady Olivia (and indeed the Duke) had consulted several physicians in Marylebone. Just recently her Ladyship had heard of a surgeon approved by the City of London Corporation, with a practice in the much less fashionable district of Shoreditch. She had also heard that the man had a distinctly tarnished reputation – not, though, she found on further inquiry, because of anything to do with his medical skills but because of his political ideas, with which Lady Olivia was not the slightest bit concerned. What did concern her was the intelligence that Doctor Parkinson had a particular interest in the shaking palsy and was assiduously ("scientifically" it was asserted) studying as many cases as possible in order to make an accurate picture of the symptoms and progress of the affliction, together with an assessment of any treatments and their efficacy. When contacted by Lady Olivia, he had written back declaring frankly that he was only in the early stages of his study and doubted he would have all the facts and evidence he needed for quite some years and therefore (with further unusual honesty) doubted he could be of much help at this point in time.

His modesty alone made Lady Olivia all the keener to see and consult him. When he declined to call at Uppworth House, repeating that he could promise little, Lady Oliva, resolved to go to his practice in Hoxton Square.

It was soon abundantly clear to everyone that Callie's appointment was an almost ideal fit. It was the Duke who voiced the only concern.

'You have, Miss Smith, undoubtedly banished any doubts I may have had,' he said, as he joined them for tea one afternoon, 'and more than justified my sister-in-law's snap judgement.'

Callie acknowledged this approval with a polite inclination of her head.

Lady Olivia, however, frowned. 'I hear a "but" coming, your Grace,' she said.

'You do indeed, my dear Olivia,' replied the Duke equably. '*But* I do believe there is a danger, a considerable danger, that your bright candle will be soon be extinguished, if it continues being burned from both ends; indeed, from all ends, if a candle can have more than two.' A small smile at his weak joke eased his lined features.

Lady Olivia gave one of her hmphs, but it was a small one and she could not meet his Grace's eye.

'To choose another, perhaps more fitting, metaphor, we need to take care not to kill off this golden goose – do we not?' His question was gentle, but it was not meant to be ignored. 'Olivia?' he urged a response.

'Of course!' came the defiant reply. 'But Miss Smith has no complaints – do you?' she demanded of Callie.

'No,' Callie said firmly.

'Precisely,' said his Grace. 'But,' his look had become a little sterner, 'the purest gold is the softest and most easily worn away.'

Lady Olivia glanced at him, shot a look at Callie, then looked down at her right hand which was shaking in her lap. She seized it angrily with her left hand and stuffed it firmly down the side of her chair. She muttered fierce words that were almost inaudible. 'What are you suggesting?' she challenged the Duke. 'I don't want anyone else,' she added mutinously.

'I know,' he said evenly, 'but surely you understand Miss Smith cannot attend you all hours of the day and night with no break? I am aware,' he cut off the retort he could see coming, 'she has done so until now, but I can see she is not quite as lively, quite as robust, quite as hale as she was. She needs,' he said, quite firm now, 'time off, regular time, to do whatever she needs to refill the oil in her lamp – to change my metaphor once more.'

Lady Olivia looked at him with one more small attempt at denial, then her face crumpled.

'Your Grace,' Callie protested. 'I really am quite well. I can manage. I ….'

A ducal hand silenced her. 'But for how long? When I was called upon to approve your employment and Lady Olivia made plain her plans, I feared it would be *she* who would become exhausted.' He added drily, 'I also believe, at that same interview, I made it known that I do not, in general, make heavy-handed use of my title and position. I am, however, at this stage going to make one very clear statement.'

He looked from Callie to Lady Olivia. 'The situation *must* be addressed and arrangements made. *You* may decide the how and when, but,' he warned, 'if you do not heed me, *I* shall issue orders.'

Discussion and some honest reflection on Callie's part had led to the admission that what she would value most would be an undisturbed sleep. What she also realised she missed greatly was the countryside in which she had always lived – the plants and trees, the open skies, the lack of packed humanity. London was exciting, thronged with interesting people and marvellous activities, but it was also crowded and noisy and dirty and stinking.

To address the first issue, it had been agreed that Maisie would work with Callie for several nights learning what Lady Olivia might need so that Maisie could take over the bed in the dressing room once a week and be on call. Callie insisted *she* must have a room nearby so that if anything arose that Maisie could not deal with, she could be summoned quickly.

There was one main shortcoming to this arrangement: Maisie, although she could write her own name and spell out simple words, was barely literate and would not be able to read to Lady Olivia in wakeful hours as Callie did. This difficulty, however, proved to have an odd answer since it turned out that Cook was not the only person Maisie could imitate; the girl had, in fact, a remarkable knack for mimicry – together with an insatiable appetite for gossip – and proved herself a very good entertainer.

The second issue – that Callie wanted some semi-rural solitude but could hardly wander around a deserted Park on her own – was resolved by the addition of a delighted Peter Giblin to the staff of Uppworth House.

22

Dob discovered only one time and place to escape constant surveillance – although it provided no opportunity for a private encounter with the Lady Alicia.

His initial hopes of a meeting with her in the St James's Square gardens or the nearby Park were dashed by his first essays: he might be able to escape the house and scale any necessary walls or fences, but Lady Alicia could not.

Moreover, an early scouting expedition ended in ignominy when Tomkin caught him on his return and escorted him to a waiting Earl.

It was like being carpeted by Old Jenkers! Dob scratched around for some sort of explanation. 'At Bromby I was used to running before breakfast each day,' he said. Had that only been a matter of weeks ago? 'Mr Jenkerson believed it good for both the mind and the body and indeed,' warming to his theme, 'I found it so.' Then quite truthfully, 'I miss it.'

The Earl looked disbelieving: surely the fencing and boxing were quite enough gentlemanly exercise?

They were quite different, Dob tried to explain; and the running helped with both.

Why had Dob sneaked out of the house?

He had not wished to disturb anyone.

The Earl regarded him suspiciously, long and hard. Eventually to Dob's complete amazement he agreed to the early-morning running – as long as it was in Hyde Park (a little distance from St James's) and one of Tomkin's "footmen" accompanied him "just in case". Dob did not bother to ask what "case" his father had in mind.

It might do nothing to solve the problem of meeting Lady Alicia, but Dob really did enjoy it – the physical challenge, the morning air, the freedom of movement, the parkland dotted with trees and usually devoid of people at that time. He also enjoyed very much tormenting the "footman" delegated to escort him. Dob gradually but inexorably increased both speed and distance, until Forster was scarlet of face and scarcely able to draw breath into his tortured lungs. Dob pretended sympathy and slowed his pace for a while before stepping it up again.

There was nothing like an overt agreement, but it soon became an established pattern that Forster would see Dob to the entrance of the Park, join in for appearance sake what Dob regarded as a gentle warm-up, then take himself to the Star near the Piccadilly Turnpike, which was open for overnight travellers.

An hour or so later, Dob would meet him in the taproom for a draught of ale before they made their way back at a brisk walk to Pentridge House.

Dob might, out of sheer pig-headedness, have continued there with the Bromby regime of a cold wash except that it was not worth the fight with Tomkin and, in truth, he did rather enjoy the hot water and Mr Harris's gentlemen's grooming products.

He did not, however, abandon the Bromby habit of plain fare for breakfast and all in all he felt healthy of body even though his mind remained burdened by the main problem in his life.

As the light strengthened, the birds anticipated spring with an increasingly loud dawn chorus.

Dob came to the end of the new circuit and toyed with the idea of a swim. The Lake had been created by damming the River Westbourne, but its irregular edges made it look very much like a natural feature. As he stood getting his breath back, debating the matter, he realised he was not alone.

On a bench was a woman watching intently the antics of a number of ducks as they dived, heads down, webbed feet in the air. Every so often they would right themselves, paddle a little distance then repeat the manoeuvre. Sometimes, two or three birds would act together and the woman laughed in soft delight.

Dob suddenly saw it. 'Like a dance,' he exclaimed. 'All that bowing and curtseying!'

'Exactly,' she said without turning her head.

They watched the anatine capers for some time, the companionable silence broken only by the odd chuckle until the birds disappeared from sight beyond the broken remains of last year's reeds.

What a complete contrast, Dob realised, with the glittering *haut monde* where men and women in elaborate dress disported themselves according to a complex etiquette.

He looked sideways at the woman and saw now that the shawl around her head and shoulders was richly patterned and of a soft fabric that he could not name but suspected was exotic and knew must be expensive.

Then all thoughts of stuffs and fashion fled as his attention was caught by the woman's face. 'Miss Smith!' he exclaimed. 'What a surprise to see you – a nice surprise,' he added hastily.

'My Lord Kelton,' she returned in a manner that suggested the meeting was not such a nice surprise for her.

'How do you come to be here?' His curiosity brushed aside her lack of enthusiasm. 'In London? In Hyde Park? At this time of day?' He saw that her dress, by contrast with the shawl, was singularly unremarkable: plain fabric and dark of colour, it might almost have been the one she had been wearing when they met near the kennels at Pentridge.

She saw his look and for a moment her grey eyes sparked then she sighed. 'I have others of much better quality provided by my employer, but I thought this least likely to attract attention. Although the shawl definitely spoils that intention.' Her lips lifted. 'It is so lovely I could not resist bringing it.'

More questions rushed into Dob's head. 'Your employer? He provides well for you but allows you to come to the Park alone? Wouldn't your parents be worried about that?'

'She,' came the quiet reply. 'My employer is a Lady. And I have no parents and have had none since I was a baby.'

'But you were living with your parents at Pentridge.' Dob was puzzled. 'Your father is a clerk there, I recall.' He almost smiled at the pile of account books; then he remembered something else. 'He was ill. I trust he is now improved?'

She shook her head. 'Mr and Mrs Smith, although I share their name, were not my parents. They were my foster-parents.'

He took that in. 'Were?'

'Mrs Smith had ailed for some while. When Mr Smith succumbed to the congestion in his lungs his wife simply gave up and followed him.'

Dob frowned at the quiet statement of such drastic news – and such a short time ago, he realised: she must have left Pentridge virtually immediately. A dark thought came to him. 'Joey talked of Mills the steward playing merry hell,' Dob said slowly. 'I don't imagine the man was very sympathetic to such a terrible turn of events.'

'No,' she said shortly.

'But you were fortunate, at least, to have employment waiting for you here in London.'

Another suspicion formed as she hesitated, but then she said firmly, 'I am *most* fortunate in my employment.' She got to her feet. 'You must be getting chilled and I should return. My Lady will need me.'

'I'll escort you.' Dob had also risen.

She shook her head emphatically. 'It's not far. Moreover,'

she added with the ghost of a smile that lit her grey eyes, 'I already have an escort.'

Dob looked around; as far as he could see, the Park was still deserted.

Then she raised her hand and a figure appeared from a small copse.

As he drew closer, Dob could see that the youth was inspecting him closely; then the hostile stare faded a little and the patched coat was allowed to fall over what was undoubtedly a butcher's knife.

'Peter'll accompany me,' said Miss Smith.

'And *you* can collect that cove from the taproom in the Star,' said Peter. 'Like you always does.'

Dob frowned. Had he not escaped the Earl's surveillance after all? 'Who set you to spy on us?' he demanded.

Peter tilted his head on one side considering his answer. He nodded at the young woman. 'I only watches out for Miss Callie,' he said. 'I don't know nothing about spying for anyone.'

Dob hoped he could believe it.

'And I'll see her home now,' the lad added darkly, 'like I always does.'

Dob took the hint. 'I'll leave you in Peter's safe hands then,' he addressed Miss Smith (Miss *Callie* Smith). 'But do I gather you frequent the Park? I go running here every morning.' He glanced at Peter who gave a faint nod of confirmation. 'Early, before other people are around – most other people,' he corrected with a wry smile. 'I like the exercise and I like to be on my own for a while. As,' he continued, 'I might presume you do.'

She said nothing.

'Has our meeting this morning spoiled that?' he inquired.

The lad was scowling at him again.

'The ducks were comical, weren't they?' she said. 'And Lady always said laughter is better shared.'

And Dob had to make do with that enigmatic answer.

23

Dob had worked out several runs to different parts of the Park and varied them mainly according to how he felt. Weather was never a consideration (as it had rarely been at school); in fact, the harder the challenge the better Dob liked it. This general rule still applied, with more circuits at greater speed easing (somewhat) moods of increased frustration, but very soon they all had a very definite ending point.

The morning after their first encounter he had looked for her at the same bench by the lakeside, but she was not there. He felt unreasonably disappointed and set off for another, harder, run. A few days later, he spotted her in a different location, standing beside a tree and studying its bare branches.

Easing his pace, Dob looked around for her watch-dog and made out Peter not far away. Dob slowed a little more and wondered whether to interrupt her. Why should he spoil her moments of peace? And he recalled the butcher's knife. He had no doubt, somehow, that Peter knew how to use it – but in what circumstances would he do so? Dob judged that with a rapier he would have more than an evens chance of disarming the lad, but he carried no weapon. His boxing skills offered more hope – he had persuaded the master to show him a number of tricks that a "true gentlemen" would never actually lower himself to use.

For heaven's sake! Invasion of someone's solitude was hardly a *casus belli* – what was he thinking?

As he came almost to a stop, she solved the dilemma for

him by calling out a polite greeting. Still, he needed to ask: 'Do you mind if I join you? Do tell me to go away if I am disturbing you.' He could sense Peter poised to spring like one of Pidcock's tigers in the Exeter Exchange on the Strand.

'No,' she replied. 'I was about to start back.' She gestured at the steam rising from him. 'If we walk together you will not cool down too quickly, I believe.' Her grey eyes danced with merriment. 'Like a race-horse!'

It was an almost exact analogy, but this mundane fact did not stop him from grinning back.

And he was sure, when he tried afterwards to remember what they had talked about on the short walk which followed, that the subjects had been hardly less commonplace but just as enjoyable.

From then on, they always set a meeting place for the following day with the understanding that either of them might not be there, prevented by some other commitment. Most mornings, however, they did rendezvous with enough time left from their separate allocations for conversation.

It was plain from the start that neither wished to spoil the interlude of diversion from the serious worries of life and the exchanges were, by implicit agreement, deliberately kept light-hearted – often about some recent event in the seething capital that they had either seen or heard about; or, as spring progressed, about the changes in the Park.

Dob introduced some anecdotes from his school days (and marvelled at how they now seemed like ancient history) but did not expand on the family circumstances behind his being there. Nor did he ever make more than a passing reference to the current circumstances that filled most of his other waking hours (and some of his dreaming ones) although he guessed Callie (as he had come to think of and call her – without her objection) must know something of the proposed match.

In return she described tales of life on the Pentridge estate that the Family in the Hall would never see – the everyday work of the countryside and those who laboured at it, the knowledge and craftsmanship, the cropping and the husbandry, the harvests and feasts. She made scant mention of the back-breaking travail that even Dob knew lay behind it all. She made no mention at all of Mills the steward and not much of her foster-parents. She had a talent for describing people and happenings, animated but without mockery, that brought them alive to his inner eye.

Sometimes she talked with enthusiasm about the latest book or play that she was reading to her Ladyship. Dob listened intrigued, although he could contribute little, Bromby having been almost exclusively concerned with ancient Greek or Roman writers.

He remembered her facility with figures. Had all *her* education come from her foster-parents? He could not imagine it and yet the tacit contract forbade him from asking.

24

It had started with the Earl's father – long before he had come by the title. At the time he had been plain Joshua Roberts, gentleman (in some sense of the word), owner of Pircombe Manor, a decidedly small seigniorial property, equidistant from Gloucester and Bristol. The house (or its original buildings) might very well be of an age with nearby Berkeley Castle, but it shared none of the fortress's great historic significance and fascination; and simple Mr Roberts never imagined for one moment that he might claim a rank equal to that of Berkeley's incumbent.

However, the complicated English mill of titles and inheritance which ground slow and exceedingly small finally produced a parchment (no less) declaring that Joshua Roberts was heir to the dormant Earldom of Pentridge and also to the lower ranked Viscountcy of Kelton. There followed (in less bold letters) a tortuous exposition of the lineage, reading rather like something from the Old Testament. Below that, some less-than skilled artist had illustrated the coats of arms. A note on ordinary paper, however, delivered with this document, added the deflating information that neither title was associated with entailed estates. In plain language, the penman explained, there was no property, no lands, no commercial value whatsoever attached to the titles.

Moreover, Joshua soon learned that some Earldoms carried more weight than others – the Earldom of Berkeley, for instance, was much older than the Earldom of Pentridge and therefore infinitely more senior. Additionally, it turned out that Pentridge, for which the Earldom had been named, was little more than a stretch of northern moorland (and Kelton a hamlet with a single turf-topped dwelling) which had been, for a short time, of some strategic importance to an embattled sovereign.

Joshua almost wondered whether to bother with the title, before recognising that even with no financial value of its own, it might, after all, be helpful in promoting his own commercial ventures.

And as those ventures flourished, he found himself in possession of sufficient funds to purchase not only a house in London and a villa in rural Richmond (which his Countess happily made her permanent residence with their infant son, Cyrus) but an estate in L…shire with a reasonably impressive house and lands, which he promptly renamed to match his title.

Cyrus had, in the fullness of time, inherited both the landless titles and the very real property. He had also

inherited the business which had made the rise from
obscurity possible.

But times had changed and the present Earl of Pentridge
sat in deep contemplation of how that had come about and
his current plans.

In the seventeen-thirties Bristol had been the major port
in Britain for the Guinea trade. At that time some slave ships
still worked in and out of London, but most merchants in the
capital made their money from other cargoes and goods:
West Africa had become largely the concern of the marine
insurers.

It was precisely in that period that young Joshua Roberts
had devoted himself to the business. His success owed a great
deal to shrewdness and hard work but also to a dose of good
luck, an important but totally uncontrollable component of
any trade on the high seas – particularly where perishable
goods were involved. He proved to have exactly the right mix
of hard-headedness and daring. He explored all the possible
details of each venture then made unequivocal decisions on
how much to invest. He looked at which ship might carry
most cargo and be least likely to sink; which captain most
likely to command her (and her crew) and make a successful
return. He explored where the outgoing goods could be best
sourced and at what cost: the cloth, the guns and
ammunition, the ironware and trinkets, the alcohol, that
would fetch the best prices in the Guinea ports. He inquired
of all returning ships about which of those ports might
currently be able to supply the required numbers and quality
of slaves and likewise what and where in the Americas the
demand for them was greatest. He kept a very close eye on
the returning cargoes of sugar, coffee, tobacco, rum and
molasses – what their commercial value was, which way
markets might be changing.

So many factors to consider but each important in its
own way and each contributing to the whole. Joshua Roberts

had a head and an instinct for every detail. His heart was never involved, nor his conscience – both were totally irrelevant.

Within twenty years Bristol lost its top position in the slave trade to Liverpool, the latter having considerable advantages in its large anchorage and nearby burgeoning industries. Joshua Roberts seriously considered moving his operations there. But he knew everything and everybody in Bristol (or those that mattered) – it was simply a matter of making sure *he* was one of the reduced numbers of traders still financing profitable voyages.

And this remained the situation for the best part of the next three decades. Over that period Joshua ensured his son had an education fit for the scion of a noble family while also learning every necessary detail of the trade that paid for it all. He was happy to discover that Cyrus had inherited both intellect and inclination; if there was a distinct element of cunning there too, Joshua could only see that as an additional talent in the deception of the press, the *ton* and the commercial competition. Joshua lived his last years happy in the knowledge that position and wealth were in safe hands.

25

As dawn made an appearance earlier and earlier, so did Dob and Callie (and the ever-watchful Peter) – in order to keep ahead of the increasing numbers of well-dressed ladies and gentlemen who would throng the walks and lawns at a more fashionable hour as the Season got into full-swing.

Even after attending some "important" ball which only ended in the small hours of the morning, Dob insisted on coming to the Park. Sometimes, indeed, he did not even bother going to bed in between. He liked his sleep as well as the next, but he also had the reserves of healthy youth to make do without it when necessary – and running in the Park had become absolutely necessary. As, he realised, had meeting Callie.

He enjoyed keeping the meetings secret from his father in the same way he enjoyed any means of thwarting his parent's control over his life. For many weeks, however, the idea that they might be clandestine or illicit never entered his head: he was not (yet) officially affianced to Alicia and had no particular affection for her, so there were no grounds for guilt on that account. Moreover, the conduct of the encounters and the nature of the friendship with Callie was entirely "proper", Peter being a fiercer chaperon than the most formidable duenna.

One morning he suddenly found himself observing Callie as if for the first time. Afterwards he realised that this had much to do with the fact that the advancing year and warmer weather meant she was no longer swathed from head to toe. He could see the whole of her face, clear skin framed by dark hair that had escaped both pins and bonnet. Her features did not have the delicate structure so-vaunted by some of the blue-blooded; and in many ways their design was rather unremarkable. What was striking, however, was how they became animated as she talked, and how her clear grey eyes sparkled. How very different from the women he had mixed with just a few hours ago at Lady M…'s rout! In the glittering, gilded ballroom, lit by hundreds of candles, the young ones (much the same age as Callie, he would guess) had been trying to look demure and sophisticated and generally only managing to look gauche or embarrassed or both (feelings he recognised only too well!). The slightly older ones who had not "taken" in previous Seasons had been trying to cover their growing fears with aloofness. The still more mature, resigned to spinsterhood and dependence, had been supporting disappointed mamas and helping younger sisters succeed where they had failed.

Some of this he had understood for himself, some he had learned, perhaps surprisingly, from the snatched exchanges with Alicia. Wondering about *her*, he realised she was an enigma – well out of the school-room but just making her society come-out; *her* aloofness not from the usual dread of not making a good match but from being forced to act on stage a role she had no desire to play (that much he knew).

But he did not, at that moment, wish to think about Alicia – she was part of a huge problem that could be worried about at any time.

He listened to Callie's voice without taking in the words and let his eyes wander over a form now also more clearly revealed. Gone was the shawl; the drab woollen dress had given way to one of some much lighter fabric – nothing bright in print or colour, but definitely of a good stuff and, he could clearly see, skilfully cut and fitted. She had the solidness of a country-girl, but he could appreciate now that her body was slim – though it had the curves of a woman: her slender neck disappearing into the high line of the bodice, the roundness of her upper-arm, the soft swell of her breast.

In a moment of revelation, he understood what had so engrossed other boys at school and provided them with hours of wild speculation; at the time, he had nodded while having no real idea what they were talking about – or why.

Of course, he knew the facts – there had even been those flings at Branksdown last summer, but they had been half-hearted, as much at Willo's urging than any particular curiosity on his own part.

Now his body was full of excitement, of joy, of energy, of fascination and his mind felt as if someone had thrown open the shutters on a mid-summer morning – everything was illuminated, outlined with brilliant clarity.

He was transfixed by the beauty of the moment and the young woman at the centre of it.

He slowly became aware that she had stopped talking and was looking at him. On her face was amusement at his distraction but also, he was almost sure of it, a reflection of his own awareness.

26

When Cyrus took over from his father, he had few concerns about the family business.

There had been the odd crackpot diatribe against the slave trade, but the judicial ruling by the Earl of Mansfield in 1772 that slavery had no legal basis in Britain generally roused little interest in the country and made no difference whatsoever to what happened beyond its shores, on the high seas or in other lands, even those territories under British rule.

There had been the usual hair-splitting by the marine insurers: the "natural death" of a slave during the arduous Middle Passage from Guinea to the Americas they deemed an "inherent vice" (the damage or loss that might occur to any cargo) while arguing that shipboard rebellion was somehow different. Even their nit-picking precipitated by the *Zong* debacle failed to raise much public interest – at the time.

Of course, the Gregson Liverpool syndicate should never have employed such an inexperienced captain on the *Zong* in the first place. He did not have a full crew and yet loaded more than twice the usual number of slaves (losing some of them on the crossing to the Caribbean as a result). The captain and his inadequate company then failed to identify their position and sailed right past Jamaica and ended up severely short of water. The dilemma facing them was one of human survival – but also of commercial consequence. There was the obvious question of how many people the remaining water reserves could support. But what about those they could not? If the slaves died on board (or indeed on land, after arrival in a dehydrated condition) there would be no insurance pay-out. On the other hand, the "general average" principle covered the loss of any cargo that had to be jettisoned in order to save the rest. There was unanimous support for this action, unanimous that is on the part of the crew. Over the next days a hundred and forty-two African men, women and children were picked out and thrown overboard. The captain died within three days of the *Zong* putting into Black River; the ship's logbook quietly disappeared; the remaining two hundred and eight slaves were sold for an average of £36 each.

News of the events finally reached Liverpool where the owners claimed for their loss; the insurers disputed the claim; the owners went to court; the jury found in their favour; the insurers appealed.

The Earl of Mansfield was again called on to form a judicial opinion. He upheld the appeal: not because there was any legal difference between a load of cattle and one of slaves but on the grounds that there should have been no need to jettison *any* cargo. In spite of confused testimony and the loss of the ship's logbook, there was, in the Lord Chief Justice's opinion, ample evidence that the prime cause of the losses lay in errors made by the captain and the crew.

Unlike the general populace, Cyrus Roberts took a very close interest in all this. As far as he was concerned, the main lesson to be learned from it (apart from confirmation of the universal truth that insurers would always seek to avoid paying compensation), was the necessity of having a sound vessel under the command of a competent captain. The Earl of Pentridge came to the conclusion that he could best

achieve this by being entirely in charge of any venture: a
syndicate might spread the financial burden and risk, but it
also led to varied and often conflicting opinions (not to
mention sharing any returns). From then on, he acted as the
sole owner, the sole investor, the sole beneficiary. He chose
which ship to purchase; he dictated how it should be fitted
out and supplied; he appointed the captain and stipulated
what crew should be taken on; he set out in which ports the
ship should load and in which it should discharge and sell its
cargo.

For five years, business went well enough. Cyrus offset
any general decline in the trade out of Bristol by ensuring
each of *his* voyages was completed as fast as possible. Quicker
turnaround enabled a greater amount of cargo to be carried
but also, very importantly, meant that bills of exchange (the
form in which slaves were paid for) were remitted sooner.
The voyage of one rival, the Earl learned with contempt, had
taken thirty-one months. *His* captains knew they were
expected to return to their home port within ten.

However, Cyrus was a lot less happy with the growing
number of sentimental voices being raised against the slave
trade: the *Zong* business had not, after all, gone completely
unnoticed. In particular the mealy-mouthed Quakers had
taken up the matter and made a number of important recruits
to their "cause". Josiah Wedgwood had made and donated
hundreds of ceramic medallions depicting the seal of the
newly established Society for the Abolition of the Slave
Trade. This portrayed, in black on a white ground, an African
in chains on one knee, his hands raised in supplication,
arching over him the words "Am I not a Man and Brother".
In no time, it seemed to the Earl, this maudlin image (and its
nonsensical caption) was adopted by women who knew
nothing of the real facts and was being sported on bracelet or
hairpin.

Of more serious concern to the Earl were the regular Anglicans who joined the Society for they, unlike the Quakers and other non-conformists, could be elected to Parliament. Before long Sir William Dolben (member for Oxford University for heaven's sake!) was leading a group of fellow MPs aboard a slaver moored on the Thames to see conditions for themselves; then leading through Parliament an Act to Regulate the Slave Trade. Its main point was to restrict the number of slaves that could be carried in any ship (relative to its tonnage); the argument being that overcrowding was the main cause of poor sanitation, inadequate food, illness and hence mortality.

The Earl seethed at the lack of understanding; like Lord Penrhyn (one of the MPs for Liverpool) he knew that captains had every reason to deliver as many slaves as possible alive and in good condition, so as to maximise sales and prices.

He was even more incensed when the Plymouth chapter of the meddlesome Society published an engraving of a slaver called the *Brookes*. It showed in minute detail how four hundred and fifty-four slaves might be stowed aboard by allowing each man a space of six feet, each woman five feet ten inches and each child one foot two inches. Before Dolben's Act the poster declared, the *Brookes* had carried as many as six hundred and nine slaves.

The Earl's first thought was of the financial loss that difference represented: up to one hundred and fifty-five units at anything up to £50 for a prime specimen – a drop of 25% in the expected profits for each voyage. Then he looked more closely at the accursed picture and grew even angrier. The artist had taken infinite care to portray each black body, but other particulars were erroneous – not least the absurd absence of any storage space for water and provisions!

The general public, however, in its gullibility, was

convinced.

Sentimental feelings had been aroused and continued to grow. There was increasing support not just for the regulation of the trade but for its abolition.

William Wilberforce, another of Pitt's cronies, tried to achieve this, introducing bills into Parliament with the persistence of a dog gnawing a bone.

On the first occasion, to the Earl's satisfaction, the bill was heavily defeated – largely due to the true nature of the "Sons of Africa" being revealed in the violent revolts in French St Domingue (themselves a reflection and fitting consequence of the bloody revolution just across the Channel).

The second time, an even larger majority voted for the counter-proposal put by Henry Dundas for "gradual abolition" – this, the Earl recognised with some relief, was a thinly-disguised ploy to postpone the matter indefinitely. However, less than a year later Wilberforce made yet another attempt which was only narrowly defeated.

Soon thereafter, the attention of politicians, press and populace was fortuitously diverted by the declaration of war between Britain and France.

A war could be disruptive to trade, but it often also provided commercial opportunities; on balance the Earl could not regard it as a bad thing. His main concern was how long the conflict might last.

27

The only mistaken investment the Earl ever made was, unfortunately, a serious one: he allowed himself to be beguiled by the appearance of a lovely woman. She had first caught his attention as a possible Countess because of her connections (albeit not quite direct) with the Berkeleys, the oldest family in the county if not the whole country. Joshua had liked his title for its commercial benefit; while recognising the reality of this, Cyrus also valued, very much, the social standing and influence it accorded. He would take for himself a bride of impeccable pedigree and breed on her a dynasty of truly aristocratic Pentridges.

It was always clear that the lady in question would bring no financial gain, but at the time the slaving ventures were making a very good return and seemed to guarantee more than enough to maintain a noble lifestyle. Perhaps, an older Earl now reflected, he had been overconfident in that; perhaps he had allowed himself to be so.

Even her name, Hesperia, appeared the perfect Classical match to his own – although soon enough its pretentiousness came to irritate him, as did many other things about her. However, on their first meeting he thought her everything that a noblewoman should be: elegant, graceful, well-mannered, impeccably groomed and dressed, educated in all the desirable feminine arts (and in none of those that were rightfully the concern of men). In addition, she was quite simply beautiful: her hair was so fair it gleamed silver; its lustre framed a fine-boned face with neat chin and nose. China blue eyes gazed passively out of a flawless complexion. Fine, white hands lay quiet on the lap of her silk dress; soft leather slippers peeped out from beneath its flounced hem.

The enchantment lasted through the months of their continental honeymoon, the news that she was *enceinte* and the birth of a healthy son and heir. Her feeble protests against the immediate need to beget "a spare" (or more) irritated Cyrus a little but were easy enough to ignore – he simply insisted on his rights and was content when she was once more increasing.

Quite when her stupid superstitions began to take hold, he was unsure. Had she already begun to fill her head with such balderdash before the second pregnancy? And how she had come to learn that nonsense about the supposed curse on Pentridge Hall, he never discovered. It was possible the journey had been unwise, but Cyrus was sure the main cause of the miscarriage was his wife's wilful melancholia. As it turned out the child was only a girl; of far greater import was the consequence that the Countess could have no more children.

After his initial rage subsided into an enduring state of bitter recrimination, Cyrus took stock of the situation. Of course, he had always intended the best for his heir, but now it was apparent that young Darius would be the sole heir, the matter of his education and upbringing became even more important.

Naturally the Earl looked to the usual form followed by aristocratic families: designed to provide the proper learning for a young nobleman and to confirm the essential elite network. In the early years this meant private tutors; later there might be a few years at one or other of the public schools, followed by attendance at either Oxford or Cambridge; and finally, the Grand Tour. Cyrus's own education had involved a series of tutors supplemented heavily by lessons in trade and mercantile investment from his father. His patrician connections had largely been forged through hunting parties at Pentridge. And, in effect, his honeymoon had been his Grand Tour. He was determined that Darius's upbringing should be entirely *comme il faut*; (certainly free of the slightest commercial taint).

The problem was that the young Viscount Kelton was wilful. He learned his lessons from a series of hapless teachers (without much difficulty but equally without much enthusiasm) then somehow always contrived to "escape" – through an attic window at night, by boat onto the river, over the high wall of the villa's garden.

The more the Earl tried to bring the boy to heel, the more Darius defied him.

Then the Earl heard about the principles of Mr Jenkerson and how they were put into practice at Bromby Manor. Further investigation persuaded the Earl it would be just the regime for his wayward heir.

A look at the school roll provided the final argument: almost exclusively the sons of leading peers.

He was never sure why he dug out the tawdry heraldic parchment with its pronouncement that Joshua Roberts was found to be the true heir to the Earldom of Pentridge, but as he went through the long list of names providing the tortuous proof of relationship, he wished he had studied it sooner. A peer might have a number of titles as well as his own baptised and family name.

This had almost obscured one name that now struck Cyrus forcibly.

And demanded immediate investigation.

28

Callie enjoyed reading to Lady Olivia, whatever the book, play or poem. She appreciated adding to her knowledge of the "classical" works but also enjoyed the more fanciful tales such as those by Ann Radcliffe whose Romance of the Forest was her Ladyship's current choice.

Nevertheless, she wanted more.

One book at a time, out loud, was too slow. And she knew there must be so many different things to read about.

Now she stood and looked at the packed bookcases of the Uppworth House library and did not know where to start.

As she moved from one shelf to another, one wall to another, there were so many enticing covers and titles. She lifted out several and turned the pages, thinking to scan the contents so she could make a decision, but each time her attention was caught and she found herself reading a whole chapter before remembering her purpose and taking up another volume.

'Spoiled for choice?' The question made her jump.

She had been so engrossed in her quest that she had not heard the door open.

At a gesture from the Duke, his man Hibbs pushed the chair into the room before withdrawing.

Callie somewhat belatedly dropped a respectful curtsey and began to make an apology.

'For what?' came the mild inquiry. 'You have permission to use the library, do you not?'

She bowed her head in acknowledgment. 'But I had no wish to interfere with your Grace's use of it. I thought it would be empty at this hour.' She glanced at the clock on the mantel and her eyes widened.

'Time can pass much faster than you think, can it not, when one is absorbed?' The Duke smiled.

She nodded.

'Should you be elsewhere?' he inquired.

'Not just yet,' she replied with relief.

'Then let us see if I can help you decide where to start.' He waved a hand around the walls. 'These are only part of the Uppworth collection; the library at Uppworth Park contains many more, acquired over the centuries by various ancestors.' He smiled wryly. 'Including, I suspect, a considerable number mainly for their impressive exteriors! Be that as it may, these are the works I wish to have to hand here in London, arranged to my order.'

Callie had not discerned any particular order – but then she knew more about bookkeeping than the disposition of library books.

Perhaps his Grace saw her scepticism for he said, 'Believe it or not, there *is* method in their arrangement.' He gestured upwards. 'On the top shelves are the books I have read but do not imagine reading again very soon. On the middle shelves are those I plan to return to. On the lower shelves – in immediate reach – are books currently in use or waiting to be read. Within those three broad categories there is some sorting by subject and author, but,' he gave an almost apologetic smile, 'I know where everything is and generally, I am the only person who needs to know.'

Of course, when he explained it, it made complete sense. As a Duke he need never be short of someone to give him the assistance he needed in so many things, but this was one way in which he could secure a small measure of independence.

'So,' he continued, 'I know where any book is located, but that does not help your problem, does it? – where to start.'

Callie smiled ruefully. 'No, your Grace.'

He frowned slightly. 'Do you have any idea what would interest you?'

'Anything; everything,' Callie said honestly.

'Fiction? History? Philosophy? Politics?'

Callie looked around helplessly.

He considered. 'I believe I know what my sister-in-law likes, and therefore what you are reading with her. I imagine you are looking for something else?'

Callie nodded. That did not seem to narrow the field very much.

'Do you enjoy your daily walk in the Park, by the way?' he asked.

The image that came immediately into Callie's mind was not of grass or trees but of fair hair dampened from running.

However, before she could even begin to wonder if the Duke knew of their meetings, he continued, 'Is it enough to make the rest of city life bearable?'

'Quite enough,' she said firmly. 'I have no wish to be anywhere else,' she said truthfully.

He nodded as if satisfied with the answer then manoeuvred his chair so he could reach a book. 'I wonder if this might interest you. Moral philosophy I suppose you might call it, though in relation to very real financial matters. Not light reading, more a challenge to a questing and sharp mind.'

Callie stared. She knew that although she was ignorant of many things, she was not stupid. But was the Duke right? Did she have a sharp mind?

'Of course, it is just a suggestion. You can choose something else.'

Callie rose straight to the bait. 'Thank you, your Grace; I am sure it will do very well.' She took the book and only then looked at the title page:

AN

INQUIRY

INTO THE

Nature and Causes

OF THE

WEALTH OF NATIONS.

By ADAM SMITH, LL.D and F.R.S.

'It took him years to formulate his ideas. He published the first volume,' he indicated the book, 'just before Sophie was born.'

A couple of years before Callie. 'Is he still alive?'

'He died six years ago; after,' the Duke added dryly, 'finishing four more.' He waved a hand. 'They are all there – *if* you find yourself interested.'

Callie was already turning the pages of the one she was holding. She could see it was a far cry from a Gothic romance or Shakespearean play. Well, she had wanted something different! And she suddenly wanted to test her mind; she could hardly wait to get started.

But wait she must: she had to get back to her Ladyship.

She closed the book and prepared to take her leave.

His Grace had picked out another book. 'The author of this has just died; there was a notice in yesterday's newspaper.' He lifted the volume. 'A most interesting fellow with a most interesting life.' He opened the cover and offered her a look. 'See.'

"*The Interesting Narrative of the Life of Olaudah Equiano, Or Gustavus Vass, The African.*" The title was arranged around the medallion of a man with a black face.

'I read it when it first came out, eight years ago, but would like to read it again. He will be sorely missed by The Sons of Africa.'

Callie had been astonished by her first sight of an African in London, but Peter had said there were plenty of others – the poor ones on the streets and others in employment, many as novelty servants.

His Grace peered at her. 'When you read about Adam Smith's ideas on creating wealth perhaps you might ask yourself about trading in human beings.'

Callie was not sure why he should put that in; there were going to be hundreds of other things she would surely be asking herself.

She nodded, however, before saying, 'I must go to her Ladyship now.'

'Of course,' he said. 'But I would like to hear your reaction to the book sometime, if I may.'

She thought that behind the polite remark was a sincere wish.

She made a low curtsey and hurried away with the book tucked safely in her pocket.

29

A date was set to advertise the engagement.

There would be a notice in The Times and a handful of the other better-quality publications, of course, but also a grand ball to celebrate the event. The house being rented by the Baron in St James's Square was not as imposing as its near neighbour, Norfolk House, but it did boast a ballroom in the Palladian style sufficiently impressive for the occasion.

The Earl and the Baron were agreed every detail should be correct – from the list of essential invitees to the décor; from the refreshments to the musicians; from the wines to be served to the livery of the footmen.

Dob racked his brains harder than ever for a way out. Alicia, somewhat surprisingly, seemed less concerned. In a quiet aside during a concert she pointed out that officially betrothed couples could quite properly claim private converse.

The elaborate preparations proceeded. Dob's days were packed with appointments; his evenings with all the right social events; his nights with too little sleep, and that often interrupted – either by nightmares where he saw himself as a bowhead whale surrounded by boats full of hunters, intent on capturing him with their harpoons; or, almost as tormenting, by dreams of Callie Smith.

Sometimes he simply could not make it to the Park; on a few occasions, she was not there. Either case Dob found devastating: instead of being in tumultuous northern seas full of icebergs, he pictured himself in an African desert, a burning landscape of sand and rock, desperate for a single drop of water to drink. And he berated himself for being a sentimental fool.

Then the next time they met, all seemed well with the world – a tiny, enclosed world of their own.

For a while their previously easy conversation had become a little stilted by self-consciousness, but that passed; sometimes they were both content to sit in silence, their joined hands sufficient communion.

They rarely made any reference to their separate everyday lives, but Dob felt he had to mention the forthcoming announcement: Callie must surely see it in one of the newspapers.

'And,' he said in despair, 'I don't see any escape. Not so much from Lady Alicia,' he continued. 'I don't find her unbearable. Indeed, I hardly know her well enough to find her anything! But all my life, my father has tried to manipulate me, force me into a plan of his making. This is a tyranny too far! And I know that Alicia's heart lies elsewhere.' He squeezed the hand he was holding in an inadequate expression of the emotion that had been growing but had never, until then, been allowed articulation, even to himself. 'As does mine.' He lifted her hand. 'I have thought of taking ship for America. I am young and strong. I could manage there, somehow.' He warmed to his theme describing what he had heard about life in the now independent colonies.

He drew to a halt as he realised Callie was silent.

There were tears in her eyes as she drew their joined hands to her lips.

'Come with me!' The words burst from him. 'In Scotland we could marry, you and I,' he said desperately. 'Then sail together from there.'

For one wild moment he thought the bowing of her head was agreement, then she resolutely lowered their hands to the bench.

'I believe my heart is as much yours,' she said softly, 'but,' she drew a breath, 'there are others who have a place there too.'

He peered at her.

'I could not leave Lady Olivia,' she said simply. 'Perhaps if we had had this conversation two days ago, I might have been tempted to agree, but we went to see Doctor Parkinson.'

He stared.

'He has an interest in the palsy that affects Lady Olivia; he has looked at a number of cases and begun to make a detailed study. He questioned and examined Lady Olivia very thoroughly. He declared with regret that so far, he has found nothing to suggest the condition might be cured or even halted.'

'So, she must have good nursing care,' said Dob a little impatiently, 'but that does not need to be from you, does it?'

'Lady Olivia,' she continued, 'asked him to describe exactly how the illness will progress. He was reluctant to do so, but she insisted: she wished to know what she must prepare herself for. When he saw that she really meant it, he did exactly as she requested.' She paused. 'Lady Olivia was quiet for a few moments then she said, "Thank you." Thank you!' Callie sniffed impatiently. 'How could I possibly consider abandoning her?'

They both lapsed into silence.

It was Peter, like Chaucer's Clerk, who reminded them that time waited for no one. He was advancing from his chosen post, glaring at their still joined hands.

Dob reluctantly disengaged his fingers.

He felt deflated, hopeless. 'Can we still continue to meet?' he begged. 'Please.'

Callie chewed her lip for a moment. 'I cannot change my mind,' she said quietly. 'I think it would be best if we don't. I will go to another park.'

She brushed impatiently at her cheek.

Peter arrived and gave Dob a ferocious scowl.

The Earl declared the ball a success: everything had passed off exactly as he had ordered – well almost exactly. His wife, commanded to leave the Richmond villa and comport herself in a becoming manner, had not quite shown the gracious radiance he would have liked, but she had managed a well-mannered dignity – there had been no repeat of the ridiculous outburst of Christmas. His son, immaculately dressed and presented, was undeniably handsome, his silver-blond head standing out from the crowd; and if his blue eyes lacked lustre then that was a welcome improvement on the glittering defiance that had been too often apparent.

Lady Alicia Tentham was impeccably turned out in a gown of moss green watered silk, as aloof as ever – the picture of the superior aristocrat, to the Earl's mind. And on her hand, she wore the betrothal ring presented by Dob at the earlier family gathering in the drawing room. The Pentridges had no family heirlooms so the ring was newly made, the brilliance (and cost) of its diamonds and emeralds sufficient to cover its lack of antiquity.

The Earl was smug in the knowledge that a perfectly matching necklace and earrings were being fashioned by the same exclusive jeweller, ready for the wedding – and that the hefty price for the set would be soon enough more than offset by the bride's dowry.

The Grand Plan was well on its way to succeeding.

For Dob, the event passed in a blur: he managed (mostly) to bury his misery in the effort of smiling, keeping up the small talk, recalling the names of the preened and pomaded guests, remembering the steps and patterns of the dances – and avoiding the strong temptation to drink himself into forgetfulness.

Forgetting himself, however, would be a dangerous indulgence: likely to destroy any last hope of thwarting his father's plans.

30

By one of Fate's ironies, the ball to mark Sophie's official
come-out took place on the same evening as the betrothal
"celebration" in St James's Square. This did not, however,
cause a conflict for any of the guests invited to either, since
there was no overlap whatsoever.

Uppworth House was not as grand or ornate as the leased
mansion in St James's (certainly nowhere near as magnificent
as Norfolk's) and from the outside only those decorative
columns marked it out in any way from its Grosvenor Square
neighbours. Nevertheless, to Callie's mind at least, it was
perfect in its deceptively simple good taste. Inside its
ballroom might lack size but its proportions were perfect, its
decor the height of classical elegance. The colour scheme of
the walls and furnishings was emphatic but did not obtrude.
The guests were the focus of any assembly there – they did
not have to compete with heavy gilt or over-intricate
plasterwork, with swathes of exotic flowers, with tables
overladen with crystal and silverware and fancy dishes. They
were received by the Duke and Lady Olivia with a genuine
warmth that made the hosts' respective disabilities almost
unnoticed.

The members of staff, in their own way, were welcoming
too. They were carefully presentable but not overdressed. All
(including the extras recruited for the event) had been
rehearsed in their tasks in taking cloaks, offering drinks and
other practical duties, but above all they were to be constantly
alert for any way that they might be helpful – in finding a
convenient seat for an older guest; in fetching a specially
requested refreshment; in ensuring that the fires at either end
were kept made-up but not over-hot (just enough to counter
the evening chill); that guttering candles were instantly
trimmed, spent ones replaced; that floor powder was ready

for use on any part of the tightly-fitting narrow oak planking that might become exposed during the evening.

Both the polished marble tiles of the hall and the shining boards at the edges of most of the rooms were beautiful to see but presented a real and constant danger for Lady Olivia (quite apart from the edges of carpets or mats). It was Sophie who had watched the string players preparing their bows at a concert and had an idea.

Mrs Ballance, justifiably proud of the gleaming floors in her charge, had been reluctant to divulge the ingredients of the polish that was made and applied to her specification and even less keen to make any change to it – a change that she saw as a criticism of her good housekeeping.

However, Lady Olivia managed to convince Mrs Ballance that her previous zeal was not in question and that her cooperation in the experiment would be greatly appreciated. It turned out that the floor polish was a careful blend of Fuller's earth and beeswax, scented with mint and tansy. Rubbing it regularly into the boards preserved the wood, kept up its deep gleam and made the rooms smell sweet.

Mrs Ballance was house-proud, but she also cared deeply for Lady Olivia and finally agreed to try something that might make the floors less of a hazard – but only if *she* had sole charge of experimenting with how fine to grind the rosin and how much to add. She was deservedly proud of the result and guarded the new recipe as fiercely as she had the old.

Lady Olivia had fulfilled her resolve to see Sophie properly presented: with Callie's constant attendance and help (not to mention enthusiastic comments and suggestions), aunt and niece had spent many days (and a considerable sum of money) in choosing and ordering exactly the right dress and accessories. The initial research had been done at home by leafing through the more recent editions in Lady Olivia's collection of the sixpenny monthly *Lady's Magazine* (or

Entertaining Companion for the Fair Sex, Appropriated Solely to Their Use and Amusement).

The articles on recent books, music and biography were of interest to all of them, but for their particular purpose they poured over the illustrations of the latest fashions and picked over the details regarding fabric, colour and trimmings. It was quite clear that the pinched silhouette achieved through fierce whale-boned corseting had gone, with the waistline moving ever higher. The full skirts, elevated and sometimes held very wide by hoop petticoats had given way to slimmer lines with gentle gathers over small crescent-shaped pads. Moreover, heavy brocade had been replaced by finer striped silks or printed cottons worn over a quilted linen "waistcoat". The resulting gown was altogether lighter to wear and dance in.

For the spring, the magazine suggested yellows and greens and Sophie chose a fabric sprigged with a small flower design in those colours. The neckline was low enough to show off her clear skin but prevented from being immodest by a trim of finest Honiton lace (Continental lace being almost impossible to come by on account of the war). More lace edged the skirt and the short sleeves. Long gloves and dancing slippers were in matching leaf-green. The hair around her face had been trimmed so that it could be tonged into curls but otherwise hung in ringlets secured at the back of her head by a wide silk ribbon of golden yellow.

The finishing touch was a single strand of matched pearls given to her by the Duke.

During the first weeks of the Season, Sophie had driven in the Park in the Uppworth carriage, had taken tea at the homes of several other young women also about to be launched and attended a few carefully chosen *soirées* and music evenings. While being impatient for her very own ball, she had been thrilled by these novel social occasions. More particularly, it had become apparent that the application of rosin was not the only thing she found interesting about string players – or one player to be precise. She begged to attend a second concert by a specific group and while she listened intently to the whole programme, it was quite clear to Lady Olivia that her niece had eyes only for the cellist.

Her Ladyship's suspicions were confirmed when Sophie over-casually suggested that that group should be engaged for *her* ball. Lady Olivia agreed to investigate – and immediately dictated to Callie a great many notes making inquiries that had nothing to do with musical skill or recital availability.

She discovered easily enough that the cellist was James Millburn, the Honourable James Millburn in fact, a younger son of the Viscount Millburn of Millburn St Andrews in the county of D .... James had originally been, as was common for a third son, earmarked for the Church. He had, however, shown himself a talented musician on both the cello and pianoforte and when he went off to begin theology studies, he proved a great deal more devoted to the organ in the college chapel than to the spiritual content of the worship taking place there. After just two terms, he had concluded that he was much more suited to being a musician than a clergyman. He had left Oxford for London's manifold theatres, mansions, gardens and salons where he had established a growing reputation. He was, Lady Olivia had been reliably advised, neither married nor engaged. While being an essential piece of information this did not answer a question of equal importance, namely the possible reason for his marital state. In a word, what was the extent of his means?

This crucial matter quite clearly needed to be discussed with the Duke even though any *liaison*, Lady Olivia admitted to Callie, was entirely hypothetical at this point.

Callie was not present at the discussion, but whatever was said led to another letter inviting the group to perform at Uppworth House. Sophie's excitement knew no bounds when an affirmative reply was received.

31

While the general tenor of the event was less formal than many other similar functions, nevertheless orthodoxy prevailed: the musicians were employees for the evening and would not mix socially with either their employers or the guests.

But that did not prevent Sophie, accompanied by one of the footmen, from playing the gracious hostess. She greeted the quartet, thanked them for coming and assured them that if there was anything at all they needed during the evening, they should not hesitate to ask the footman. With just the smallest of hesitations, she went on to deliver the carefully phrased speech that she had composed and rehearsed: she played the pianoforte herself; she very much liked the works of Mr Haydn and was currently working on some of his compositions with her tutor.

The musicians were, naturally, familiar with all Mr Haydn's available works. Which piece, the leader inquired politely, was Sophie's favourite.

She thought she managed not to blush, nor to let her eyes wander as she named it: the piece was, of course, for cello and pianoforte.

The violinist did not even consult the cellist but responded immediately that they would be more than happy to include the piece in the *tafelmusik* scheduled for the supper interval. He himself would perform the keyboard part on the piano in the connecting music room.

Sophie had known this would be the most likely outcome of her scheme and was prepared to accept it as second best, but she still hoped for more.

The instrument was, as she was sure he had noticed, from Garcka's manufactory.

One of the talented "Twelve Apostles", commented the violinist with approval.

Newly tuned, Sophie stated, with a gesture towards the square instrument of mahogany with decorative satinwood inlay. And the three pedals for buff, damper lift and swell in perfect working order, she added.

Was she as familiar with the Haydn concerto as she obviously was with the fortepiano?

The cellist's inquiry held amusement but, thought Sophie, also a genuine interest. She replied firmly that she was – and tried to conceal her glee when the cellist wondered then if *she* might like to play it with him? After all, added James Millburn with a smile that sent a shiver down her spine, the evening was being held in her honour, was it not?

With a shiver of a different kind, Sophie wondered if she might just have set a trap for her own humiliation and downfall.

With that most important goal achieved, Sophie set out to enjoy the first part of the evening to the full. The mix of excitement and apprehension made the skin on her arms rise in gooseflesh whenever she thought of what was to come, but mostly she managed, fairly successfully, to bury it under the pleasure of being feted and courted and partnered.

There were long-standing acquaintances and distant relations of her family, "old" school friends with a scattering of single brothers, chosen members of the *ton* with eligible sons.

The last dance before the interval was a lively one and Sophie found herself flushed and somewhat winded.

'We have recently come by one of Mr Handel's lesser-known compositions from Mr Granville Sharp's collection. If we play that while everyone gets arranged, it will give you a chance to catch your breath,' James Millburn put to her.

Sophie managed a grateful thanks with only the hint of a gasp and by the time the piece came to an end she was seated at the pianoforte with her hands almost steady and her pulse only racing a little.

James Millburn adjusted his chair and his cello. His dark eyes were warm with encouragement for a moment, then he was all professional. The routine of tuning calmed Sophie further. She was able to ignore everyone else, the movement as the last guests settled into their seats, the murmur of voices. She concentrated on the music and the playing – anything else could wait.

They nodded their readiness to each other and commenced the piece.

The familiarity of the music carried Sophie through the moments of nervousness until she was able to play with her accustomed ease. She felt the usual enjoyment steal over her – enjoyment of her ability, enjoyment of Haydn's composition, enjoyment of the interweaving sounds: the throaty bowed notes of the cello counterposing the piano's hammered complexity.

They reached the end of the first movement and it seemed perfectly natural to go into the second then the third.

The final notes faded into an appreciative silence, eventually broken by a collective sigh and applause.

It was deserved. James Millburn was a consummate player, but Sophie knew she had not disgraced herself. She beamed happily at the audience as she acknowledged their approval; she turned a slightly more self-conscious smile on her partner.

'Thank you so much,' she said to him.

'Thank *you*,' he responded. 'It was a pleasure to perform with such a genuinely able player.'

Her heart fluttered – she had not turned out to be the deluded young miss he must have feared.

'Indeed,' he added softly, 'I should very much enjoy doing so again – if it is not impertinent of me to suggest it.'

For Sophie, the rest of the evening passed in a cloud of pure bliss, and she found it hard not to giggle like a schoolgirl every time the word "impertinent" came to her.

32

Callie enjoyed the evening very much. She stood close enough to Lady Olivia to provide help when needed whilst keeping a tactful distance. Her gown had also been made specially for the occasion; of a muted colour and simple design, it explained exactly to those attending who she was and why she was there: she was a servant, albeit one of superior status, but at nobody's beck except Lady Olivia's; the plain declaration would save everyone from possible misunderstanding and embarrassment.

The dress allowed her to fade into the background just as a sparrow's plumage made the bird almost impossible to spot in a bush. It was as if she could survey the whole room and those in it from a private spyhole, she reflected, as she took in the scene. Being beside her ladyship and his grace when they welcomed the guests, she had heard each name and recalled it as one marchioness bent her head in gossip to a countess; as one young viscount begged a dance from a young lady; as two honourable gentlemen took themselves off to the adjoining card room.

She recognised most of the dances and watched with approval as the sets moved and flowed, the dainty dresses of the ladies contrasting with the dark superfine evening clothes of the gentlemen, the coloured slippers and the dancing pumps treading out the measures lightly (and securely!).

She listened with pleasure to the string quartet and was delighted that the duet Sophie had contrived with the cellist went so well.

She really did not mind being a bystander. She did not resent her position. It did not bother her that she would never be the one dressed to perfection being presented to the *haut monde*. During the whole time she had lived in Wicklow, the magnificent ballroom there had its shutters closed and its furnishings shrouded in Holland cloth. No by-blow of the Marquess could ever expect to see it otherwise.

Callie was in attendance as the guests took their leave. Sophie was understandably euphoric with the success of the event and her personal ploy; she whispered in an aside that she wished the evening could go on forever.

Lady Olivia smiled at her indulgently, but Callie could tell that her ladyship was tired. She hoped her employer was not *too* tired for then she would not get the sleep she so obviously needed.

Indeed, it took some time for her ladyship to settle and in the morning, she announced that she would have a lie in. She would send for Callie in due course.

Callie had told Peter Giblin not to expect her after such a late night, but he had evidently been looking out for her. 'Fancy a walk after all?' he inquired.

She shook her head. 'Her ladyship'll need me in a while. So how did it go last night?' she asked, referring to his allotted part in the proceedings: meeting the carriages as they arrived with guests and directing them where to go and wait. 'I trust you carried out your duties politely.'

'Hof course,' he said archly.

'And not too exhausted to get up for your breakfast as normal?' she inquired with amusement.

'Of course not,' he returned. '*And* I already went out.'

To avoid being called to help in the massive clean-up operation, she did not doubt. 'You simply *had* to get some fresh air in the Park?' she teased him.

'Not *our* Park,' he said. 'The one we used to go to.'

She stared at him. 'And why would you do that?'

'I likes to keep up with things,' he answered.

She frowned. 'Things in General,' she pressed, 'or any Thing in Particular?'

'Both,' he responded, meeting her look.

She knew she should not pursue it. 'And?'

'He was there, doing his running.'

Callie did not need to ask who Peter was talking about.

'At his usual time, even though,' Peter's eyes narrowed, 'their ball went on even later than ours.'

Callie had never tried to discover how Peter knew such things. She did not want to know now; nor what the ball had been about.

He told her anyway. 'Announced the engagement.'

Of course, they had. But still Callie's heart sank.

'Put out notices too.'

33

Lady Alicia had been right.

After weeks, months, of their every move and every moment together being minutely monitored, the betrothed couple were at last permitted to walk side by side in the park – with the Baron and Baroness following but not within hearing.

'Keep going,' urged Alicia. 'Keep your voice down and look as if we are discussing the weather.'

Dob glanced at her face, as devoid of emotion as usual, and tried to mirror it. 'If I took your arm,' he said, 'it would look good – and help to talk quietly. May I?'

She tucked her hand into his elbow and leaned into him a little. The gesture was entirely devoid of intimacy.

'Do you have any plan?'

'What should we do?'

They both spoke at once.

'You first,' said Alicia. She was not being submissive; Dob had realised she never was, however compliant she might seem. In fact, he suspected, she was taking the lead.

'At worst,' he said succinctly, 'I can simply run away.' Quite literally! 'I could go overseas somewhere. I don't care a jot for the title, the family, the estate. Even with nothing in my pocket I believe I could fend for myself if I had to. But for you that must be different.' He invited her to respond.

'Yes,' she said. 'A woman with nothing in her pocket is powerless. And,' there was unusual emotion in her voice, 'why should I even have to think of it? I am heiress to a fortune – a fortune,' she said deliberately, 'which I will not hand over to anyone.' She looked at him for his reaction.

'I do not share, *in any way*,' Dob said fiercely, then hastily lowered his tone, 'the ambitions of my father.'

She nodded slightly. 'Good. I thought that was the case, but I think we need to be quite clear with each other in order to act in concert.'

He agreed.

'My father believed that marriage is the natural, the only, state for a woman; furthermore, he agreed absolutely with the legal assumption that women are by constitution quite unsuited to dealing with financial affairs. Since a cruel Fate had denied him the chance to pass on the Tentham fortune to a son, the only thing to his mind was to ensure that I made a suitable marriage so that, on his death, the family fortune would pass into the capable hands of a man, namely those of my husband. I managed to resist all the suggestions he made on that score, having my heart *and mind*,' she glanced defiantly at him, 'set elsewhere.'

Dob had good reason to know that she was not the only woman with a mind at least as acute as any man. He smiled to himself at the thought of Miss Callie Smith.

Lady Alicia was continuing, 'When he realised that he would likely die before the matter was settled, my father changed the terms of his will: he stipulated that the Tentham fortune should be put into trust; he charged Baron Stickling with securing my marriage to a suitable husband and thus the future of the Tentham estate – on the successful completion of which the Baron would receive a handsome payment for services rendered.' She used the language of trade with deliberate contempt.

That explained some things, including the Baron's determination. 'Was it not possible for you simply to marry the person of *your* choice?'

She started to shake her head, then quickly stopped herself. 'No,' she said instead, giving him a sideways glance. 'I do not wish to marry anyone. I wish to live entirely as *I* please, on *my* money.'

An unusual resolution in a woman, but Dob could completely sympathise with the desire to order one's own life!

'However,' she continued, 'in the event that I did *not* marry, my father could not block me forever from inheriting. He did argue that twenty-eight was the very earliest age that a female was likely to have anything approaching maturity, so he set that as the condition. Although, he clearly expected the situation would never arise.'

'When exactly is your birthday?' he asked.

'The fifth of November.' She gave another humourless laugh. 'When a famous plot spectacularly failed!'

'And our wedding is set for the last week in September,' he mused. 'So, what should we do?' he repeated his earlier question.

She kept her eyes on the path in front of them. 'I believe the best thing is to go along with the marriage nonsense until as late as possible. If we try and obstruct it before then, they will think of unpleasant ways of trying to force us.'

That was certainly credible.

'We would only need to find the means to hide for a few weeks.'

He frowned, considering the possible problems.

Her green eyes glittered. 'Don't worry,' she said, at his continuing silence, 'you'll be reimbursed – once I secure what is mine.'

Dob flushed and nearly wrenched his arm away. 'Let us "be quite clear with each other",' he hissed. 'We have a common purpose. If working together seems the best way to achieve it, then let us do so. I shall not be your paid lackey.'

The frost turned to ice – then thawed. For the first time Dob felt her smile was genuine. 'I believe pretending to like you for the next months might not be so hard after all.'

'Don't try *too* hard!'

34

The Season progressed, gathering momentum. Sophie was occupied from morning to night: she was invited to so many functions she had to write polite refusals to many of them. And still there was hardly an hour in the day when, assiduously accompanied by Lady Olivia (and Callie), she was not receiving guests or visiting, or taking carriage rides, or attending a ball or the theatre, helping host a select dinner or eating at some grand house elsewhere in town. Several young men showed an inclination to court her; one even made an offer.

Sophie enjoyed the attention but gave her would-be suitors no false encouragement. She had been promised that the ultimate choice would be hers and, quite simply, she had already made it.

With the blessing of both the Duke and Lady Olivia, into the hectic social programme were scheduled precious hours for visits to the music room of Uppworth House by James Millburn, whenever his professional commitments permitted. Lady Olivia and Callie were, of course, there too, but often Lady Olivia allowed herself to doze off in her armchair while

Callie would take up a book. She very much enjoyed the music, but she could hear it just as well from near the French windows and the distance gave the pair the opportunity for some private conversation.

One day James arrived with a very smug expression on his face and several dog-eared sheets of paper clutched under his arm – it was, he announced, the only piece Haydn was known to have composed "*Zu vier Händen*". James had heard of the work and had finally tracked down this one copy, from the friend of a friend who had visited Vienna.

James usually played cello and Sophie the pianoforte. Sometimes he would offer her advice on her technique; sometimes he took her place and played a piece for her.

This latest find, of course, demanded they sit very closely side by side, their four hands in concert on the keyboard.

As a consequence of all this, there had been no opportunity for Callie and the Duke to discuss Adam Smith's book. Finally, the chance arose. The Duke invited Callie to join him in the library, from where the warm weather of early summer lured them outdoors. Hibbs pushed the wheeled chair out onto the terrace then retired.

For a while the Duke looked out at the small secluded garden but seemed more absorbed with his own thoughts than with looking at the flowers in their neat beds.

Finally, he gave a small shake of his head and turned his gaze on Callie. 'Please tell me what you thought.'

'I found his ideas very interesting,' said Callie truthfully. 'Some of what he says makes sense: people not only specialising in a particular trade but then specialising in making the various parts so as to speed production; the use of money replacing exchange or barter. However, when he goes on to suggest there is some law that naturally balances supply and demand and prices, and *must* bring about the best for everyone if only it were allowed to work freely, I find that hard to believe. Would it really end the practices of unscrupulous landowners and their stewards?' The Duke's eyes narrowed. She continued quickly, 'Or of companies trying every means to make the most profit and pay the lowest wages? Would everyone, manager or worker, master or servant, receive a fair share? Who is to say what is fair?

'I really cannot believe the self-interest in human beings could be so "magically" balanced or corrected!

'He stresses the importance of money being invested in order to bring about wealth. Will those who do so, not want to make as much as they can for themselves, as they do now – regardless of the conditions of all the people who actually do the labour?'

The Duke's face, marked by pain lines, softened. 'You have not disappointed me,' he said with a smile. 'You have a mind as questing as I suspected – and even sharper! That was a most succinct summary, Miss Smith, with questions as perceptive as I could have wished.' His smile faded. 'Are all landowners, factory owners, merchant adventurers as selfish as you cast them? Are there not any with principles?'

Was he speaking as a landowner himself? 'I realise my experience is limited,' she added quickly. 'And mostly I know of factories and mills and cities only through what others have said or written.'

'But you have direct knowledge of country life.'

Callie worried he would pursue the matter of her background, but with a pensive look he spoke of his own. 'I was neither Fate's nor my father's first choice as heir to the Dukedom,' he said wryly. 'I was definitely "the spare". My older brother fitted the part so perfectly, coming up to every expectation of preserving the ancient family name and holdings. He learned all his lessons, comported himself with unfailing politeness, accepted absolutely the way things had always been done.

'I, on the other hand, questioned everything. I applied myself most diligently to the study of every controversial work I could lay my hands on.

'I was barely nineteen when my father purchased a commission for me. The war with the American colonies had already started and within the year I was with the expeditionary corps in the southern-most port of Savannah. While we awaited our next orders, I learned a little of the town we had taken and became curious to see something of the estates it served. How, I wondered, did they compare with Uppworth? I knew in theory, of course, about slaves being shipped from Africa to work on the plantations, but I was totally unprepared for the reality.'

Callie realised then why his Lordship had asked her to consider such trade when reading about the wealth of nations.

'It was not just the conditions under which they lived and worked,' he continued. 'It was the underlying assumption that these were simply beasts of burden, harnessed (literally!) and driven to labour for the benefit of the landowners.

'The plantation owners were more than willing to give me a tour. Perhaps they did not disclose all – indeed I know they did not, from what I later learned – but what they did reveal with no compunction whatsoever was that they did not regard the slaves as fellow humans, even those baptised Christians!'

'*Where there is neither Greek nor Jew, circumcision nor uncircumcision, Barbarian, Scythian, bond nor free: but Christ is all, and in all.*' Callie quoted a verse from Colossians that had struck her – albeit in relation to a different state of inequity.

The Duke's gaze snapped back. 'Very much what the Quakers believe: the equality of all before God. Mind you,' he added, 'while there are Quakers here in London very much involved in the Society for Effecting the Abolition of the Slave Trade, there are still Quaker slave-owners in the now independent United States despite the grand declaration of Jefferson (himself a slave owner incidentally) that "*all Men are created equal, that they are endowed by their Creator with certain unalienable Rights, that among these are Life, Liberty, and the Pursuit of Happiness*".'

Callie thought about that. 'Our parson certainly did not believe that: he preached the *unalienable right of his Lordship* over all those things! And, in any case,' she hurried on as she realised that she had, yet again, referred to things she did not wish to talk about, 'the declaration hinges on what one understands by "*Men*", does it not? Humans of the male sex? What of the female? Do American females have any more unalienable rights than those in Britain where few women have any independence and may lose that at the whim of a male relative?' She should not think of Lady. 'Or lose all legal identity on marrying.' She flushed: his Grace would assume she was referring to Sophie. 'And what,' she said rather desperately, 'of those human creatures you talked about, regarded simply as beasts of burden?'

He frowned. 'I fear you are *too* sharp Miss Smith.' He held up a hand to cut off her apology. 'I take full responsibility for encouraging you to be so. But now I must caution you about talking in such a free way with anyone but myself. Have you heard of the Two Acts?'

Callie did not think so.

'The Seditious Meetings Act and the Treasonable Practices Act were passed last October.'

She stared. 'Sedition and treason?'

She almost laughed until she saw that his Grace was serious, very serious.

'There are others, apart from the Americans, who are very concerned about Rights. Strictly for discussion between us,' he said earnestly, 'I shall give you Mr Burke's thoughts on the matter and the response of Mr Paine. The revolution in France – with its slogan of Liberté, Égalité and Fraternité –

has made our King and his government fear a similar uprising here, whipped up by seditious speeches and pamphlets. Dr Parkinson was lucky not to get caught up in the Popgun business.'

Callie recalled then that Lady Olivia had said something about the surgeon's political reputation.

'James Parkinson,' explained the Duke, 'is a member of the London Corresponding Society, a group of artisans, tradesmen and shopkeepers who wish to see reform of the political system, principally the institution of annual parliaments elected through universal suffrage – universal for men, naturally.' He acknowledged Callie's earlier comment with an ironic lift of his lips. 'It is probable that James Parkinson wrote the articles attributed to "Old Hubert", but it was four other members of the Society who were arrested for the so-called Popgun Plot, "*a pretended plot to kill the King*" with a poisoned dart.'

An attempt on the King was certainly treason.

'If you are interested – and have the time! – there's another book I could lend you. One of those accused was Paul Thomas Lamaitre; he published a book last year in which he describes the ridiculousness of the accusation and details the atrocious way he was treated by the law and those supposed to uphold it. It is quite evident that the whole thing was a complete fabrication.'

'So, he was acquitted of the charge?'

'Finally!' said the Duke. 'Two days ago, in fact. That's something else for you to read – the reports in the newspapers. Have you heard, Miss Smith, of *Habeas Corpus*?'

'It sounds like Latin,' Callie said 'Some other Act of Parliament?'

'A good guess. It is indeed Latin; it is short for the phrase "*habeas corpus ad subjiciendum*" and means the body of someone accused must be brought before a court. I think we agree there is a sad lack of fairness in our society (whoever defines it!). The principle of *Habeas Corpus* addresses one great injustice: no exploitative landowner,' (Callie shifted uncomfortably), 'no autocratic steward, no tyrannical king, no government can have someone imprisoned arbitrarily – that person must be charged with an offence and brought to trial in a court of law.

'However, at times the principle has been suspended, when it has been argued that the danger to the state is so great nothing should hinder its protection – as it was last year when the Popgun plot was "uncovered".'

'So that's why it took so long for this Paul Thomas Lamaitre to get the chance to defend himself in court?'

'Indeed.'

'And there was no plot, you think?'

'I think,' said his Grace, 'that somebody who sees the members of the London Corresponding Society as dangerous contrived a way to silence them.'

'Then before there was any chance of proving in open court that the Plot was false, these Two Acts had been passed?'

'Exactly: preventing just about all public meetings and greatly curtailing what matters may be spoken about. Hence my warning to you, Miss Smith.' He frowned. 'It was, I think now, selfish of me to encourage you.'

Callie had been grateful to the Duke for his offer about using the library and his recommendation of what to read – it had seemed rather like the encouragement Lady had once given her. Only now did she wonder why he should have bothered. 'Selfish?' she queried before she gave herself time to think of things such as prudence.

'Well, perhaps not entirely selfish,' he said. 'It's true I hoped I might share a little of the brightness you have brought into the lives of Lady Olivia and Sophie.' Callie felt her face grow warm. 'But I did also think you might benefit. However, I wonder now if I have done you a disservice.'

Callie could see that the treasures she had been offered were about to snatched away again. 'Not at all, your Grace,' she said more passionately than good manners dictated. 'I had to leave the best of teachers before my education was anything like complete. I always knew there was so much more to learn and now I realise I did not even know how much I did not know.' The words tumbled over each other. 'I swear I will not speak a single word that might be thought seditious; except to your Grace, of course.'

'How could I deny myself that?' he inquired with a chuckle. 'Nevertheless, I believe we should stop now.'

'But there will be another time, won't there? I may read Mr Burke and Mr Paine mayn't I and tell you how I find them?'

'Yes, Miss Smith, to both your questions.'

Callie heaved a great sigh of relief.

Both provoked lively discussions and both led to his Grace mentioning other writers. Callie demanded to know who had first had such ideas, anyway, and found herself referred back to the ancient Greek Aristotle. After that, as she understood it, the "Thinkers", like Thomas Aquinas and Thomas à Kempis, had mostly thought about religious ideas which she and the Duke agreed, they *might* explore some other time.

Italian Machiavelli was shocking but fascinating in his treatise on what made an effective "Prince": *It is better to be feared than loved, if you cannot be both.*

English More painted his picture of "Utopia": *The ordinary acts we practise every day at home are of more importance to the soul than their simplicity might suggest.*

There were other Englishmen like Hobbes: *The condition of man ... is a condition of war of everyone against everyone.*

And Locke: *I have always thought the actions of men the best interpreters of their thoughts.*

There was Scottish Hume: *Beauty in things exists in the mind which contemplates them.*

There was French Descartes: *It is not enough to have a good mind; the main thing is to use it well.*

And Genevan Rousseau: *What wisdom can you find that is greater than kindness?*

So many people and ideas to think about; to compare with each other and with how life was now – most particularly in Britain and France.

Callie devoured it all.

35

The Duke occasionally joined them for a visit to a concert or a play, although access, with or without his chair, was usually undignified and sometime hazardous, despite the strength and skill of Hibbs.

On one evening, the Duke insisted on accompanying them to a ball, although he spent the evening surveying the scene with something very akin to repugnance.

When he and Callie met the following morning, he was still distinctly out of sorts.

'Perhaps I should come back another time,' she said, although she would be sorely disappointed to miss their discussion.

'No,' he said. 'But I do not believe I feel up to talking philosophy today.'

'Are you in pain, your Grace?' she asked, noticing there was more grey in his hair and the lines on his face seemed deeper.

But he shook his head. 'Not in my body,' he replied.

Callie was puzzled. 'Would you like to talk about something else?' Perhaps he might be diverted from whatever was ailing his spirits.

'Such as?'

'What happened after Savannah,' she said on impulse. Her considerable curiosity had been left unsatisfied. 'Or is that presumptuous of me?'

His eyes gleamed. 'Perhaps it is,' he said, 'but refreshingly honest!' The amusement faded as he regarded her for a long pondering moment. 'We got side-tracked, I recall, by more recent matters of treachery and sedition.'

He looked at her intently again then picked up the tale.

'We had taken Savannah in the south of the Colonies, but in the north things had not gone well: the Patriots, as the colonial rebels called themselves, had proved very difficult to pin down let alone defeat. The British forces had retreated to New York and there was a virtual stalemate.

'In an attempt to break this, General Sir Henry Clinton, then at Philipsburg Manor House, proclaimed the freedom of all slaves belonging to Patriots, regardless of whether they were willing to fight for the British Crown or not. Furthermore, any slaves who left their masters were to be granted protection and land.

'Needless to say, when word got around, thousands of slaves took the opportunity to flee.

'I met some of them when we took Charleston the following year. That is when I heard of the real conditions behind what I had been shown: the terrible crowding, disease, starvation and abuse on the slave ships that brought the Africans from Guinea; the degradation of being marketed like cattle; the use of chains and collars and irons to suppress the least dissent; the harsh punishments inflicted at will on men, women and children; the long hours in the fields in the burning sun, being flogged when they tired. So many died, that new batches of slaves from Africa were needed regularly to make up the numbers. If slaves did marry and have children, the youngsters were routinely sold as slaves on other plantations. The African women were constantly abused by the white overseers and plantation owners, with the law also declaring *their* offspring slaves.

'How could one possibly not see these as fellow human beings? How could one not share their pain and humiliation? How could one not feel deep shame that the British law allowed this and British merchants profited from it – and still do?'

Callie could give no answer; she knew then how truly little experience she had of life.

'And,' he shook his head, 'there were so many slaves who sought their freedom that Sir Henry urged some to go back to their masters!'

'What about the promise of protection and land?'

The Duke pulled a sour face. 'That was kept in a way. When we evacuated Charleston not long afterwards, some ten thousand ex-slaves were transported too.'

'Where to?'

'Some became Black Pioneers in Nova Scotia, despite the completely alien cold and harsh conditions there. Some went to the West Indies to work on the plantations as free men. Some came to England and added their numbers to the Black Poor already here in London.'

'Were there not many who would have liked to return to Africa?' she asked. 'Not as slaves, obviously, but to have land and live there.'

'There were, and are, some who would like that,' agreed his Grace. 'And,' he frowned slightly, 'also some English people who think they *should* like it. Have you heard of Sierra Leone?'

Callie had not, but when he described where it was, she could immediately picture the globe in Wicklow that she had loved to turn and study.

'A town has been started there, Freetown they have called it, and some land has been settled, but I have heard of discontent and unrest. How it will turn out I do not know. And I have burdens of my own to see to.'

Callie glanced at his legs, their withered distortion apparent even in the immaculately-tailored breeches and hose.

He saw where her eyes were turned. 'Yes, my legs are my main burden and what they have prevented me from doing. And I have still not explained to you about them, have I?'

She should be ashamed of her inquisitiveness, but she was not. And somehow, she sensed that he felt the need to tell her.

'After the withdrawal from Charleston I sailed to New York where I found an urgent letter from my father. My older brother had died of a sudden inflammation of the lungs.' Just like Callie's foster-father, George. 'He had been engaged to a very suitable young lady but had not yet married – so there were no children. However much both my father and I disliked the situation, I was, quite inescapably, now the Uppworth heir. I was required to resign my commission immediately and return to England, to do my duty.

'For the time that my father was still alive, it was very difficult, for both of us. I resented my position and determined to be just plain obstructive to anything my father favoured. Although,' he smiled, 'I had to concede defeat when he found a bride for me: I just could not pretend to dislike her! She was such a sweet-natured woman, a natural Duchess. She gave birth to twins, a boy and a girl who gave my father both pleasure and consolation in his last illness.

'Illogically, when I had charge of everything, it all seemed much easier. The sense of responsibility was heavy, but the chance to try out some innovations was exciting.'

His face had lifted at the memory; now it fell again.

'My twins came into the world together and scarlatina took them away together. For eight years they were the delight of everyone who knew them. The boy was the more solemn; his sister the more forthright.'

Callie could hardly imagine the grief, let alone make any suitable comment.

'Worse was to come.'

How could anything be any worse?

'My wife and I decided to go away from Uppworth for a while: there were too many painful memories there. We had only travelled a few hours when the carriage lost a wheel and overturned; we were crushed inside. Sometimes I can believe it was a small comfort that my beloved wife died in my arms.

'When they pulled me out and carried me back to Uppworth, I felt completely numb. I thought it was the shock. It was only when I finally found the will to rise that I realised I no longer had command of my legs: my back, the doctors said, had been broken in the accident; *perhaps* some movement might return. It did not.

'I cannot pretend that life, at that time, did not seem entirely pointless, but since its bleakness is indescribable, I shall not try. And, gradually, bit by bit, against all reason, some point returned.' He gave a small smile. 'It started when Lady Olivia came to manage the house bringing Sophie with her. Into the darkness they brought a spark of light which grew into a steady flame.

'And I realised that I could still order matters for all those who depended for their livelihoods and wellbeing on Uppworth; for the past few years I have found ways to do so.

'Other challenges, however, remain.'

Callie looked at him enquiringly.

'Even after Sophie is happily settled, as I believe will soon be the case, Lady Olivia and I will be left with our particular challenges. You know as well as anyone what faces my sister-by-law. My own nemesis has only recently revealed itself to me.'

Callie started. 'Your health, your Grace?'

He shook his head. 'No,' he said. 'Although the immobility forced on me is likely, the doctors say, to lead to its own ill-consequences. They may shorten my life,' he said frankly, 'but anyone may be cut down at any time.'

Callie did at least know that much.

'No,' he repeated. 'It is not my health which has come to concern me. Although, in a way, of course, it is central to the matter.'

Callie frowned.

He gave that half smile. 'I do not mean to set riddles.'

Callie was thoroughly puzzled and bothered by now. What was he talking about?

36

The spring gave way to a hot, dry summer. Windows were flung open in an attempt to bring some breath of air into the ballrooms and salons. Often, that only served to permit the ingress of gritty dust raised from un-dampened streets by the passing of wheels, hoofs and feet. In the evenings, myriad candles added their heat to that of the day

In the Park, flower beds were assiduously watered by teams of gardeners who disturbed Dob's early-morning peace. The leaves on the trees turned from fresh bright green to a much deeper hue, many of them sticky with protective glaze. The gravel paths crunched beneath parasolled amblers. In the evenings the water fowl paddled wearily into the reeds, leaving the lake to the swallows and martins and their swooping raids on the clouds of insects hanging over the unruffled surface.

The Countess of Pentridge had been allowed to retreat to rural Richmond where the villa enjoyed cleaner air and a peaceful ambience, even if the sun shone just as strongly. She dutifully came into town when ordered to do so, but this was infrequently.

It became clear to Dob that the brief flame of defiance would not be rekindled. When they did meet, they exchanged greetings, but there was scant trace of their brief closeness at Christmas.

Dob and Lady Alicia attended all the proper functions, showing off themselves and their impending alliance to the *monde*. They exchanged polite talk with all the right people.

They were presented to anyone who was anyone – that is to say, anyone with aristocratic connections.

The only one of that description in whom Dob had the slightest interest was Lord Willoughby Landston. His school mate had duly finished at Bromby and was to go up to Oxford at Michaelmas. The Duke of Branksdown had brought his son to London to introduce him to Society and to see how it worked – although it would be some years before Willo would be required to enter the marriage mart.

'Lucky you!' muttered Dob in a voice low enough to escape the ever-hovering Stacklings but within distinct hearing of the statuesque lady right next to him.

Willo raised a somewhat astonished eyebrow at that perfectly composed figure.

Lady Alicia raised an equally patrician brow – while her hand on Dob's arm tightened in warning. 'Luck, as you will no doubt appreciate Lord Landston, has nothing whatsoever to do with making a suitable match. Viscount Kelton and I both apprehend the essentials and are in total agreement about them.'

At this, Willo turned back to Dob and his eyebrow lifted further.

'Lady Alicia is quite correct,' Dob said, summoning the false smile he had perfected for the benefit of the Stacklings, and adding with only the faintest hint of irony, 'We find ourselves happily in accord.'

'Do you so?' Willo's eyebrows now knitted themselves.

All at once Dob had had enough of simulation. 'That the whole thing is a total disaster!' The admission to his oldest friend came out as a low hiss.

Willo's mouth opened in astonishment and Dob could see the next questions that would pour out.

Alicia's angry murmur accompanied an urgent tug at his arm.

'Meet me at the Keeper's Lodge as soon as the Hyde Park gates are opened in the morning and I will explain all to you,' muttered Dob. 'Do not approach us again this evening and *say absolutely nothing to anybody.*'

'Aha,' murmured Willo. 'Righto.' He made a polite bow to Lady Alicia and promptly excused himself to greet someone he had spotted across the room.

'That was exceedingly rash and stupid!' Lady Alicia's normally veiled eyes flashed.

'Willo won't tell,' said Dob firmly. 'And,' he added with a confidence that was based on no more than sudden and desperate hope, 'he can surely find the cash we need. The plans we have made could work but not without money.'

That was so undeniable that Lady Alicia's anger faded a little and she carefully loosened the grip of her gloved fingers on his sleeve.

She rearranged her flawless features into their accustomed calm. 'It really is quite warm and I understand iced lemonade is being served in the refreshment room. I believe I should greatly enjoy some.'

'Of course,' said Dob. 'I shall be honoured to fetch you a glass immediately.'

The meeting the following morning gave Dob greater hope than he could ever have expected: Willo was more than eager to help in what seemed to him a glorified prank – the young man saw no difficulty in securing the necessary funds, nor in making the required arrangements for transport and accommodation. What difficulty could there be for the son (and heir) of the Duke of Branksdown, leading member of the upper House and of His Majesty's diplomatic corps?

As they talked through the details, Willo became more and more enthusiastic. 'Dashed, if I'm not more than half-minded to come with you.' He grinned at Dob. 'Sailing across the sea to face adventure in a new land sounds a good deal more thrilling than going up to Oxford!'

Dob had had much of the schoolboy knocked out of him since Christmas. He knew enough of life now to realise that reality could be *very* different from expectation. In his more optimistic moments, he could feel excited about the choice thrust upon him, but often, especially at the night, he saw only too clearly what he would be leaving behind – not an earldom; he did not care a fig for that, still less for its present title-holder.

However, he did care, a great deal, about Miss Callie Smith. If only any future could include her! By his side, in his arms.

37

It was patently obvious to everyone, not least the couple themselves, that there was a serious and shared attraction between Sophie and James Millburn; what was less obvious to the cellist was how that attraction might be taken to its logical (and most desirable) conclusion. As the end of the main Season approached, James grew increasingly despondent at the thought of the Uppworths leaving the capital, taking Sophie with them. What made the prospect even more melancholy was the realisation that their return to London was by no means assured – the health of both Lady Olivia and the Duke being so uncertain.

Since Easter had heralded in the warm summer, the French windows of the music room had often been flung open. Like those in the adjoining ballroom (and the library beyond), they gave access to the terrace which ran across the back of the house. In the private garden, the flowers were a riot of colour. As James Millburn arrived for what would be one of his last visits, however, he had eyes only for the woman at the centre of the room: Sophie was seated at the piano playing a sonata written by Beethoven the previous year.

He drank in both the magnificent musical composition and the young woman bringing it to life, her elegant hands dancing across the keys, her body following them slightly.

It was only as the piece drew to an end that he realised there was no one else there: there was no comment from Lady Olivia, no clap by Miss Smith. There was only the faint murmur of voices, from *beyond* the French windows, their owners presently out of sight.

James seized his moment. Grasping both of those beautiful hands, he poured out his heart to their owner – his love, his longings, his despair that he could not offer marriage: he had not the means to support her in the manner she was both accustomed to and deserved.

Sophie returned his grip – and his sentiments of love – but foreswore his despair. She would, she declared, gladly give up all comforts to be with him.

James longed to believe this was enough but knew it was not.

He lifted their joined hands, gently unfolded each of her supple fingers and kissed them one by one.

There was a small cough.

The couple sprang apart as they realised the Duke was at the French windows in his wheeled chair.

James hastily began to excuse the gross breech of etiquette.

A sharp gesture stopped him. 'Mr Millburn,' said the Duke. 'Sophie,' he included his niece. 'It is I who should apologise – eavesdropping is not, in general, something I approve of, but it seemed a necessary part of Lady Olivia's plan.'

Two puzzled faces stared at him.

'My Aunt's plan?'

'Neither she nor I have the luxury of time to let things take their natural – well-mannered! – course,' the Duke said drily. 'There are things we would like to hasten along – but only if they are the *right* things.' He added, 'We could not make assumptions – we needed an unreserved declaration of your mutual affection.' He half smiled. 'Which I have now heard.'

James felt a flush of annoyance at their being manipulated, but the feeling was almost immediately eclipsed by the hope raised by the Duke's words – then, almost as quickly, that feeling was doused by reality. 'Your Grace, what you heard was indeed the unreserved truth: I love Sophie, with all my heart and find, to my joy, that my love is returned. However, what you also heard about my circumstances is similarly the simple truth. Whatever Sophie says, I could *never* see her give up respectability and comfort for my sake.'

The Duke nodded. 'Neither could I,' he said. 'Nor need it be so.'

James flushed again as he guessed the Duke's meaning. 'But no more could I give up my own *self*-respect – what kind of man would that make me?'

'Pride,' commented the Duke shortly, 'is a two-edged sword. But,' he prevented James's riposte, 'this most serious affair deserves the dignity of proper discussion, not an exchange through a window like a verbal *jeu de volant*. You would oblige me by helping my chair over the weather-sill.' He turned to Sophie, 'While you, my dear, might go and tell your aunt and Miss Smith that their presence is now required.'

When all were assembled, the Duke spoke. 'It is the usual form for the financial arrangements of a match to be sorted out between the father or guardian of the bride and the prospective groom. However, I believe it will best suit *our* particular situation if all those concerned are present.'

Callie rose to her feet. 'It being a family matter, I do not believe that I need or should be here, your Grace.'

'But have you not been concerned all along, Miss Smith?' He looked around. 'Does anyone feel Miss Smith's presence would be *de trop*?'

Nobody did and Callie sat down again – still not entirely sure of the proprieties but agog to hear the outcome.

'And you, Mr Millburn – will your pride allow open discussion of your circumstances, indeed all the circumstances of the matter?'

Taking all those circumstances fully into account, agreement on the essential principles was reached.

The engagement of the Lady Sophie to the Honourable James Millburn could therefore be announced immediately, with the wedding to take place soon thereafter, before the coincidence of the Parliamentary recess and the end of the high Season.

What might in general have been seen as unseemly (or suspicious) haste would be explained by the plain truth: Lady Olivia wished to see her niece settled before *she* became too disabled to participate in any of the proceedings. The Duke wished to do everything he could to make this possible.

38

The marriage of Sophie and James had as good a chance of happiness as any, more than most. His Grace hoped that she and James would know the additional happiness of children.

If only his own plans could be so easily and happily expedited! Without doubt, they were quite mad. What sane woman would accept a marriage proposal from a man well past his prime, in age and health – with such an outrageous rider?

As the energetic figures pranced and paraded around the dance floor in a whirl of coloured silks and satins, broadcloth and buckskin, perspiration and pomade, his Grace reflected that in spite of all the finery, the basic function of the occasion was almost exactly the same as the livestock market in any local town. The aim was to match seller and buyer. Well, he had the means to buy whatever he wished – didn't he? What sane woman, he reversed his earlier thought, would decline a man of his very considerable resources?

Although, his mind offered yet another question, did he want a wife who only agreed to marry him because of his money? Did he really want another wife at all?

But he quashed all those treacherous thoughts as he recalled the alternative.

He simply could not, would not, leave matters as they presently stood.

For the greater part of his life he had never really expected to be involved in the matter of title and succession. Fate had rudely demonstrated the folly of such an assumption with the sudden death of his older brother. On inheriting, the new Duke had taken the precaution of confirming who was next in line. Baron Richleigh, a first cousin, seemed an unobjectionable character. In any case, the existence of the twins at that point made the matter academic.

Even after Fate intervened, not once but twice more, with supreme malevolence, the matter was not the Duke's greatest concern; not even when he realised that the road accident had robbed him not only of the use of his legs but of any chance of begetting another heir. The law of the land dictated how titles and entailed estates should be disposed; the matter was settled.

The news of Baron Richleigh's death the previous year, at the hands of highway robbers, had unsettled it again.

The manner of the Baron's demise was shocking but since they had not been well-acquainted, had little personal impact on the Duke. In regard to the succession, he knew that the Baron had a son who would inherit the barony, and, in due course the dukedom; but following that thought came the awareness that he was even less-acquainted with young Nestor Richleigh than he had been with his parent. Although the Duke could do nothing to change the legal state of affairs, the responsibility for Uppworth and its many dependents weighed on him heavily; he felt impelled to inquire about the person who would assume this charge after him.

The information discovered by his lawyer had been disquieting in the extreme. It had all been hushed up, of course, but even so the Duke was deeply chagrined at missing it – he had allowed himself to become too engrossed in his own problems.

Nestor Richleigh was a fellow possessed of both vanity and a quick temper: not a happy combination. After one perceived insult he had called out the offender and put a ball between his eyes. While duelling had once been regarded as little more than aristocratic hijinks, it was no longer so. In recent times participants had found it wise to make themselves scarce for a period. And in this case, someone had died; the authorities had decided to make an example.

Baron Richleigh had sought help from every possible contact, but in truth he knew few people of influence. Finally, he had recalled someone in the Home Department and contrived a deal: Nestor would not be brought to the Bow Street court to face the capital charge of murder on condition that he put his undisputed skill with firearms at the disposal of king and country. The Baron would buy his son a commission that would not be surrendered until the end of the present hostilities, *in any circumstances* – even accession to the barony.

Nestor's regiment had been posted to defend the island of Jamaica and its hugely wealthy sugar plantations against invasion by the French or indeed against any further internal insurrection. The news of his father's death had been sent to Kingston but, given the terms of Nestor's commission, it was hardly surprising that there had been no response.

The Duke recognised the irony of the man who was his heir supporting a British colony built on slavery. Quite apart from that, his Grace knew enough about the Caribbean conditions which afflicted both Africans and Europeans – fatal diseases that flourished in the extreme heat and humidity – to realise that the survival of that heir was heavily against the odds.

Who then, was next in line *after* Nestor Richleigh?

That information, when confirmed by the Duke's lawyer, had been not merely disquieting. It was totally unacceptable.

In addition, the matter was of supreme urgency. Nestor's life might well be shortened; the Duke's own days were almost certainly numbered.

Furthermore, the Duke finally learned that while *he* had only just caught up with the situation, the next in line had evidently done so some while before and was even now contriving to make the very most of an increasingly likely outcome.

The Duke had seriously put his mind to finding a way around what, though highly regrettable, he had previously accepted as unavoidable. Very soon, he must secure the hand of some woman who was willing not only to become his wife but one who would collude with his plans. Although, even if or when that was achieved, an awful lot lay in the hands of Fortune.

Still, it *had* to be essayed.

39

Fortune at least smiled on the arrangements for the marriage of Sophie and James: the acquisition of a special licence was no problem; nearby Grosvenor Chapel was available on the desired day; James's parents and eldest brother could make it (the attendance of his second brother, a naval captain, was unlikely whatever the date). The only other guests for the marriage ceremony, the Duke and the Lady Olivia, were, of course, already in residence.

Position and means favoured the practical details: requests, commands and orders to clergymen and postal agencies, tailors and dressmakers, tradesmen and craftsmen, were complied with instantly – other, existing, customers notwithstanding.

The Duke's sense of manners bothered his conscience a little – but only a little: a few people might be inconvenienced; many would benefit from the ducal largesse.

Celebration of the event, as was entirely to be expected, took the form of a musical evening. Naturally both James and Sophie performed; as did the quartet of which James was a part.

There were, in addition, a collection of other professional musicians and singers of his acquaintance who contributed, but all guests were urged to participate, however untaught or untalented they might feel themselves. Callie sang a song learned long ago in Wicklow, the lilt and tune still perfect in her memory, the words adapted to the occasion. Several of the musicians joined her, embroidering the melody with enthusiasm.

There was a break for informal refreshments then the evening concluded, equally unsurprisingly, with dances from Playford's Dancing Master.

James had a number of musical commitments to fulfil so there would be no immediate honeymoon as such, although both he and his bride very much hoped to journey down to Millburn St Andrews in the county of D ... later in the summer.

Still, they would have two days (and nights), before James's next concert, to enjoy both each other and the house that was to be their new home.

The house stood in a quiet street near Berkeley Square. While nowhere near as luxurious as Uppworth House, it was well-appointed. Its main attraction for the Duke was its location: true, it lay not far from Grosvenor Square, but of at least equal importance was the fact that it was roughly midway between the Rotunda in Ranelagh Gardens and the Hanover Square Rooms, venues where high-class concerts were given and where James often took part in public performances. Furthermore, it was convenient for New Bond Street, where the Duke had made another purchase, namely a majority share in a business that made musical instruments and published sheet music.

Number Three would remain the property of the Duke and the Millburns would pay rent for it – a modest rent for that part of Town but not a peppercorn.

The share in the music business, meanwhile, was an outright gift, a wedding present. Earning a living might be regarded as downright vulgar by those who had enough money not to, but for James it was a matter of personal pride, an essential part of his self-esteem.

He would continue to perform and teach music; he had a small inheritance from a great aunt; with the additional income from the New Bond Street enterprise, he could expect to keep Sophie and any family they might have in perfectly adequate respectability and comfort.

40

Callie had enjoyed every moment of the preparations for the wedding and every minute of the day itself.

In the week that followed, however, she became aware that it had all taken its toll on Lady Olivia. Her ladyship had also relished the whole thing, had refused to miss any part of it and of course, she said impatiently, it had been a little tiring. What else could one expect? And now there was time to take things more quietly. And Callie should stop fussing!

Callie tried: that is to say, she managed to fuss more covertly. She kept a curb on her tongue and made efforts to hide the help she had to provide. She had seen her ladyship's condition go up and down; often being tired made it worse, then it would improve again – more or less. Nevertheless, Callie was concerned. She wondered if it was worth mentioning to the Duke, although she was not sure what he could do; and in any case he seemed distinctly out of sorts himself. He sent messages postponing their talks on the books he had recommended, which Callie missed acutely.

When she took her daily early morning walk in the park, she also missed the meetings with Dob. Rather ridiculously, he reminded her of one of Lady's yearlings, born to finely-bred sire and dam, shining coat covering muscles and sinews that were perfectly formed but as yet immature; legs still a little too long. But at the same time, he was undoubtedly handsome: his hair, often darkened by sweat when he had been running, was actually strikingly blond, shining silver when it dried. And his eyes were so blue they matched the heavens.

Callie, a child of the countryside, recognised well enough the frisson that ran through her as they had sat side by side and he took her work-worn hand in his strong slender fingers. But it was more than that; she knew it was. For those all too short, and too few, interludes it could flourish as they met as individuals, untrammelled by the expectations of the wider society which ruled the rest of their lives. She was baseborn, working as a servant (albeit a comfortably placed and respected servant). She was strong and healthy: useful attributes in a servant but the opposite of the ethereal qualities valued in *Lady's Magazine*. She was more literate, certainly more numerate, than most of her sex born into the upper classes on the right side of the blanket; and that too made her an oddity. Furthermore, the practicality and breadth of her knowledge would have perplexed, likely repulsed, the elegant, perfectly-mannered young ladies she had observed while attending soirées and balls with Lady Olivia and Sophie.

Dob, she was convinced, felt equally a misfit in his own particular situation. He looked every inch the young lord but had no airs or graces; made no play on either his looks or his position. He accepted her entirely for herself.

But just as day must end when night falls, their brief idyll had had to end when real life intruded. There had never been any future for them; they had both known that and wittingly ignored it. The announcement of Dob's engagement had made that no longer possible.

Callie deliberately avoided reading the society pages of the broadsheets; was heartily glad that Dob and his affianced were not present at any of the events she attended; managed, mostly, to avoid seeking out his distinctive lean, fair person among the fashionable crowds parading the streets of the capital. She suspected Peter probably had information on Dob, as he did on a remarkably wide number of people and happenings, but she never asked him.

The plan had always been that the Duke and Lady Olivia would travel home to Uppworth as soon as Sophie was settled and Callie was looking forward to being out of the constant noise and smell and bustle of the city.

She was also profoundly relieved that she would not be in London for what was widely dubbed "the match of the year" (even though the actual wedding would take place out of Season).

However, the weeks passed and although some of the nobility left to spend the rest of the summer on their country estates (or at the seaside), no mention was made of a date to pack up and close Uppworth House.

Callie assumed it was because Lady Olivia did not feel up to the journey; certainly, her ladyship continued to be more down than up. Callie could not hope to replace the excitement and activity of Sophie's launching, engagement and ultimately wedding which had undoubtedly kept her ladyship going, but she tried her best.

Her efforts, however, were not helped by the Duke's absence – both in the literal and metaphorical sense. He was often out of the house and when he was at home, he was distracted. There had been no meeting in the library, not even by chance. Whenever Callie went there in search of a new book for Lady Olivia or for herself, she found herself alone.

There had been some visits to the very happy mistress of Number Three, then in August Sophie and James departed for Millburn St Andrews.

41

Among those who had left the capital was the Duke of Branksdown, with his son Lord Willoughby Landston. Dob had bid Willo an emotional farewell that would have undoubtedly caused derision among their erstwhile school fellows: Dob was hugely grateful for Willo's help in financing and planning The Escape as they called it; he also realised he would not see his closest friend again for a long time, possibly never.

Meanwhile there was nothing to do except hide his impatience as the sweltering days of high summer dragged on towards autumn. He would have liked at least to spend the time at the villa in Richmond with its much more pleasant situation, but his father had vetoed the suggestion, even accompanied by the ever-watchful and loathsome Tomkin.

He saw Alicia on most days; was required to see her. When they took tea in the drawing room in the St James's house or in its perfectly manicured private garden, the Stacklings were always nearby. When he escorted her to the park, there were fewer people of quality to meet and greet, and the Stacklings somehow felt that was reason to walk closer behind them. Conversation of any meaning was snatched.

Nevertheless, Dob thought they had exchanged the essential details.

On the days when they did not meet, Dob's time was allocated to visits to the tailor, the hatter, the glover, the bootmaker. He would have been impatient of the nonsensical fashions and frippery in any case – knowing that they were all for nothing made it even more difficult.

The only thing that helped make life in any way bearable was his daily run – for the fencing and boxing lessons had been terminated.

Even though it no longer included the prospect of meeting Callie, it gave him a blessed hour to himself. And the exertion eased just a little of the frustration.

Alicia was also required to attend endless sessions with those commissioned to fit her out for the wedding and the life which would follow: travelling dresses for the journey to Tentham Court; morning dresses to receive all those who would come to meet the new owner of the wealthy property and estate; afternoon dresses for the tea invitations from neighbours; evening dresses for dining with select guests. Fine nightgowns to wear in the four-poster bed that had been her mother's, where her new husband would visit to exercise his marital rights.

Alicia had great skill in concealing her true feelings, but she had great difficulty hiding her shudder when asked to give her opinion on which cotton lawn and which kind of lace she favoured for the nightgowns.

She likewise had difficulty suppressing a shiver when visiting the milliner's – although *that* was a shiver of excitement.

But they must be very careful, she whispered. Just for a little longer.

The Earl of Pentridge and Baron Stackling cooperated for mutually beneficial reasons; for both the stakes were very high.

For the Earl, however, the value of the Grand Plan went far beyond the monetary. By turn he was impatient and self-congratulatory.

At night, he sometimes lay trying to spot any problem he had not foreseen, any let or hindrance from any quarter; wishing it was all settled.

By day, he sometimes indulged in gloating over the way he had contrived the whole thing: Fate had lent him a helping hand, granted, but he had improved on it with both of his own.

The Duke of Uppworth had known anguish and despair, sorrow and loss, but never until now had he indulged in abject railing against a Fate which had brought matters to such an ignominious pass.

The chase had gone cold, although in truth it had been barely warm; never warm enough to broach the outrageous rider; and still, the lady had cried off.

And, the Duke could not really blame her.

42

Of course, Callie was aware of Lady Olivia's various difficulties; very aware. Along with problems controlling her hands and legs (the first constantly moving, the latter often freezing – whether the lady willed it or not), her ladyship sometimes found it hard to swallow. Callie carefully cut up or mashed her food.

Loss of dignity was only one of the consequences of the inexorable illness: irksome but not the worst. Primed by the talks with Doctor Parkinson, Callie was alert to something "going down the wrong way". It had happened once and only Callie's immediate and vigorous intervention had prevented her ladyship from choking.

When she had finally recovered, Lady Olivia had remarked that she supposed she should be thankful.

What did the final damage, Doctor Parkinson concluded, was most likely some of the chocolate Lady Olivia so much liked to sip from a cup held for her. But her ladyship had not choked – Callie was certain she would have noticed.

Doctor Parkinson reminded her that, sadly, all the body's usual reactions faded one by one, even those of self-defence. It was almost certain some morsel of food or drop of drink had entered the lungs and caused them to become inflamed.

And none of the things that might aid other people could help Lady Olivia. She could not take in gasps of steam; she could not drink the herbal tea; she could not expel the vile puss that built up, however hard Doctor Parkinson slapped her back. Within hours the fever was raging through her body; before morning she could no longer draw breath.

Callie was distraught. She had lost, all of a sudden, a woman she had come to care about a great deal. And she blamed herself – whatever Doctor Parkinson said and however kindly the Duke spoke to her.

She was also exhausted from many days and nights without sleep and the terrible emotional upheaval.

She really must go and rest, the Duke told her. There was nothing more for her to do. Later, when Lady Olivia had been laid out, Callie might, of course, come and sit with her.

But Callie could not seek the blessed oblivion of sleep; she did not deserve it. She slipped out of the house and walked in a daze through the gradually lightening streets.

It was only as she saw the keeper unlocking the gate that she realised where her feet had taken her – not the park where she now went but the other one. The one where she used to meet Dob.

Did he still run here? She had no idea.

She sank down onto the familiar bench and the misery and emptiness washed over her. Perhaps she half dozed.

He did not take her hand. He put an arm around her. And she turned into him and wept.

It was an impulse as old as mankind. An impulse arising from human need – the need to find comfort, the need to provide it; the need to express the emotions of the moment – out of a certain past but unknown future. Two individuals seeking togetherness.

It was inexpert, with scant privacy. Still it was essentially tender: a communion of body and soul, a consummation of love.

It changed everything yet could change nothing.

The plans for The Escape had been made; there could be no last-minute change. Dob swore he would send as soon as he could for Callie to join him in America. Their difference in station would not matter there, he said; they could be man and wife and make a life together as they wished.

She told him to write to her at the Giblins' address: her employment with the Uppworths must surely come to an end, just as soon as the obsequies were complete – now there was no Lady Olivia to serve.

She had no idea what she would do next, or where, but she would keep in touch with the Giblins. And wait to hear from Dob.

43

Lady Olivia's funeral was held in the Grosvenor Chapel, the happy scene of Sophie's and James's nuptials such a short time before. Following the sombre service, the cortege made its sad way to the burial ground that had been consecrated near the fields of Bayswater.

The gathering afterwards at Uppworth House was small. The Duke spoke of his sister-by-law and how much he had valued her, for her practical help and companionship, her determination despite her encroaching illness. He particularly reminded them of her lack of self-pity and her almost never-failing good humour. In the event, her death had shocked them by its suddenness and her absence was most keenly felt, but now he had had a chance to reflect he was convinced that for *her*, knowing full well what otherwise lay in store, it was undoubtedly the choice she would have made, had she been offered any. He was equally convinced that she would like to be fondly remembered by those she held dear – not grieved over.

Both Sophie and Callie knew in their heads that he was right, but neither could yet accept it in their hearts. Sophie lifted an already sodden kerchief. Callie had no tears left – she stared at the lovely carpet, with its roses, daffodils, crown imperials, morning glories and tulips, and could only think of the hazard its deep pile had once posed.

Lady Olivia's will was soon read; she had made it years ago when she realised she would never marry and had felt no reason to change it. She had had no estate and few belongings of any value. Everything that was legally hers she left to Sophie.

When Sophie had dried her eyes yet again, she declared that Callie should choose a book for herself from her ladyship's small collection. Callie, familiar with every one of them, knew instantly that it would be Twelfth Night.

The state of unreality persisted.

Callie continued to meet Mrs Ballance daily, but it felt strange: she was no longer acting on Lady Olivia's behalf and, in any case, Mrs Ballance could make perfectly well any household decisions that were needed for the modest style of living required by mourning.

She and Sophie spent painful days sorting through Lady Olivia's belongings, packing up the things to be carried to Number Three; bundling up clothes to be donated to some charitable institutions Lady Olivia had supported.

With Maisie, Callie stripped all the linen and furnishings to be washed and beaten. When everything was once again in order, they swathed the furniture in Holland cloth covers.

Finally, there really was nothing left for Callie to do. She was certainly not too proud for menial work anymore, but it was abundantly evident that she simply was not needed. In fact, Mrs Ballance had already paid off all the extra staff recruited at the beginning of the Season. Others would follow, once all the other rooms had been cleared and closed, leaving only those who maintained the House whenever His Grace was not in residence. When would he return to Uppworth? wondered Callie, with increasing concern.

Peter Giblin was still in post, although quite what he did with his time Callie did not know nor bother to investigate. But ultimately, he had a family to return to and, in all probability, his old job working with his father.

Would the Duke give her a reference so that *she* could seek other employment?

Her attempts to secure a meeting with his Grace, however, were strangely unsuccessful.

In fact, she began to wonder if he was deliberately avoiding her.

44

It was the first Monday in September. Callie managed to eke out until noon a few bits and pieces that really did not need doing then made her way to the library. The Duke was not there, but there was evidence that he had been: the day's *Times* lay on the table and on top of this a broadsheet of the kind aimed at readers much more interested in social scandal than the latest doings of the French general Napoleon in northern Italy. Callie's fleeting surprise at its presence there was eclipsed almost immediately by the headline: "Aristocratic couple 'elope'". Even this particular publication did not quite dare name precisely those involved, but the public would know perfectly well who was meant. "It seems that Society is to be denied the most anticipated event of the year, *viz* the joining in holy matrimony of the Viscount K and the Lady T, planned with *no expense spared* for later this month." Callie read on, her pulse quickening. "It has been most strenuously denied by both the Earl of P, father of the putative groom and Baron S, guardian of the intended bride, that the couple, *incontinent of a moment's further delay*, have run off to seek a blacksmith's wedding." She scanned the following columns that described every ball, concert or promenade where the couple had been observed during the Season – quite obviously "struck down by *Cupid*". All of it patent nonsense and pure invention, she knew. But it seemed likely the main point was true: Dob had made his Escape.

She had no doubt there would be "*no expense spared*" in trying to find and retrieve the couple. She had no idea what Lady Alicia planned to do, nor did she much care, although she vaguely wished her success. But she desperately hoped Dob would make it, not to Scotland (that was a false trail) but over the sea. She hastily laid down the broadsheet as the door opened and Hibbs wheeled in the Duke.

His Grace looked a little put-out to find her there. He sat for several moments in silence, as the pain lines on his face deepened into a frown. Then his innate manners took over. He declared himself glad to see her, asked if she had time to sit and talk to him a while; inquired if she would like any refreshment; despatched Hibbs to order the tea that she requested.

After the tray arrived, they conversed easily enough for a while, about the weather, how well the garden looked; how nice it was to hear from Sophie and James who had resumed their interrupted visit to Millburn St Andrews and made an enjoyable excursion to Weymouth. Then it grew more awkward. The Duke mentioned a book or two but with no real enthusiasm and Callie could pretend no great interest. She had been unable to lose herself in reading since Lady Olivia's death; her emotions were too raw; her life too unsettled.

'Have you,' said Uppworth eventually, 'given any thought to the future, your future that is.'

Of course, she had! 'I was wondering, your Grace, about registering with an agency in order to seek another position.' She took a breath. 'I was hoping you might see your way to providing me with a reference.' Even though Lady Olivia had died in her charge.

Perhaps her lingering sense of guilt showed on her face. 'Why would I not?' he replied. 'I can hardly think of a better example of a "gentle woman of impeccable credentials".'

She managed a small smile.

'But that, you see, is exactly the problem.'

Callie gaped. She did not see at all.

'My problem,' he added hastily as if to reassure her.

It only increased her bewilderment.

'I was rather hoping you might take up a different position – here.'

Callie stared at him. What was there for her to do? Now that …

'Well, perhaps not here, perhaps at Uppworth. Yes, more likely at Uppworth.'

Callie had never seen the Duke so ill at ease, so unsure of himself.

'But perhaps it is too soon: you are still upset over the death of dear Olivia; and there is the mourning period too, of course, to consider.'

What did that have to do with anything?

'But,' he inclined his head towards the newspapers, 'life goes on; events happen, overtake us. I cannot afford to wait.' Wait for what? 'This is all coming out terribly badly. I was not expecting to see you this morning. I shall endeavour to set it out better another time. But please, Miss Smith,' he said earnestly, 'do not think of leaving before we have spoken again. Try to recompose yourself; take more walks to the park with young Giblin!'

45

Callie did exactly that – the second part at least. She spent many hours walking not only in the park but elsewhere, Peter seeking to divert her with places that she had never seen before.

Although they also visited his family near Smithfield. She was very happy, of course, to see Ruth Giblin again; she was even pleased to renew her acquaintance with the ever-garrulous Widow Fletcher.

And she was excited to find not one but two packets just received. She looked first at the letter delivered by Royal Mail. On her arrival in the capital she had let Lady know, with the briefest of details, about the deaths of the Smiths and her subsequent move; she had sent another, more fulsome letter, telling Lady Horatia of the position with Lady Olivia and relating some of what she had been doing. However, she had stressed that Lady should send any reply to the Giblins', as Callie had not informed anyone at Uppworth House of her Wicklow connections. Lady Horatia was more than happy with Callie's prudence: the nobility were all related, in many and unexpected ways, and it remained imperative to keep the Marchioness from knowing Lady kept contact with the Marquess's by-blow. Lady Horatia was not aware of any kinship with the Uppworths, but one never knew! And, she freely admitted, she had always been much more interested in equine bloodlines – and went on to describe with great enthusiasm a colt born recently.

Callie smiled as she read the details.

She turned to the other packet which had been delivered by hand. She guessed who it was from – and was almost too nervous to open it.

It appeared to have been scrawled in great haste – but perhaps those strong slender fingers always produced such impatient script: she had no way of judging. It stated in bald prose that The Escape had been effected – which she already knew. He had seen lady Alicia installed in her place of concealment with a well-born female companion – neither named. He had made his way to the docks but found the ship would not sail for a week; and the time, hidden away in a waterfront cellar, had passed very slowly and uncomfortably. There had been a couple of alarms when he feared discovery, but now he was about to board *The Katherine*, ready to sail on the morning tide. The captain reckoned with a decent wind to make the crossing in six weeks. Dob reiterated his confidence that he would soon get himself established and repeated, in block letters, his promise to send for her shortly. Until then … there were several blotches and crossings-out at this point as Dob attempted to express more personal feelings, clearly a little practised exercise. In the end he simply signed himself her most devoted D.

She could not stop herself asking Peter to take her to the docks. His eyes narrowed, but he did not argue.

There outside the various shipping offices were boards announcing both recent and expected arrivals and departures. *The Katherine* had left before dawn, bound for her homeport of New York.

A shiver ran down Callie's spine; a memory from long ago came to her, of the cook in Wicklow looking at her sadly and speaking of people who set off over the ocean to distant lands and were never seen again.

It was several weeks before the Earl of Pentridge stood outside the self-same office. He cursed to himself yet again about the time wasted on the false trail to Scotland, then on the tedious search of every possible shipping agency in Bristol, Liverpool and London. The announcements of past sailings had been erased and replaced many times over, but the clerk recognised the Earl's description. Yes, there had been a young man, tall and lean, with silver-blond hair and striking blue eyes. He produced a neatly kept record of *The Katherine*'s passengers and pointed to the one listed as "Robert Smith".

The Earl laughed silently and completely without humour at the name: so obvious!

He was most familiar with the triangular route operated by his ships, but he knew well enough which way *The Katherine* would have taken to make use of the winds. He confirmed with the clerk what the crossing time was likely to be.

Although, the clerk, put in, there had been reports of stormy weather soon after *The Katherine* had set out.

The Earl frowned. He knew the winds could be fickle at any time of the year, but around the autumn equinox they could be both violent and contrary.

Had *The Katherine* run into these?

The clerk did not know. There had been no news of her, either way.

But the ship was headed for New York; even if she had had to run before a storm, she would eventually resume her course across the Atlantic.

The Earl needed to find a vessel bound for the same destination and follow as soon as possible; then personally direct a search of the American port for his errant son. A fast packet was due to depart on the morning tide in five days' time.

The Earl used the interval to set his affairs in order.

Impatient to be off, he took a cab to the docks.

There was a new announcement chalked up outside the shipping office: *The Katherine*, bound for New York had foundered with the loss of her cargo and all her passengers. Three surviving members of the crew had been picked up by the inbound East Indiaman *Royal Dragon*, which had docked the previous evening.

The clerk could give no further details, however furiously the Earl shouted at him, but the rescued sailors presently lodging at the Good Queen Bess would undoubtedly be able to say more.

They were doing exactly that when the Earl pushed his way into the packed tavern. Encouraged by the mass attention and the free-flowing drink, one seaman was embarking on yet another account of the wreck and their miraculous escape.

The Katherine had not even cleared the Bay of Biscay when the storm had overtaken them. There had been nothing they could do except reduce the sails to the merest rags and fly before the wind, pray hard – and bail even harder: for several boards were sprung and the ship's carpenter could do no more than patch them. Every hand on board, crew and passengers, desperately pumped and bailed.

All the passengers? demanded the Earl.

Every single one of them – yes, including the lean young man with the fair hair, Robert Smith.

Then the tiller broke loose and the same passenger helped in the efforts to make it fast again. A huge wave thundered down on the ship and swept Smith overboard. Yes, two of the survivors saw him go into the heaving black waters; no, they did not see him come up again, although they peered hard into the churning ocean.

No, he could not possibly have survived.

The ship somehow endured through the next day and night. Just before dawn a huge crash, louder even than the wind and the waves, announced the end. The triumphant sea tossed aside the weakened boards and flooded the vessel.

The strengthening light revealed only a mess of smashed timbers. The sole recognisable parts afloat were the bowsprit and the curiously untouched figurehead, her gleaming hair still glossy black, her fair cheeks white, the dress swathed around her comely breast still blue. The only living beings to observe these things were the three seamen clinging to them.

It was little short of miraculous that the lookout on the East Indiaman spotted them on the still heaving waves.

There were several hackney writers noting every word, composing in their heads articles that the broadsheets would pay for. One, however, knew he would command the best of prices for he it was who had written the piece under the banner "Aristocratic couple 'elope' ". He had recognised the Earl of Pentridge and immediately understood that Robert Smith, the passenger with the fair hair lost at sea, was none other than the Earl's missing heir, Viscount Kelton.

46

The Duke of Uppworth read the broadsheet with great interest but little sympathy; that is to say he was sorry for the loss of so many people but felt nothing for the son in whom the Earl's terrible ambitions had been vested.

While pertinent, the news made no difference in the end to what the Duke needed to do, what he had so far failed to achieve. As he put aside the publication and left the library, he knew he must prepare himself to speak to Miss Smith: it could not be delayed any longer.

Callie read the same piece and sank into an armchair.

At first, there was the numbness of shock, then the stabs of bewilderment, finally the agony of grief and loss. There were images of a vital young man, a living being, animated by plans for the future, their future; eyes fixed only on her: clear blue in their interest, amusement, concern, tenderness; stormy in anger and frustration. How could that person be no more?

It just could not be true.

She roused herself and went in search of her cloak – and Peter.

He seemed unusually loath to walk with her.

'Then I'll go by myself,' she declared.

'You mustn't go down the docks alone,' he said.

She stared at him. 'Why do you say the docks?'

He shuffled from one foot to the other. 'I heard the news,' he said reluctantly. Peter could not read well, but he had ears sharper than most; of course, the street-hawkers would be crying the latest. 'It's him, isn't it.' He did not even make it a question. 'Your lordling.'

She was so taken aback that she made no objection to his choice of words; although she really should not be surprised, she realised: Peter always seemed to know everything.

Everything? she suddenly wondered, thinking of her last meeting with Dob. Tears threatened for the first time and she had to work hard to force them back: crying never achieved anything, never washed away the sorrow.

The Earl's first reaction on hearing of the wreck of *The Katherine* was a disbelief and dejection such as he had never before felt in his life.

The Grand Plan into which he had invested so many years of careful planning and preparation and which had seemed *certain* to deliver huge dividends, both financial and social, had come to nought. In his life, the Earl had encountered setbacks, even some major ones, and he had always overcome them (with the exception, of course, of his wife's failings); but what was he to do now? What was worth doing anymore? The failure of the wedding to Lady Alicia Tentham had been a bitter blow, ending his high hopes of achieving financial independence from trade-tainted income; but the other part of the Grand Plan depended entirely on bloodline, and with the death of his son, the bloodline had come to an abrupt end. For that there simply was no substitute: several very expensive lawyers had long since confirmed it.

The Earl had drunk heavily on occasion but had never, once, allowed himself to become incapable; that night he drank himself into a stupor. Next day he nursed a sore head and brooded on how things could have come to this pass; he thought particularly of those who had failed to impose discipline on Darius – like that school, for all its claims! *Mens sana in corpore sano* – Latin nonsense! Physical activities – what did they have to do with an aristocratic mind?

He recalled the ridiculous prank Darius had played at Pentridge, outrunning the hounds. He recalled the boy's insistence on running every morning here in London.

And the Bromby boys had been required to swim as well, not to mention play hockey … swim. Had Darius become as good at swimming as he clearly was at running?

The Earl himself had learned to swim as a boy in the Little Avon. The river, generally a placid waterway, had strong currents in time of flood, but swimming in the sea, especially in a storm, would be completely different. And the surviving sailors had seen Darius go under and not reappear.

Still.

The following morning the Earl was awake early, totally sober and full of purpose once more.

Royal Dragon was still unloading at one of the East India Company's warehouses. Her captain, summoned from nearby lodgings, lost his ill-humour the instant his eyes lit on the coins being proffered.

In the ship's main cabin, he drew out a map and pointed to the spot where they had picked up the survivors from *The Katherine*.

Yes, he could be quite sure of the coordinates: *Royal Dragon* had all the latest navigational instruments, including a marine chronometer.

The Earl studied the chart; he inquired about the distance to the shore. Where, the Earl asked, would the wind and tide tend to cast up any – flotsam?

The captain peered at him. There would be little enough of that, he said bluntly.

Nevertheless, he indicated a length of the coast, where the largest port appeared to be Rabat.

The Earl spent the rest of the day searching the docks and shipping offices for a boat willing to take him there. In Rabat, there would surely be seamen who knew the waters and coast intimately.

Perhaps appropriately, the boat he found was a slaver, bound for West Africa and due to sail in two days' time.

He was rational enough to realise he was most likely embarking on a totally futile mission, but he simply had to pursue even the faintest of hopes; there was no other point to life.

He had already ordered Pentridge House to be closed. Apart from the couple charged with the caretaking, all the staff were to be dismissed – with the exception of one footman, whom he ordered to accompany him. After all, Forster knew Darius and must be fit with all that running in the park.

He sent a note to Richmond restating simply that he was going away for an unknown period of time; he did not explain why or where. Nothing would change in the arrangements for the support of the Countess and her life there. It never occurred to him to wonder if his wife had seen the news of the shipwreck or how she might be affected.

He visited his bank and drew out what he imagined would be suitable and sufficient funds.

47

Where once Callie had sought an interview with the Duke and felt frustrated when he avoided one, the shoe was now on the other foot: it was she who was keen to forestall a meeting and declined his invitations to join him. His third note, however, was quite clearly a command.

She pinned her hair securely. She tidied her dress and reflected how much Lady Olivia would hate knowing that *her* demise was the cause of such sombreness, how she would undoubtedly have wished Callie to don the richly patterned Indian shawl in which Sophie had wrapped the treasured copy of Twelfth Night; but propriety could not be defied.

And in any case the bright colours of the shawl would undoubtedly have only made Callie's pallor more evident. She tried, with little success, to pinch some colour into her cheeks, drew a few deep breaths and set off for the library.

She drank her tea; she nibbled a biscuit as slowly as possible.

The Duke spoke of the weather. Would it be as warm a winter as the previous one, he wondered? Or would there be one of the severe frosts that had frozen the Thames at intervals over the past two centuries?

Finally, there was no more small talk. Not even a crackle of burning wood broke the silence for the coal in the grate glowed quietly.

'Miss Smith,' said the Duke eventually, 'do you remember that I spoke to you of my nemesis only recently becoming known to me?'

She nodded.

'I do not wish to insult you, but can I presume you know the meaning of the word?'

She nodded again.

Nevertheless, he continued, 'To the ancient Greeks, Nemesis was the goddess of retribution who dispensed divine justice in the form of inescapable ruin and destruction. However, I think that is not after all the right allegory for my situation: what fate and man have contrived has nothing to do with divine justice, quite the opposite. Moreover, I do not accept that it is inescapable; I must at least try to resist it.' He pulled a wry face. 'Which I imagine has done nothing at all to enlighten you as to my purpose.'

'No, your Grace,' she agreed.

'To put matters plainly,' he said, 'I had come to accept too readily what seemed inevitable, without really looking into the consequences. And that,' he grimaced, 'is still not very plain, is it?' He drew a breath. 'The blunt facts are that I lost my son, then in the carriage accident I lost my wife; more than that, I lost my ability to create another son, even with a new wife.'

The facts were indeed blunt, but Callie knew at least a little of the huge depth of human grief behind them.

'I knew who would inherit both the Uppworth title and estate but was too wrapped up in my own affairs to investigate properly.'

Callie opened her mouth, but he held up a hand. 'Let me finish,' he said, 'for it has taken me long enough to get started.

'Then I discovered that things had changed; that another man was now my heir; a man who appeared to me increasingly abhorrent the more I learned of him. For the sake of both divine and earthly justice, I could not just accept that. I thought and thought about a solution but could not discover one, until I had an idea – a ridiculous idea, one that would take almost a miracle to realise, but the only one even remotely possible.'

'I don't see …,' began Callie dubiously.

'It involves a certain legal sleight of hand but – if it works – would be for the greater good.

'You see, if I remarried and my wife had a child, the law would recognise that child as mine.'

'But,' Callie had to point out, 'you have just confirmed that you cannot consummate a marriage and thus hope to create a child. Is that not commonly known?'

'It well may be widely speculated on, but it is, at the end of the day, only supposition,' he said shortly. 'And if there was evidence otherwise, who could *prove* differently? A wife cannot give testimony against her husband; a reputable doctor is bound by his professional oath.'

'But,' she said carefully, 'who would actually father the child? And,' she added, 'what if it were a daughter?'

'Some healthy fellow might surely be bribed to such employment,' said the Duke frankly, 'and to keeping the matter private. And if the child *were* a girl, it is true she would not solve the conundrum, but she would delay matters considerably, and,' he smiled wistfully, 'she would surely bring as much delight as my own daughter and Sophie.'

There was another silence as Callie thought furiously.

'You are, Miss Smith, an acute and sensible young woman. You will guess why I am telling you this.'

Of course, she did. Her mind raced.

'I have to tell you that I attended several balls with the intention of seeking out a suitable woman for my scheme; none appeared. I now think that by far the most suitable is right before me.

'But,' he added hastily, 'that is from my point of view. What I am proposing is unusual in the extreme and you may well find it quite objectionable. We have, I believe, dealt with each other quite well up to now and I fear my hare-brained scheme might bring that to a regrettable end. However, I made up my mind that it had to be ventured.

'Before you reflect on all this and make your decision, I must add that it is quite possible that my paralysis will shorten my days. In any event, my widow would, of course, be most generously provided for, regardless of whether she can produce an heir.

'Please,' he said earnestly, 'take whatever time you need to consider.'

But Callie had already considered. 'I cannot,' she said with resolution, 'fulfil the part.'

He stared at her. His face fell in disappointment. 'It is too much to ask,' he said heavily, 'of any respectable woman.'

'It is not that, your Grace' she said. 'Not at all. For, the world cannot regard me as a respectable woman.'

'Because you were born the wrong side of the blanket? That is hardly your fault.'

She shook her head. 'It is not that either.'

She took a deep breath and told him.

48

He stared at her in shock.

As well he might, she thought. She had been shocked at the realisation herself. There had only been that one occasion and in spite of the circumstances, the raw emotions, the shared lack of experience, they had known enough to part at the last moment. According to Mrs Hunt, who had passed on to Callie her extensive knowledge of the subject, "falling" should have been nigh impossible.

In the weeks that followed, Callie disregarded what should have been obvious signs, putting them down to sorrow over the loss of Lady Olivia and the impending departure of Dob.

Then, just days ago, had come the devastating news of the wreck of *The Katherine* and the stark fact that there would be no future with Dob, ever. As she sat through the dark hours of the night, she could no longer deny the other facts and could not imagine what she was going to do. She remembered her thoughts when faced with leaving Pentridge: an equally bleak future but definitely less complicated.

Now there would be a child. Her child. Dob's child.

And Callie knew that she would do anything, anything to protect it.

But what *could* she do?

She would sell her body and her soul if necessary but only as long as the child was not harmed.

There would be some months before her condition became evident. What employment might she find until then? What way might she earn some money? If she could save enough to keep herself until after the child was born, she might then move somewhere and present herself as a widow.

And here was the Duke offering her the almost perfect solution – almost.

The possible, probable, Society reaction to such a marriage sprang into her mind even as he talked. A Duke could be as eccentric as he pleased – marry somebody not only decades younger than himself but devoid of all social standing – while she would be adjudged a scandalous money-grabber and treated accordingly. It would be painful but a price worth paying: her child would have a legal name, security and – she was sure of it – the affection of the Duke, even if it was a girl.

But the child would be born too early for his plan.

And, as he continued to stare at her, she knew he must be revising his opinion of her – and regretting his proposal. He must surely feel disgust at her wantonness, revulsion that he had allowed such a person into his household, to have intimate care of Lady Olivia, to associate with Sophie.

She found that she hated losing his good regard, but at the same time she could feel no guilt about her feelings for Dob, nor her actions. She herself was the result of a young nobleman using his position for no other purpose than the gratification of his sexual appetite. She did not blame her mother for succumbing – how much choice did a housemaid have? Although the world might very well see Callie's present position as a case of "like mother like daughter", she knew it was nothing like.

She lifted her chin another inch and held the Duke's gaze.

'When?' he asked.

He was not dismissing her from the room, the house, instantly?

She gave him the date she had worked out.

There was another silence as he patently did his own calculation, counting back to the time of Lady Olivia's death. 'You were in need of comfort.'

That was true but misrepresented matters.

'Was that all there was to it?' he pursued.

'What point is there in discussing it?' she asked.

He considered a few moments. 'You have presented me with news that does not seem to match what I thought I knew of you, Miss Smith. I wish to understand before I make any judgment.'

Which was worthy of the man; she bit her lip with determination.

'I cannot believe you would indulge in casual intimacy; yet if it was not casual then there must be a relationship behind it which you have kept – private. Is that the case?'

There was nothing casual about the love that had called their child into being. 'Yes,' she said.

'Does the father know?'

She shook her head and before he could ask the next obvious question, she hurried on, 'He is no longer here.' She swallowed. 'He is gone forever.'

The Duke narrowed his eyes at her choice of words but did not challenge them. After a moment, he asked with almost a note of apology, 'Might I assume he is as upright as you? In body and in person.'

She recalled the tall leanness; the fair head; the startling blue eyes; the unfinished youth infused with an oddly mature human sympathy. She blinked hard. 'Yes,' she managed.

'A man fit to be the father of *my* child?' the Duke asked deliberately.

The marriage by special licence, at a very unfashionable little church, was attended only by those required by law to be present: the clergyman and the witnesses (one of whom was Hibbs). Even Sophie and James Millburn only received a card (from which the date had oddly been omitted) announcing the union – although both bride and groom much regretted the absence.

The covertness was explained by the fact that the family were in mourning for the death of Lady Olivia; the hastiness was left to conjecture.

And at Uppworth Park, in the county of G …, to where the couple immediately retired, any surprise was largely eclipsed by relief that the succession might yet be settled – and by curiosity about the new Duchess.

49

The Earl regarded the port of Rabat and recalled what he knew of it. He was well aware that it (in common with other ports all along the coast) was used by the notorious Barbary corsairs. It was true that the old Sultan Mohammed had made, some twenty years before, a treaty of "Friendship" with the then newly formed United States of America: that had declared Moroccan ports open to American ships at the same time as efforts were made to curb the activities of the corsairs. Attacks had nevertheless continued; they had grown more numerous again during the recent years of civil war over the succession and for the new Sultan Sulieman the corsairs were only one of many areas in which he had yet to establish his authority.

The Earl's first task was to find someone who spoke English. Ahmed claimed that qualification, having sailed for a while, he said, aboard an American ship (in what capacity never specified).

Ahmed was then tasked with using all his local contacts for news of a castaway. On the third day, he introduced his cousin who claimed to have heard something. Dark eyes looked out keenly from weathered features, flicking between the Earl's face and the coin held between finger and thumb.

What had he heard?

He had heard of a boat finding someone on the shore.

When?

Back around the equinox.

What boat?

Belonging to one of the corsairs.

What did he look like, the castaway?

The dark eyes sought another coin. Fair. A glance. Very fair.

Where was the boat now?

It had been over in Salé; but it had sailed – bound for Tangier, it was said.

With the castaway?

A third coin. Yes.

The Earl was faced with a dilemma. Should he linger and hope for more news, for confirmation? Or hurry to Tangier on what might turn out to be no more than a wild goose chase?

His cousin would continue the search in and around Rabat, most assiduously, Ahmed assured the Earl; while Ahmed himself would accompany the Earl to Tangier. Both for an appropriate fee, naturally.

The Earl made his decision. At dawn the next day he headed north with Ahmed and Forster.

50

Although the prime purpose of the marriage was quite clear to both of them, they had not talked about how that would translate into daily life.

For his Grace, the country mansion and estate were full of memories: of a childhood not unhappily spent in the shadow of his elder brother; of a later time with the reluctance to inherit balanced by joy in his wife and children; of a period of complete desolation made just bearable by the arrival of Lady Olivia and Sophie. Now circumstances had changed once more; past events could not be forgotten, but he could choose how much part they played in the future – at least the immediate future.

And most immediate was the disposal and running of the house. His tentative suggestions about this on the first morning were interrupted by the less than tentative remark by his new wife that she had not even seen the place yet. It would be most practical – would it not? – if he gave her a tour so that they could discuss just such matters as they went around.

Most practical? The Duke glanced down at his wheeled chair: there were parts of the mansion he had not visited in years, not wished to visit.

Hibbs might, she conceded, need some help, but surely it could be contrived?

And so it was, that they passed along numerous corridors and into manifold rooms, the Duke's chair being lifted up and down one staircase after another, around sharp turns and past obstructive furniture; Hibbs and another burly manservant retiring tactfully after each successful manoeuvre but remaining within call.

The style of the mansion at Uppworth Park, the Duke informed her, owed much to consultations between his grandfather and Robert Adams (as in the London Uppworth House) with its classical lines and proportions, its graceful fireplaces and plasterwork, its high windows letting in light and views of the gardens and countryside (once the heavy brocade curtains were drawn back and the close-fitting shutters opened).

The furnishings, revealed from beneath Holland cloth covers, included cabinets and decorative pieces from all corners of Europe, mixed with elegant pieces by Chippendale, matched to the carefully rolled Wilton carpets. Washstands held ceramic dishes and bowls from China; walls displayed large silvered mirrors within gilded frames and numerous paintings of all sizes; niches contained clocks in intricately worked cases, statues from far-off times and places.

Along the corridors and galleries were more portraits and landscapes, some so darkened with age it was almost impossible to make out details or features. The Duke confessed he did not know the subject or origin of all the house's contents, although, he assured her, there was a *meticulous* catalogue, which had been made on his grandfather's orders and which now occupied a sizeable and very sturdy shelf in the strong-room beneath the butler's pantry.

At first, Callie found it more than a little over-awing: even the Wicklow mansion, its proportions exaggerated no doubt in her childhood memories, was not as grand. Back then she had understood little – and Lady had had scant interest in such things. However, fascination soon overcame any misgivings. The Duke looked at her quizzically, as she put one perceptive question after another.

After several days viewing, only the nursery wing remained. His Grace took a deep breath. 'This was where my brother and I spent our tender years.' He continued, 'And where my twins were cared for; where,' he could not keep the tremor from his voice, 'they died together and were laid in small matching coffins.'

Impulsively, Callie put a hand on his shoulder. 'I can hardly imagine the pain of that,' she said quietly. Losing Dob was a constant grief, but to lose a child, two of them …

The Duke's hand brushed hers, recognition of her sympathy. 'Nevertheless, life goes on; against all reason. If it is God's will, I fear I cannot see His purpose. But now there is the prospect of a new child and everything must be done for its greatest benefit. The furniture and furnishings could be completely changed; all gloom and doom driven out,' he said with more determination than conviction.

Callie pondered. 'I cannot say whether that is possible, even desirable: their memory should surely endure. But I have another consideration.'

He looked up at her.

'Nurseries are placed, as is this, in a far corner of the house so that all childish noise and behaviour is unheard and unseen. However, I wish to have this child by me, to feed and tend, to comfort and to enjoy. Yes,' she saw him about to object, 'I do know – by close observation! – what is involved. And no doubt will be grateful enough for *help* in the care. Still, I cannot imagine the child here, separated by such a distance.'

His frown deepened.

'But perhaps the sounds would disturb you.' So far, they had occupied adjacent rooms in the suite adapted for the Duke on the ground floor. 'I could remove upstairs, to the rooms that look out over the gardens,' she offered.

'No,' he said sharply.

'Or other rooms,' she added hastily as she recalled that those rooms had once been occupied by the Duke and his first wife.

'No,' he shook his head at her misapprehension. 'Those are the nicest rooms in the whole place, by far the most pleasant for you and the child, but,' he added, 'with a little alteration they could once more accommodate me too. If,' he peered at her quizzically, 'that is an acceptable arrangement. For I believe I should not mind any childish noise and behaviour; quite the contrary.' He nodded towards the nursery rooms. 'A proper use for these rooms will perhaps become apparent, but might we consider that some other day?'

Behind the mansion, attached in fact to the storerooms and sculleries, was the carriage house and stable-block. It was difficult for the chair across the cobbles, but the Duke was glad Hibbs contrived it when he saw the pleasure and admiration in his Duchess's eyes as she viewed each occupant of the spacious and sweet-smelling boxes, putting her surprisingly knowledgeable questions to the head stableman.

The paths and walks of the gardens were much easier. It was possible in many places for the Duke to move the chair himself. Callie offered to push him, but he would not hear of it. There should be no question of her straining herself, and, in any case, he should exercise his arms and shoulders.

While the mansion reflected the ideas of Robert Adams, its setting showed those of a young Lancelot Brown. Near the house there were formal flower beds, everything presently cut back and tidied. There was a canal, devoid of lilies at this season, but reflecting in its dark surface the orangery that the Duke's grandmother had fancied. Beyond the ha-ha, as far as the eye could see, was gentle parkland dotted with trees, their branches stripped bare by the strong autumnal winds.

There was still more to see, but that involved the use of a double-chair shay specially adapted to carry the Duke. Callie climbed into the seat beside him, while Hibbs perched on the dickey at the rear.

'Perhaps,' his Grace said, with an almost mischievous smile, 'I might let you take the reins later, for I am convinced you are quite familiar with horses, but for the moment I intend to be selfish and drive myself. It is an irony of life that one does not value one's independence until it is lost.'

And with that he urged on the dun mare between the shafts.

Concealed by Capability Brown's perfectly naturalistic manmade hill, was the road which led north to Gloucester and south to Bristol, and across that lay the Home Farm. Once upon a time, before the Uppworths outgrew it, said the Duke with soft irony, this had been the family manor-house.

A huge granary and wool store were in the same Tudor style; as also were the adjoining cowsheds and dairy. Other buildings of indeterminate history were for tools and implements, pots and buckets, ropes and chains.

Nearby was a large kitchen garden with some beds still sporting a few vegetables such as leeks and cabbage; there were fruit bushes, their buds already formed for the next year but tight and hard against the winter. Trained against the high stonewalls which faced the sun and trapped its warmth were espaliered apples, pears, peaches and apricots.

When the weather next permitted, they drove a little further to the village of Uppworth, its cottages arranged either side of the main road. Here, the Duke informed her, the White Horse had income from both local and passing trade, but otherwise the residents depended almost entirely on the House of Uppworth, as he termed it: the gardeners and farm labourers, the baker and the blacksmith, the butcher and the candle maker, the washerwomen, the seamstresses, the parson and the doctor, those maids and servants who did not live-in, the saddler, the cooper, the furniture maker, the school teacher.

Not forgetting those in the outlying farmsteads and tied cottages, he added, such as the gamekeeper, forester and fowler.

Was there a map? asked Callie, showing the whole – the acres, roods and perches; the land use. As there was at … on other estates.

The Duke confirmed there was one in the estate manager's office. But it might well need amendment, his Grace added. He had not seen it for years as estate business was these days discussed in the mansion study.

What kind of man was the Uppworth estate manager? she wondered. From what she had seen, the estate looked to be reasonably well run.

The question she asked out loud, however, lifting her arm, was a query about the surrounding lands.

The Duke pointed in one direction. 'The Earl of Berkeley, in his ancient castle, is the main landowner between Uppworth and the River Severn. And,' he turned the other way, 'the Tentham estate lies between Uppworth and the Cotswolds, with very fine grazing for its sheep.'

'Lady Alicia Tentham?' Callie said in astonishment.

'She holds the title and the land,' he confirmed with a slightly odd smile.

51

Dob tried to find a position comfortable enough for sleep – although "comfortable", he had realised, was a relative concept and had virtually no meaning in his present circumstances.

The shackles on his legs had caused festering sores. Under the iron collar, his neck was raw. He shifted again trying not to disturb the men on either side of him. There were, he thought, twenty in the chain.

He understood now his dreadful mistake in swearing to the corsair captain that he had no wealthy family, nobody willing to pay a ransom for him. At the time the only thought in his sea-soaked brain had been to avoid anyone contacting his father. He had naively assumed that he would simply be put off in a port somewhere.

His next mistake had been to admit to the slave trader that he was not Catholic: he had not seen the relevance. Apart from fencing terms, Dob had been an unenthusiastic student of French at Bromby – which he realised with a shock he had left less than a year before – and too late he had understood from the heavily-accented words that Catholic slaves might hope to be redeemed from funds raised in Catholic churches in Europe. Apart from the Catholics, the trader had informed him, he sometimes had other Protestants – mostly Americans with a few German and Dutch – but at present, Dob was the only one.

At the first market, Dob was barely conscious – days walking in the sun exhausted him, but the hard ground at night kept him sleepless. Innumerable times he stumbled, twice he blacked out and fell – only to be brought back to awareness by the shocking pain of a perfectly-directed lash across his back.

The thought of staying there on the gritty ground forever seemed appealing: since death looked inevitable why not simply give in to it? But it seemed Dob's body was not yet ready to surrender: in spite of himself, he staggered to his feet, at the end of the day as greedy as his fellows for life-sustaining water and food.

By the time he was pushed into the ring, he was once more on the point of collapse. Later, as he replayed the scene with a clearer head, he thought he should be grateful that his senses had been numbed to the full degradation of being paraded naked before a circle of potential buyers; of being prodded and pinched, of having every part examined – from teeth to genitals.

He became aware that he was an object of considerable curiosity – the paleness of his skin and hair made all the more apparent by the darkness of his fellows. At the same time, his colouring together with a scarcely mature body suggested a lack of strength.

Several buyers looked at him with prurient interest, but none made a bid.

He pulled close the noisome *burnoose* which provided a cover at night and watched the slow dance of the stars, statelier than the most old-fashioned minuet, he thought. Which brought into his mind memories he usually kept at bay: shining ballrooms of silk-clad figures, refreshment tables laden with artfully arranged cakes, bowls of fruit punch never allowed to become empty; Lady Alicia with the ever-present Stackling hounds on her heels. How was she faring? It must surely be past the fifth of November, with its bonfires filling the dank air with wood smoke. Had she avoided discovery? Was she now in control of her fortune? Free to live as she wished – with the love of her heart …

And the love of *his* heart? How was she?

He recalled their last bittersweet meeting – and his promise to send for Callie as soon as possible from America.

What would she do when that summons never came?

52

As well as being stormy, the winter turned out to be one of the really cold ones, with a hard, unrelenting frost adding its unwelcome Christmas gift.

The fires in the occupied rooms of the mansion were constantly fed, with coal carried across the Severn from the Forest of Dean and with logs from the Uppworth woods.

The long library had a hearth at each end. Except where windows interrupted, its walls were entirely hidden by stacked book shelves. The recommendation, reading and discussion of books resumed. Often the conversations spread into other topics and over the weeks it felt less like tutor and student, more like companionship.

Callie was enormously grateful for the fortunate circumstances in which she found herself; they could so easily have been very, very different. If she felt uncomfortable with the unaccustomed ease, chafed to be busy with something herself instead of merely meeting with the housekeeper or cook and confirming arrangements, she reminded herself that the most important thing in her life at that time was the unborn child which announced itself with increasing vigour.

When she really could sit still no longer, she wrapped herself up warmly and walked briskly through the unheated parts of the house. At the odd un-shuttered window, she scraped ice from a pane and looked over the glittering landscape, the frozen surface of the canal, the rimed paths, and accepted it would be unwise to venture out.

In spite of the fires, of the attentiveness of Hibbs and numerous other servants, the Duke caught a chill.

Although Callie summoned the doctor immediately, she could already detect the terrifyingly familiar sounds of creaking leather as his Grace laboured to breath.

Dr Wells was a country doctor but one with experience and common sense. He decided not to let blood for the moment. Instead he approved what Callie had already done, using an extra bolster to keep the Duke almost upright, encouraging him to breath in the steam of herb tea as well as drinking plenty of it. Callie had been thankful to find that the mansion kitchen had quantities of dried peppermint and Dr

Wells promised to send willow bark to relieve the chest pain and help with the fever.

His homely face furrowed in thought for some moments. 'Of course,' he said eventually, 'it goes without saying that his Grace should get complete rest; sleep is one of nature's greatest healers.

'However,' he paused, 'I heard once from a colleague in Bristol that he had found coffee efficacious in easing congestion of the lungs – although it also tends to stimulate both wakefulness and the workings of the bladder.' He looked at Callie. 'I apologise your Grace, for mentioning such things, especially to someone of your tender years.'

Callie assured him that she might indeed be young, but she was no stranger to tending the sick – although the awful thought would not be dismissed that George, Margaret and Lady Olivia had all died.

His Grace directed a scowl at the swell of her belly.

'There is little danger,' she repeated Dr Wells' earlier assurance, 'to me or the baby. And,' she said with determination, 'I will simply not allow another death.

'Furthermore,' she interrupted whatever he might have wanted to say, 'the child needs you; Uppworth needs you. For you to die now, in fact,' she declared, 'would be nothing less than selfishness!'

He managed a crooked smile and a faint echo, 'Complete selfishness.'

That exchange probably had little to do with the eventual outcome, the harvest of the Grim Reaper patently having nothing to do with logic or indeed fairness.

Nevertheless, the fever finally surrendered to the willow bark tea and the constant application of a cool cloth to the

Duke's burning brow. The congestion of his lungs gradually eased, the vile phlegm made its way out of his tormented airways and was hawked into the patiently held spittoon. The evil humours of his body were flushed out, time and again, into the waiting bottle.

Hibbs certainly did more than his duty in all of this, but there were long hours, of the day and in the night, when Callie did whatever was needed.

At first the Duke was barely aware of her ministrations. When he became so, he protested but weakly.

Indeed, he remained seriously weak, despite the chicken broth stoutly endorsed by Doctor Wells which was spooned between his reluctant lips in turn by Hibbs and Callie.

Even before that crisis was over, another arose: the estate manager, riding along an icy track, was thrown from his horse.

His clerk could see immediately the grotesque angle of the fallen man's neck; Doctor Wells' confirmation was hardly needed – death must have been instantaneous.

Doctor Wells' other pronouncement was also absolute: on no account must his Grace be informed or in any way bothered with such matters.

Callie's first meeting with the clerk was not promising. John Wilson, it turned out, was a man not much older than herself; an orphan and charity scholar from the Crypt School in Gloucester, he had been recruited by the deceased estate manager barely a year before. He looked bewildered when Callie asked to see the accounts.

Bewilderment turned to surprise, surprise to suspicion and anxiety as she perused them carefully, ran a knowing finger down and across the figures and put even more knowing questions.

For Callie they confirmed two things: John Wilson had an adequate grasp of figures and the manager had indeed run the estate competently.

However, things would arise, sooner or later, that required a decision, direction. She had no doubt the Duke would want to engage a new manager, but he was not fit to do so at present and she could not presume to do it for him – even had she known where to start.

It was also clear that John Wilson did not have enough knowledge of the estate to fill the post even temporarily.

Who, she wondered, might have that knowledge?

And be willing to work with the Duchess, a woman, of tender years, increasingly heavy with child, new to her position and to Uppworth, unable, for who knew how long, to call on support from the Duke?

53

As he lay on the rocky ground, Dob picked out the Pole Star, one of the few he could name and recognise. Using this and the course of the sun during the day, he knew they had been moving generally southwards. If ever he managed to escape, he supposed he should head west, towards the ocean.

The main problem, of course, was that he was never unshackled from the others, except when being paraded at market; and then the chain attached to his collar was firmly held by a burly guard.

It was in a small town, very much like a dozen others, that Dob suddenly realised he had been sold: a buyer had decided that the price over which he had haggled so vociferously was good enough for his purpose, whatever that might be.

Strangely Dob had almost ceased to consider the

possibility: the unrelieved misery had seemed endless.

He viewed his new circumstances with a completely unfounded glimmer of hope.

Traipsing along, chained to a dozen other slaves, however, seemed all too familiar; although Dob did realise they were now heading up into the hills. Soon they left all settlements behind and the trail became increasingly steep. In the distance rose a plume of smoke. As they drew nearer, Dob could see that part of the hillside had been excavated; on the rock face were figures hacking out stone; at the base others were breaking it up, hauling it away towards the source of the smoke: a fire, encouraged by the rhythmic wheeze of a large bellows, under a crucible.

The work was gruelling and inexorable. Dob often staggered to a halt and slumped to the ground, only for the lash to drive him back into action. As the sun began its swift descent of the sky, he forced down some unrecognisable food before exhausted sleep overtook him.

As one terrible day followed another, however, against all the odds, he found himself growing stronger. His bare feet grew soles harder than any leather boot. His body, where it was not covered by the filthy cloth around his head or the one over his loins, turned, very reluctantly, to ever deeper shades of brown. The muscles of his arms and shoulders grew into whipcord, those in his legs strengthened and built. The torn skin on his hands mended into great callouses; his bare fists could strike almost as hard as the hammer they were required to wield – a useful asset in holding his own against fellow-slaves (as were those ungentlemanly boxing tricks).

Time revealed itself a two-faced creature. Every day passed with dreadful slowness; each morning the evening appeared an unattainable destination on a distant horizon, every stone took an eternity to break up; then suddenly the new moon showed another month had elapsed.

The same moon measured the passing weeks for the Earl. At Tangier he found any number of corsair ships, but even the promise of considerable reward failed to identify which was the one, if any, that had sailed up from Salé.

In a two-storey mud and stone building housing the American Legation, the United States consul, Mr James Simpson, was aware only of the foundering of *The Katherine* and the rescue of the three seamen the Earl already knew about. There had been no news of any other survivors; although he had recently been apprised of an American sailor being held in the dungeons of Tétouan for whom he hoped to negotiate a release. The Earl would be very welcome to accompany him and search there.

54

Her relationship with Hibbs had improved in inverse proportion to the state of the Duke's health. His Grace's manservant had connived over the sudden wedding and removal to G…shire but remained very reserved with the new Duchess. He knew, as well as anyone in Uppworth, why an heir was hugely desirable but, unlike anyone else, had known Callie as Lady Olivia's employed companion and knew for certain that the child she was carrying was not the Duke's. He kept both things to himself – but not always a suspicion bordering on outright distrust.

However, with their shared care for the Duke, Callie *thought* the distrust was beginning to dissipate; and she felt, oddly, that just because Hibbs knew so much about her, he was the only person she could possibly talk to about the estate management dilemma.

'Old Walter,' said Hibbs with a small gleam in his eye.

'Who's he?'

'Born on the estate,' came the answer. 'He's lived here all his life; he worked for both the previous Dukes in the fields, the woods, the gardens, the stables; knew everything and everybody in Uppworth – still does,' said Hibbs with another odd sign of amusement. 'He's not as spry as he was,' he added, 'but as sharp as ever – in the head and with his tongue: constantly giving his opinion to the company in the White Horse.'

There was definitely something Hibbs was not telling her, but he would not conceal anything harmful to Uppworth and its Duke – would he? 'And is that opinion balanced? What,' she prodded, 'did he think of the late manager?'

There it was again: definitely a smile. 'Why don't you ask him yourself?' suggested Hibbs.

Walter Hibblett could have been the old countryman in any of a hundred sketches and engravings: bent from years of physical labour in all weathers, face lined, white hair sticking out from a battered hat, pipe protruding from one pocket, red kerchief from another. He addressed her as 'Your Grace' in a broad country accent but respectfully enough, although his eyes (most certainly not rheumed with age) flicked over her with unveiled curiosity before he lowered them to study the boards beneath his boots.

Callie had given quite some thought to the meeting. She needed to make the right impression: she did not doubt that Walter Hibblett's opinion of *her* would be shared very soon at the White Horse and thereafter in every corner of Uppworth, and indeed the whole county.

It was her first real test. If she got this wrong it would take a lot to redeem herself.

She still wore the dark, discreet dress of mourning which she hoped would add a little gravitas to her youth. By habit her hair was simply styled. She had suggested the mansion study for the appointment: very patently taking over the Duke's place – although she had rearranged the large desk and chair so that she commanded a view both of the door and the window out towards the stable block; perhaps, she reflected sourly, the only strategy for which she could possibly thank Mills, the Pentridge steward.

The difficulty was to project dignity and authority without being aloof; to be respectful of the man without seeming immature; to listen with interest without appearing to flatter; to seek information while showing she was not a complete ignoramus.

Dob had several times tried to explain to her the subtleties of fencing, the fascination of pitting both wit and body against an opponent, even if it was only in a friendly bout (a seemingly misnamed "assault"). Many of the terms were French, she had learned, such as those used to set a match in motion: en-garde, pret, allez. And there were three types of weapon: epée, foil and sabre. Callie felt that the match with Mr Hibblett was very much in earnest and launched straight into allez without the niceties of either en-garde or pret. Metaphorical forms of all three weapons (and probably others) were deployed in the bout of verbal feint and parry, lunge and riposte, attack and counter-attack.

At the end of half an hour, Callie felt satisfied that perhaps the points scored were about even. She was convinced that the man did indeed know a great deal about the estate but knew enough too, about the world beyond Uppworth's boundaries, to make astute judgements. His opinions, in a word, were not hot air. It was abundantly evident as well that the welfare and continuing prosperity of Uppworth were of great importance to him.

She inquired, neutrally, if he had the time for further discussion? She herself felt in need of refreshment and perhaps he might like something?

He would be pleased to take a cup of tea, he said, a gleam challenging her to suggest ale.

And suddenly she recognised that look. Hibblett to Hibbs, of course! As obvious as Caroline to Callie!

'Now, Mr Hibblett,' she said when the tea was finished, 'I would be most interested to hear a little of your family.'

'Always as thick as thieves, they were, my grandson William and the Duke – only he weren't Duke then, nor like to be. Inseparable as lads, into all the things that boys do. And when his Lordship went off to fight in America, our William went as well. Been through the good times and the bad together – especially those since the accident.'

No wonder Hibbs was so protective of his Grace. And thank goodness the Duke had such an old friend as well as a devoted carer.

But Callie had to establish her own place.

She inclined her head in acknowledgment, in approving acknowledgment – and brought the conversation back to business, the business of running Uppworth.

It was the first of what became regular meetings.

Callie, Walter Hibblett and John Wilson made an unlikely team but one that quite quickly fashioned itself into a reasonably effective board of management.

John Wilson brought a list of matters that needed attention, then reported subsequently on progress. Walter

Hibblett disbursed his treasure of knowledge about Uppworth, its every corner and every inhabitant. Callie sat and absorbed it all, fascinated; sometimes overwhelmed as she realised the extent of Uppworth's wealth and resources. John Wilson listened with commendable concentration and scratched a multitude of notes.

Finally, Callie summed up, dictated to John Wilson what was agreed and authorised the actions he should see put into effect. Signing herself as Caroline Duchess of Uppworth had felt very strange at first but soon became second nature.

Callie longed to go out and about with Walter Hibblett to see the things he spoke of, to meet the people who were only names; to accompany John Wilson as he rode around the estate (as she once had with Lady); to compare present reality with the somewhat dated map that she had now seen and studied. But even a well-sprung carriage would be an unnecessary risk given the frozen landscape and, in any case, she could not spare the time: there was an enfeebled Duke to cajole, to cheer up, to read to or simply to sit with.

55

For Dob every day, regardless of the heat or cold, wet or dry, was the same unending labour. Even on Fridays when the Musulmans took themselves off for prayer, Dob and the other *kafirs* (as the Arab work-masters contemptuously called the non-believers) were kept working.

Why the owner of the quarry had to purchase replacement slaves at regular intervals was obvious. For the moment Dob's young body had responded to the huge physical demands put on it, but death was an ever-present reality: one man would simply fall asleep one night and not wake in the morning; another would drop dead at work;

another would suffer a fatal lapse of attention. Accidents received minimal treatment: some men recovered from their injuries, more did not. All too often there were outbreaks of illness – fever, ague and the bloody flux – for which there was equally little care.

Foot-whipping was used for what the guards regarded as minor offences, for even on hardened feet this caused great pain (but little loss of the ability to work); more serious disobedience was punished by flogging; trying to run away by hamstringing.

Dob could not risk failing in any escape attempt.

56

It was a great relief when the spring sun finally relieved the winter's icy siege and drove away its clammy rear-guard fogs; when the early flowers broke through; when the faintest green began to adorn the black branches.

His Grace was encouraged by Doctor Wells to leave his room; well-wrapped in warm blankets, he was carried down the stairs and into the sitting room where a blazing fire had managed to reach even the furthest corners. From the depths of an armchair he could gaze out upon the wakening garden, watch the frantic antics of the birds busy about their delayed mating and nesting.

The change of scene seemed to have the desired effect and a few weeks later the Duke had enough vigour to suggest a visit to the library where he and Callie picked up a new book and a new discussion.

One morning in early summer he announced to Hibbs that he felt well enough to meet with the estate manager and catch up on matters.

He looked at Callie in astonishment as, responding to

Hibbs's urgent message, she recounted – a little defiantly – exactly how those matters stood.

'You!' he exclaimed, his gaze taking in her youthful and now very round figure. 'With old Walter? And that charity school lad, Wilson?'

'I believe you will find,' Callie said steadily, 'that everything is in order, good order.'

He stared at her as if searching for any trace of false assurance or half-truth; then more closely for signs that she might have been overtaxing herself.

'I am perfectly well,' she anticipated him. 'Indeed, I have found it all very interesting, invigorating even – such things being much better suited to my abilities,' she added dryly, 'than fine needlework or delicate water colours.' She glanced meaningfully at the book on the side-table. 'I believe it can be no surprise to you that I have an active mind.'

He was on the verge of being angry – at the deception, at his own impotence. And Callie would not blame him for either. But she would *not* pretend to be simple or docile – however much she might owe to his generosity of spirit.

For long moments he continued to glare at her, then the corners of his lips lifted. 'Has a termagant hatched in the Uppworth nest while I was too ill to notice?'

Callie could not help but laugh. 'That, your Grace, would be a ptarmigan! I promise you I am neither a *hot termagant* nor a feather-brain.'

'No, most decidedly neither,' he agreed. His mouth quirked again. 'Might I be permitted to attend the next estate board meeting, do you think? Or will that have to be put to the vote?'

'Enough quizzing, your Grace. Of course, it was always obvious you would resume control, if only to appoint another manager.'

'But …?' he prompted.

She hesitated. 'I will miss it,' she said frankly. 'The child will come soon and will provide plenty to occupy me. But I have come to know a little of Uppworth by report and would dearly like to know more first-hand.' She paused again. 'Moreover – do not think me brazen or uncaring, for truly I am not – if the child is a boy, or even if it is girl, it will need to know all about its heritage, the heritage you are bequeathing to it but,' she swallowed, 'may not live to hand on in person.'

'I could reply that, on recent experience, you are not going to permit that to happen!' he said wryly. 'However, one cannot divert all the unpleasant truths of life with facetiousness. You are quite right to face them and speak them.' He smiled but spoke earnestly. 'I would very much like to attend the next meeting. After I have caught up a little and seen how it works, we could come to some decision about the future, couldn't we?'

Advertising for a new estate manager was delayed until such time as the exact details of the position became clear. And such exactitude, in reality, proved elusive. When the Duke was well enough to attend meetings, he contributed his points and opinions but respected the input of the others. He never overrode them, although he might suggest other factors to take into consideration. He made it clear that when he was *not* well enough to be present, he was quite content to let the trio decide and act. In particular he spelled out that he both supported and authorised the Duchess. What would happen on Callie's confinement, like the advertisement, was shelved.

The exact date of the marriage having been obscured by Hibbs's unlikely poor memory, when a robust baby boy made his uncomplicated appearance in the world just before midsummer nobody at Uppworth made any comment other than to express felicity – for the safe deliverance of the child to their new, unusual but already respected Duchess; for their long-suffering Duke; and for the prospect of a settled succession (unlike that of the Fifth Earl of Berkeley who had somehow omitted to obtain proof incontrovertible of *his* marriage until after the birth of his fifth son).

The child was Arthur Robert, his Grace acquiescing without demur to Callie's wishes: the form of a name did not matter – not a single one of the figs produced in the orangery. The baptism of the lusty new heir was entered in the church register and the appellation duly added to the leaf of the family bible.

57

Among Dob's fellow slaves were groups from different regions; some were taller of build, some darker of skin, some finer of feature; all were from beyond the borders of the Moslem lands. As well as their native tongue, quite a number knew Arabic; in practice, it was often their common language. From them Dob had learned enough to converse, and to understand what the guards said between themselves.

He saw the loaded carts being lined up; soon mules would be harnessed to the carts and a train would set out, as had happened several times over the past year or more: to carry the copper down to the plains, to the markets, to the traders, to the smiths. He knew the heavily laden carts had to be prevented from careering down the precipitous hillside and slaves, chained to the rear, were used to provide the necessary braking. He listened now as he was mentioned as one of those to be so used – and wondered if, at long last, there might be some chance of escape.

If a cart ran out of control, however, the only escape would be in certain death.

The winter rains had left the hillsides verdant and every plant and shrub eager to flower before the heat and drought of summer. Dob could almost have admired the loveliness had he had the leisure to do so – which of course he did not.

The rains had also washed away parts of the roads and on some sections the straining slaves were hard put to prevent cart and mule from tipping over or, worse, careering over the edge. By the end of the first day, Dob's feet, hardened as they had become, were bruised and bloody; every muscle in his back ached; his calloused hands were cut from heaving on the chain tethering him to the cart. The other men on either side of him were in no better state, but at least they were all still alive. On another cart, a chain had snapped, flying back into the face of the man on the other end of it. The cart, no longer adequately braked, had gathered speed and hurtled off the road, spilling its load at the bottom of a steep gulley. The muleteer had leaped to safety; the mule and the other two slaves had not had that option.

Two days later they reached more level ground. Most of the slaves were released from the carts, chained into a line and herded by some of the mounted guards back up towards the mine. To his relief, Dob was one of those required to continue with the carts. There were deliveries in several towns, but the train continued southwards, both the empty and the still-laden carts.

One town was altogether more impressive; perched on a small hill, the road approached it through fields and orchards. Dob was not sure what the twisted trees with fine silver-green leaves were, nor indeed the plants: some bright green with newly sprouted blades, others dark-green bushes, white or purple flowers dotted amongst the feathery foliage. It seemed the soil here provided abundance. Moreover, there was the bleating of sheep not far off. Dob thought longingly of thick mutton stew with vegetables and hunks of country bread – what had seemed such basic fare at Bromby now appeared like a royal feast, so vivid in his mind's eye that he felt his mouth begin to water. The slaves were invariably served a boiled cereal, dollops of it heaped into their eager, cupped, filthy hands.

The town itself proved to be equally well-laid out, arranged under the protection of the impressive casbah which had been constructed, Dob gathered, on the orders of Sultan Moulay Ismail. This was a name he had heard before, more than once, as the guards swapped favourite tales of the old "Warrior King" as they called him: of his prowess as a leader of a huge army; of his construction of forts and mosques, grand citadels with lush gardens and vast palatial stables; of his extreme cruelty – particularly that, infinitely more imaginative than mere foot-whipping, flogging or hamstringing.

Dob realised that the town lay at a crossroads and goods from north, south, east and west were brought there and traded in the bustling souk. The empty carts could now be filled with supplies to take back to the mine: sacks of grain to feed the slaves but also beans, olives, almonds, dates for the guards; oil for cooking and for lamps; leather and woven fabric; ropes and harness.

The purchasing was done by the guards, but the goods were carried by the slaves, chained in line. Dob happened to be last and as the guards concentrated on loading the broad shoulders of his neighbour, Dob seized his moment: in one swift move he picked up a slim iron bar from a neighbouring stall and stuffed it into his loincloth.

58

His Grace joked that his continued good health most certainly came from copying little Arthur's example: drinking plenty of milk and eating good, plain fare; going outdoors whenever the weather permitted; retiring early to bed.

'Perhaps I am not so round of cheek, but certainly I burble,' he chuckled at the child on his lap, who obligingly laughed back, revealing a perfect pair of pearly teeth.

Callie smiled.

But both of them knew that the comparison had its limits: while the boy would hopefully grow in strength and stature, the Duke could expect no more than a temporary remission. They were thankful for each day granted to them, but they were under no illusion and worked with urgency on arrangements for a future in which the Duke would have no part, a future where Callie would be left to shoulder responsibility for Uppworth and its heir.

Callie's life was full to the brim: every day and some nights too, when she simply could not bear to leave her beloved son to the care of his perfectly competent nurse.

The advertisement for an estate manager had eventually been placed, but so far every applicant had failed to satisfy the interviewing quartet. Indeed, not one had even cleared the first hurdle: they had all greeted Callie courteously enough then proceeded to completely disregard her; when specifically asked, most had looked astonished at the idea of taking direction from the young Duchess; some had even laughed.

There were those among the Uppworth tenants who still queried her authority too, but after a few difficult challenges Callie was largely accepted, her appearance greeted with respect, even warmth; especially when, on fine days, she began to take along Arthur – just as Lady had done with her.

Callie did not mind how busy her life was: she had so much to be grateful for, to enjoy. Moreover, it distracted her from the underlying worry about the Duke's health and, beneath her heart, the shard of ice which no amount of summer sun managed to melt.

59

At night the slaves were unlinked from each other and locked in a windowless room. Dob took care to lie himself near the door and managed to ward off sleep until he was certain all his fellows were oblivious to the world. He had not tried to share with them what he intended: he had no definite plan; he was simply desperate to try something, anything. He knew very well the terrible price for failure. He would not invite the others to take that same risk.

Now his heart was thumping so hard he feared it would waken them anyway; but the regular heavy breathing was unbroken. Dob rose cautiously from the stone floor and felt around the door. It was locked of course from the outside, but Dob had spotted that although it was heavy, the door seemed to have shrunk over time leaving a sizeable gap between it and the frame. Most particularly this meant there was an increased distance between the lock and the box let into the jamb to receive the bolt. Both lock and box were of solid iron, but *if* only the tip of the bolt rested in the box then *perhaps* there was a chance.

Dob inserted the stolen metal bar into the space between the door and the frame, shifted it upwards until it met the bolt and tried to manoeuvre the tip into the box. Nothing moved. Dob tried harder, clenching his jaw in the effort to keep silent. He changed the angle slightly; he repositioned his body so as to direct his strength – almost a parody of some fencing move, a detached part of his brain suggested bizarrely.

There was a scraping sound that to Dob's ears seemed thunderous. He paused, hardly daring to breathe. One of the slaves turned over, mumbled something in his own language and became still.

Dob forced himself to count slowly to a hundred, then applied himself to the bar again. He summoned every ounce of strength in his work-tempered shoulders and arms, braced his legs. The bolt shifted, slipping free of the box. Dob hastily stopped levering, fearful that he would drive the bolt crashing back into its cylinder. Blessedly, it stayed extended. Dob pushed very gently at the door, hoping the hinges would not squeak. Inch by inch there was more starlight. When there was just enough space, he slipped out and took a deep gulp of the night air. He eased the door to, so that at a casual glance it would appear fastened.

Turning his head, he could make out the wall which surrounded the yard. To his right was the building where the guards slept; no light showed; there was no sound. He drew another breath of relief.

The door to the street was barred but this one from the inside. With infinite care Dob lifted the bar, fighting the urge to hurry.

Then he was outside, keeping to the darkest shadows, heading out of town.

Once in the countryside he took a bearing on the Pole Star and set off westwards, towards the distant ocean, walking fast, running where he could, aiming to put the greatest possible distance behind him before dawn and the inevitable discovery of his escape.

He never knew if they tried to follow him; certainly, he saw no sign of pursuit. He was fortunate to find a djellaba spread over a thorn bush. This hid both his unusual fair colouring and the wretched slave collar that he had no way of removing. His feet were so blackened by sun and filth he did not think their natural pallor would betray him, but it was often difficult to keep his face in the shade of the hood and on the few occasions when he could not avoid people, he kept his tell-tale eyes firmly fixed on the ground as he muttered a greeting that just could be the local Arabic.

Of equally grave concern, was that he could not maintain a steady direction: the roads followed the ridges and valleys laid out by some ancient god; in any case, he often had to divert across fields in search of something to eat. Sometimes he found crops that he could pick; many times, he was unsure what they were, but desperate hunger drove him to try anyway. He had no way of cooking anything, but on a few occasions, he was able to steal from an untended pot.

Water was also a problem. There were wells aplenty, but there were always people around those. Sometimes he was lucky enough to find an irrigation channel.

He had no idea about any of the myriad settlements he skirted, often in the dark, desperately trying to avoid twisting an ankle or worse; and even if he had learned a name, it would not have helped him know where he was. He lost count of exactly how many days had passed since his escape, but he knew the moon had grown full then waned and started to wax again. He became increasingly convinced he was getting no nearer to the ocean he so badly wished to reach.

To the east a high mountain range loomed ever closer and to the south he could make out the fortified walls of a large city. Surely such a place would be at a crossroads: from there, there must be a route to the west.

He set off to walk around the walls, but in the end the

thought of markets with food stalls was too tempting. He chose the busiest time of the day and joined the throng passing through the ornate gate set in the red stone walls.

And here his luck ran out.

60

Callie realised that sooner or later she would have to meet their neighbours, that is to say, the landowners and others with claims to gentility: after all the Uppworths were senior peers, entrenched for generations in the local hierarchy. For more than a year she was able to put this off. Everyone speculated, of course, about this unknown whom the crippled Duke had married and who had, almost miraculously, produced an Uppworth heir. However, in his youth, as the second son, the present Duke had never really been part of the social scene and when he unexpectedly inherited the estate and title, the county *ton* could not be truly comfortable with his unaccountable views which they referred to as "liberal" but privately thought of as eccentric, verging on the revolutionary. Thus, they had not pushed to resume contact after the terrible series of events that took in quick succession his children, his wife and his power to walk. Now they vacillated between fascination and reluctance and were as thankful for the combined excuse of mourning Lady Olivia and the confinement as was her Grace.

Callie was busy with concerns much closer to her heart, but she was, after all, now the Duchess and her son would one day, God willing, be the Duke. And since there had to be a reckoning, she decided it would be best if she took the lead.

The Duke pulled a rueful face when she discussed it with him. 'For myself,' he said, 'I would not care if I never had to attend another ball, dinner or soirée, let alone host one! But I fear you are right: it should be done for Arthur's sake and any soldier knows it's always best to seize the initiative, put the enemy on the back foot.'

She smiled. 'I was thinking of it as a kind of military campaign too.' She added wryly, 'Recalling, in fact, what Machiavelli advised.'

He lifted a quizzical eyebrow. 'Which bit in particular?'

'That "a captain should endeavour with every art to divide the forces of the enemy",' she said. 'In this case, go and face them separately *before* they have the chance to square up en masse at some grand function.'

'And have you decided which *enemy* to take on first?' he inquired with an appreciative chuckle.

'I was wondering about our nearest neighbour, Lady Alicia Tentham,' Callie said. 'I have heard that she is not altogether the "conventional" sort. Perhaps,' Callie added quickly before he could inquire where she had heard this, 'she might prove to be an ally.' As she had, oddly, to Dob.

'Ah yes,' said the Duke, more soberly, 'our nearest neighbour. Her lands indeed border the Uppworth estate. They would, of course, go to her husband – if she were ever to marry.'

'She remains unmarried?' Callie prodded.

'She was engaged, a year or two ago, but there was something of a scandal – shortly before *we* married.'

'Scandal?' Callie hoped she did not sound *too* casual.

'She and the putative groom disappeared.' Callie swallowed. 'His father,' there was definitely a sourness in the tone, 'and her guardian sought high and low but to no avail. Some weeks later there was news that the fellow had perished in a shipwreck en route for America.' Callie's heart contracted painfully. 'In the middle of November Lady Alicia coolly appeared at Tentham Court, announcing that she was now of age to come into her fortune; that she would live as she wished, as the fancy took her; that she had no intention of surrendering her independence to a husband, ever.'

Callie contemplated taking Arthur with her. When visiting the Uppworth tenants, any tension was usually broken by the child's artless babble and actions, but Callie feared there was just a chance Lady Alicia might see something familiar in Arthur's features. Perhaps the blond curls would mellow with age, but the blue eyes would not change now. At present the chubbiness of infancy hid any possible resemblance to Dob's square jaw and the snub nose had yet to assume any determination. Still, she would go alone.

She picked out from her largely unused wardrobe a gown of the finest wool, modest in style but excellently tailored; and gave to her usually disappointed maid the joy of deciding on the hat, gloves and half-boots to complement it.

As she entered his room to advise him of her plans – and more importantly of those the nurse had for Arthur – the Duke studied her.

'Do I look well?' she asked, suddenly a little uncertain.

'*Very* well: a veritable Duchess!' He added in a tone of amused wonder, 'So was Descartes correct that human attitudes and attributes are innate, whichever side of the blanket we may be born? Or was Locke correct that we come into the world as a *tabula rasa* on which life inscribes our form and character?'

Callie had questioned that long before the Duke introduced her to the works of the philosophers. She had even broached the subject with Lady (although in simpler language). The reply, in Lady's usual brisk fashion, was that it was quite obviously a mix – just look at any foal! Its physical characteristics were bred from its sire and dam, its ultimate body formed by how it was fed and treated; at the same time, each one came with its own distinct personality, evident from the moment it struggled onto its wobbly legs. This pithy summary had been more than confirmed by Callie's later observations of the succession of Hunts.

Lady Alicia, Callie decided, very much shared the aura of independence that she remembered in Lady, but while Lady's freedom had been so effectively snuffed out by the Marchioness, that of Lady Alicia radiated strongly.

She was a handsome woman, beautifully attired to show off her perfect creamy complexion and immaculately arranged deep brown locks. Every detail was just right. Did she always dress so? Or was it to impress Callie? Or – Callie tried not to stare as Lady Alicia introduced the other woman in the room.

'This is my dearest friend, Miss Berriston.' Emerald flecks in Lady Alicia's eyes flashed with an emotion she made no effort to conceal: a mix of pride and defiance and admiration and – quite unmistakeably – love. 'Theresa and I were at school together,' she said. 'Society dictated that we should be separated thereafter by marriage, but we swore to each other that if the Llangollen ladies could set up house together, so could we!'

Callie had heard something of the pair of Irish women who lived together in north Wales and who, in spite of their unconventionality, received visits from many a well-respected literary figure.

'It was difficult of course,' joined in Miss Berriston, 'particularly because of the conditions imposed by Alicia's father's will, but we found ways to meet. Even when her dreadful guardian, Baron Stackling, forced her into an engagement with a schoolboy,' (Callie managed to keep a straight face), 'and kept her virtually under lock and key in London, I found a position with a milliner near St James's and nobody thought to forbid Alicia to come in search of a new hat !' She chuckled.

The account was explaining some of the riddles for Callie. She wondered, for a moment, at the frankness – but then, why not? Lady Alicia now had the position and wealth to do as she liked, to live exactly as she wished.

The humour suddenly struck her and she responded with a small laugh of her own: while Lady Alicia was contriving covert meetings with Miss Berriston, Dob was doing the self-same thing with Callie in Hyde Park.

'But,' Miss Berriston continued, 'it turned out that the schoolboy had been forced into the match too and was just as keen to avoid it; so, he and Alicia made a plan together which succeeded splendidly. Only,' she conceded, 'not so well for him in the end: he took a ship for America which went down in a storm.'

'But you, your Grace,' Lady Alicia said, 'were not, I hope, forced into marriage with the Duke of Uppworth?'

Callie, made vulnerable by the pain of recalled loss, could not prevent a flush of anger. There was also an unreasonable feeling of guilt because of the subterfuge involved. But above all she was stung by the implied criticism of a man she had come to recognise as "noble" in the true sense of the word.

She was prevented from making a probably unguarded retort by Lady Alicia adding hastily, 'Please excuse my bluntness I promise you that I have only respect for his Grace and sympathy for his unfortunate state, but, as you will have gathered, I am much vexed about the question of marriage – the assumption that it is the *only* state for a woman and the law that then deprives her of identity and property.'

'On that we can agree,' Callie allowed, but adding firmly,

'however, I can assure you that my marriage with the Duke is one entirely of mutual consent and esteem.'

Miss Berriston nodded. 'I am glad to hear both of those things. Although,' she said, 'you will need no warning that *everyone* will pry into the same matter.' Her face brightened; transforming what was in truth a rather plain face. 'Take this as your first rehearsal!'

Callie managed a wry smile. 'Thank you. In similar vein, I can tell you to expect an invitation to the full, dress performance at Uppworth Park, later in the summer.'

61

Dob sneaked a flat bread and a handful of olives and went in search of a private spot to devour his feast. But he had been spotted.

He ran down alleys and streets, twisted back on himself. And ran again. Each time he thought he had managed to throw off his pursuers there would be cry of recognition. He sprinted down a narrow lane. He rounded a sharp corner and drew back into the shadows. If he stayed still, there was a chance his pursuers would run past and not notice him.

He drew in great gasps of breath and listened to the sounds of running feet.

At the same time his eye was caught by movement: not down in the street but high above him, on the wall edging the roof of a tall building.

Two figures, one taller, one shorter, were evidently enjoying a bird's eye view of the hunt. There were excited shouts then a high-pitched scream as the smaller figure fell.

Self-preservation dictated that Dob stay where he was; some insane contrary impulse made him plunge forward and stretch out his arms. His last, strangely detached thought was to wonder if this was how it felt to be hit by a cannon ball – then he hit the ground and an agonising pain erupted in his skull, light flashed in his brain, fizzled and went out.

With returning consciousness came terror. He was laid sideways, his head extended; only one eye would open and that revealed a hammer poised above him.

He tried to jerk away, but his body was sluggish – and the hand gripping him held fast.

'Be still!' The words were almost like a rebuke to a child.

Dob made another effort to free himself, equally fruitless.

'Be still!' the man repeated sharply then sighed and added, 'This is to ...' He lifted the hammer.

Dob jerked back wildly, ending up on the floor as his captor suddenly released him.

'… remove the collar.'

Dob peered up at him suspiciously. 'Why?' he managed.

'Ah, you understand!'

Dob ignored the sarcasm. 'Why?' he repeated his question.

'Because,' came the answer with exaggerated patience, 'Sidi Khalid has ordered it: to take off the collar and make you clean.' The man pointedly held his nose.

'Why?' Dob was still baffled. 'Who is Sidi Khalid?' he added.

The reply was another question. 'Do you want it off or not?'

Did Dob really have a choice?

The collar had gone, his foul clothes likewise. The man who said his name was Ali had carefully sponged the blood from the headwound and from the eye which Dob was relieved to find had merely been glued shut; with an evil-looking razor he had expertly shaved away every lice-ridden hair from Dob's infested person; in the warm water of a tiled bath, he had tackled with determination the filth ingrained into all parts of Dob's stringy body. And after a final soap and sluice with fresh water, he had indicated Dob should emerge.

Dob grimaced and staggered out with great reluctance. Was this the feeling that Adam and Eve had on leaving the Garden of Eden? The ache in his head as Ali bound it, emphasised the return to earthly reality. A sweet-scented salve did little to sooth the damage now exposed on his neck.

There was a clean striped djellaba and there were shoes. The gown of fine wool felt good, but Dob's feet, in spite of Ali's best efforts would not fit into the shoes. They were coaxed instead into soft leather slippers but still felt uncomfortable, indeed downright odd.

The eternal craving for food had somehow been driven into the background by the pleasure of Ali's ministrations, but now it declared itself with renewed vigour. Had this Sidi Khalid also ordered that Dob be fed? He looked hopefully at Ali.

An obliging and extra-loud growl from his stomach, no doubt provoked by the thought, saved Dob from the ignominy of begging.

Ali nodded, but his dark eyes regarded him seriously. 'Food, yes. But only a little.' A brown finger pointed at Dob's hollow belly. 'Too much would make you ill. However,' he added, 'there will be more later.'

There was to be a "later" then? Dob dismissed speculation about that as he gave himself over to the present. The pottery bowl held the familiar cereal – but accompanied by a stew of some kind: beans and other vegetables. And meat.

'Tagine.' Ali said.

Dob could not care less what it was called: it smelled divine.

Ali stayed his hand. 'Slowly.'

Dob tried to obey, tried to hold the delicious mass in his mouth, to chew and savour, but it was simply impossible. In a few seconds he was scouring the pot, licking every scrap from his fingers.

'Tomorrow there will be more,' Ali repeated the promise, 'but first some sleep.'

Dob's stomach was disappointed and further disappointment came as Ali led him to a small chamber with a mat – and a lock on the door.

'Sidi Khalid wishes to see you in the morning,' Ali said pointedly. 'He would not wish you to leave before then.'

Of course, the thought of escape had occurred to Dob: it had never been out of his mind since he had first realised the corsairs' intentions.

But there seemed to be a future – at least a tomorrow; and there would surely be a better chance of success after food and sleep.

62

Dob did not hear the door being unlocked. He did not even hear Ali's voice. But the smell of food woke him.

After the still too-small meal had been devoured, Ali renewed the bandage, scowled at Dob's battered feet and eased them back into the slippers; then led the way.

Dob stopped as they came to a courtyard, shaded by its surrounding buildings. In the middle a fountain splashed and the paths were edged with plants, many in flower. 'It's beautiful,' he exclaimed, not an Arabic word he had had much use for.

It was also very impressive: this was surely the residence of someone rich and important, a conviction that only grew as they proceeded along corridors lit by pointed windows, fretted wooden screens across the lower part giving glimpses of that central garden. The plastered walls were skirted with deep earthen red; the doorways had intricately painted wooden surrounds. At one particularly impressive door stood a servant who made little effort to hide his curiosity as he admitted them.

The room within was breath-taking. Dob stood still and stared. Flowers and birds in yellows and greens and pinks decorated the walls below a frieze of elaborate script on a bright blue ground; the high wooden ceiling was intricately carved and painted. On the baked tiles were rich carpets.

Into his mind came the image of a London salon. This was comparable and yet so different, so exotic. He drew a deep breath and stared some more.

A voice recalled his attention to the present. It was not Ali but another man who had risen from within a small alcove.

His djellaba and matching turban were of a plain beige material, but its sheen suggested silk, not wool. There was elaborate embroidery in pale ivory thread down the front and around the wide sleeves. This was a man of wealth and consequence – and he was greeting Dob with deference.

Dob, bemused, hastily recalled himself. An elaborate "leg" seemed totally absurd. 'Salam alaikum,' he said, wondering even as he uttered the words if they would be regarded as sacrilegious from the mouth of a non-believer.

But the man only responded gravely, 'Wa-alaikum salam.'

To Dob's further bemusement, the man beckoned and a small figure emerged from the alcove, also well-dressed but wan of face.

At a gesture from the man, the boy said, 'Salam alaikum,' then at another prompt, offered his right hand to Dob.

Dob regarded the small smooth hand and then his own, scrubbed as well as Ali could manage but the nails broken, the scarred and calloused surface criss-crossed by the black lines of deep cracks. It would be almost a desecration, he thought. But to ignore what was quite clearly an act of great significance would be an insult.

The boy came to his rescue and lifted his little finger.

Dob linked it with his own and could not help smiling. How long had it been since there had been anything at all to smile about in Dob's life? Although smiling might also be an insult.

However, after a moment the boy smiled back. Then, evidently having performed as instructed, he withdrew his hand and the man invited Dob to take a seat with them in the alcove.

Dob lowered himself onto the coloured leather cushion beside a low table where Ali placed a tray loaded with brass pot and beakers before quietly withdrawing to the far side of the room – unobtrusive but strategically positioned, Dob noted.

'May I offer you tea?' said the man.

Dob was sure such an impressive personage did not usually serve runaway slaves.

'I understand,' said the man, glancing towards Ali, 'that you speak Arabic.'

Dob had become aware that there were many forms of Arabic throughout the huge area covered by Islam, some definitely more refined than others. What he had acquired was undoubtedly unrefined – and his vocabulary equally so. 'Yes,' he said shortly.

'Although evidently it is not your native language.'

It would not take a genius to work that out.

'Perhaps English would be better?' The query came out fluently, the accent slight.

Dob gaped and the man smiled. He turned towards the boy. 'I fear we have neglected the proper introductions, have we not?'

The child had been staring at Dob with undisguised curiosity but now announced grandly, also in that softly accented English, 'Allow me to present to you Sidi Khalid ibn Abd al-Salam. And I,' he added, 'am Slimane ibn Khalid ibn Abd al-Salam.'

'Sidi?' Dob queried.

'My father is a most important man: in the city, in the district, in the whole land,' the boy declared proudly.

That important. Dob took a sip of tea.

'And you are?' The boy finally broke the silence.

His father reproved his manners – but only mildly.

'Robert Smith.' Dob could see no point in saying anything else.

To his surprise, Slimane immediately demanded, 'Are you Irish too?' Before Dob could work that out, Slimane continued with enthusiasm, 'Your skin is white where the sun has not burned it and your eyes are light like my *eima*, my aunt, although yours are blue and hers are grey.'

Aunt?

'Not really an aunt,' said Slimane, looking at his father.

'But respected as much,' said Sidi Khalid firmly. 'She took care of me after my mother died.'

'*Eima* tells of the land where she grew up: a land of misted lakes and green hills,' put in Slimane. 'Ireland.'

That explained the soft accent. 'Does she live here?' Dob asked, intrigued.

'Yes,' Slimane answered. 'She calls me *a stóirín*, her "little treasure",' he confided artlessly. 'And she would very much like to meet someone who might be Irish …'

'But I think you are not,' interposed Sidi Khalid. 'Perhaps Scottish or English or American?'

Dob took refuge in finishing his tea. It seemed he had earned Sidi Khalid's gratitude, but how much was it wise to reveal?

'Forgive me – and my son – for our inquisitiveness when we have so much to thank you for.' Sidi Khalid considered for a moment then continued, 'Slavery has long been part of our country. Everywhere there are towns and walls and palaces built by slaves. Our religion condones the enslavement of non-believers, who may nevertheless regain their freedom by giving up their misguided views.'

Dob tensed: was this the option he was being offered?

Sidi Khalid saw his reaction. 'As a True Believer I would welcome any conversion, but that it not my immediate point.' Dob waited. 'The Prophet enjoined on slave owners the duty of kindness.' Dob could hardly suppress a snort. 'Too often, however, slaves have been regarded, and treated, as less than human – and too often in response bestial conditions have reduced men, and women, to beasts. Even so,' continued Sidi Khalid, 'in some, the flame of humanity is not extinguished.' He looked straight at Dob, who was suddenly uncomfortable: he knew that if he had stopped for an instant to think, logic would surely have made him act quite differently. Did that make him inherently humane or plain stupid?

He became aware that Sidi Khalid had put him a question.

Yes, Dob answered cautiously, he had heard of Moulay Ismail. What did that have to do with anything?

'Of his great cruelty and ruthlessness, no doubt. Also perhaps, of his great fecundity?'

The guards had discussed it, with coarseness and envy.

'They say he fathered over a thousand children during his lifetime – on his wives, on the hundreds of concubines in his huge harem. In his palace in Meknes there was also an enormous stable, for twelve thousand horses.'

For a moment Dob's thoughts were diverted: he recalled the stables at Pentridge which housed his father's cherished hunters, more than a dozen of them, and almost laughed.

'And he had a further interest in breeding.' Khalid raised a dark eyebrow at Dob. 'He would have instantly acquired someone as pale of skin and hair as you – and put you to stud with his African slave women.'

Dob started. Where was this leading?

'And the fascination with European fairness continued: Mohammed III, the father of our present Sultan, became infatuated by the white skin, red hair and green eyes of a Scottish woman who became his fourth and favourite wife. Through her influence, others taken by the Salé pirates were saved from slavery – including an Irish woman, not particularly fair and in any case not able to bear children. She had been worked almost to death before the Sultan's principle wife redeemed her and offered her the choice of leaving the country or taking over the care, as a free woman, of a motherless boy, the son of a palace official.' He smiled. 'Fortunately for me she chose not to leave. For she had not lost her humanity – either.'

63

She was in Moroccan dress and a veil hid the lower part of her face but her eyes, grey as Slimane had said, studied him closely. It was not, however, their scrutiny that unsettled him – it was the most curious feeling that they were familiar.

'Would you prefer to talk in English, Mr Smith?' she inquired, the soft accent confirming where Sidi Khalid and Slimane had acquired theirs. 'Although *a stóirín* here,' she indicated the boy, 'tells me you speak Arabic.'

'I'm sure he also tells you how poorly I speak it,' said Dob drily.

The boy grinned.

She smiled back then looked at Dob. '*A stóirín*, my treasure,' she repeated softly, 'our priceless treasure which you saved for us.'

Dob shifted awkwardly.

'Slimane, I believe your studies await you?'

The boy pouted.

'You may talk to our guest again later.'

Slimane departed reluctantly.

The woman gestured towards the door which had been left open. 'You will realise that Ali is close by. Khalid does not yet trust you,' she said. 'Not to do harm – but not to run off!'

Dob was all too aware of Ali's constant presence and purpose.

'But Ali will not understand what we say. Please be seated.' She continued when he was settled on another brilliantly-dyed leather cushion, 'Smith is a very common name,' she commented. 'Some are born with it, others choose it.' There was that penetrating stare again.

Dob made no comment and she did not press the point.

'I am Amina,' she said instead. 'Do you know what that means? Trustworthy and faithful. I have tried to live up to it since God gave me a second chance.'

'A second chance?' Dob was puzzled.

'You see I conceived and bore my own child out of wedlock and my punishment was to be unable to conceive another.'

Khalid had not mentioned the first part. And why would the woman now tell Dob such a personal thing?

'You are shocked?'

'It is not for me to stand in judgement,' said Dob. 'In the past two years I have seen and heard things that I could never have imagined before – not in my wildest dreams, or nightmares! I thought before, that I had troubles, but they are nothing to what others have to face.'

'You are fully young to have learned that,' she commented.

'It has been a brutal school!'

'And it is not the lesson all would have learned.'

'I am not at all sure,' said Dob frankly, 'that I would not have lost any last shred of humanity in time, perhaps a short time. When the new slaves arrive, it is impossible to know who will crack and who will, against all the odds, retain some decency.' He shook his head. 'I'm lucky to have escaped when I did,' he said simply.

'Luck, God's hand,' she said, 'call it what you will. I was blessed with the chance to have another child, other children: first Khalid and then Slimane. I have seized that chance with both hands and thank God for it, every moment of every day. But,' she said slowly, 'one day I came to wonder if I would have felt the blessing so keenly if there had not been the terrible suffering before. Perhaps God's hand was in that too.'

Dob frowned. 'I have come to see many things,' he said, 'but I cannot see any beneficent God having a hand in slavery.'

'No,' she said. 'I cannot understand it when you put it like that, but there are many things I cannot understand. Often, I simply have to accept how I feel. And,' she looked at him once more, 'I have the very strong feeling that I have to know how my poor abandoned child fared. You will leave soon enough,' she said with half a smile. 'Either you will stay and allow Khalid to help you leave or you will find your own way. The first would be best,' she said earnestly.

Dob would make no promises.

'But,' she said, 'I would like to put my request to you immediately, in case you suddenly disappear.'

Dob made no commitment about that either.

'To understand it, I shall tell you my story.' She unfastened her veil, evidently so her expression might add weight to her tale. The lines on her face made it difficult to guess her age, but she had probably been pretty once, he thought. 'When I was a little girl,' she began, 'my name was Roísín Mac an Ghabhain.'

However, it was not her history, fascinating as it was, which persuaded him. It was the sudden, heart-stopping realisation why her eyes seemed familiar.

64

'*Eima* Amina has worked her magic on you, I think,' said Sidi Khalid.

Dob stiffened. The man was right of course, but how had he known? Had Ali understood after all?

'Ali does not have to eavesdrop,' Sidi Khalid said with a smile. 'He has observed that since you visited my aunt, you have not been watching for every means to leave the house.'

Dob pulled a wry face.

'And,' Sidi Khalid continued ruefully, 'she has naturally told me off – as if I were still a little boy like Slimane, not an official of the Sultan himself!' He grimaced. 'I think we need to start again – you and I; not with my gratitude to you, that can never be ignored or forgotten, but I must make clear that the hospitality offered to you is free, as it would be for any visitor under my roof. You may, in short, leave at any time, although,' he paused, 'I *invite* you to stay at least a while longer. I would like to hear more of what happened to you and offer you my help.'

Dob let his scepticism show.

Sidi Khalid sighed. 'I shall if you permit, say a little more about our sultan, Moulay Suleiman. You know something of Moulay Ismail, who ruthlessly suppressed anyone who opposed him: from outside Morocco, from any of the tribes within, from his own family. In that way he achieved peace throughout the whole kingdom, but eventually he died and there were years of war again between those who wished to succeed him. Only when his grandson Mohammed became sultan was there peace once more.'

'The sultan with the red-haired, green-eyed favourite wife,' Dob recalled.

'Quite so. As well as peace within Morocco he wished to have peace with foreign countries – provided they abandoned their claims to Moroccan soil, which the French and Portuguese were "persuaded" to do. At the same time, he invited European architects and technicians to work on his building projects; and he recognised the United States as an independent country.'

'Despite which there has not been an end to the activities of the Barbary pirates against American ships or those off them,' put in Dob acidly, realising even as he spoke what he had revealed about himself and wondering precisely what official position Sidi Khalid held. Whatever it was, he suddenly believed that the man truly was as important as his son had claimed.

The sharpening of Sidi Khalid's dark eyes showed he had not missed Dob's disclosure, although he continued his account. 'When *he* died, there was another struggle for the throne. His son Yazid killed off as many of his rivals as he could, including several of his half-brothers. His father's favourite wife disappeared along with her two sons.'

Dob frowned.

'*Eima* Amina was heart-broken – and scared. She feared Yazid would send his black troops to seek out and persecute anyone his father had favoured, as he had done to the Jews who had been invited to the country. For the two years he ruled, she lived in terror – as did many.'

'But now Sultan Suleiman is securely in power?'

Sidi Khalid prevaricated. 'Secure on his throne and here at the heart of government, but there are certain regions – and activities – on which he has still to stamp his authority.'

'Such as?'

Sidi Khalid sighed. 'International diplomacy is a complicated matter.'

'Complicated?' Dob pressed.

'The Sultan is in the process of reaffirming the terms of the Treaty with the United States.'

'And the continued corsair activity gives him more negotiating power!'

Sidi Khalid looked pained. 'Why should the United States not recognise any help towards keeping their ships safe?'

Dob presumed the Sultan wished that recognition to be expressed financially.

'Although the corsairs know American sailors are usually ransomed.' Sidi Khalid looked pointedly at Dob. 'They did not offer that to you? They learned, perhaps, that you were not American but British?'

Dob pulled a sour face.

'And that there was nobody in England to redeem you?'

Dob shook his head. He thought he had paid dearly for that omission, but Sidi Khalid's next words undeceived him. 'Although that would not necessarily have kept you from slavery: hostages are usually put to work until the ransom is delivered – and that can take time to achieve.'

He regarded Dob for some moments. 'As well as relations with the United States,' he said at last, 'the Sultan is concerned about relations with other powers much closer to his kingdom.' He was suddenly quite direct. 'What do you know of Gibraltar?'

The Katherine had sailed nowhere near it, but thanks to lessons at Bromby, Dob knew where it was on the map; for the same reason he also knew that the small territory had been acquired by Britain under the terms of the Treaty of Utrecht some eighty-five years earlier. Furthermore, he had a vague memory of Willo's father talking of its strategic position.

'You will not, of course, know how the war in Europe has been going.'

Dob had in truth taken little enough notice even before he left England.

'Over the past two years, the French have taken control of Europe; it looked almost certain that under their general, Napoleon Bonaparte, they would next turn to invading Britain.' Dob started. 'But instead, in the spring, the French fleet left Toulon and sailed for Egypt, taking Malta on the way. The French army soon took Alexandria then Cairo.'

Dob racked his brain to recall more of those Bromby maps. Egypt was some way from Morocco – although from much more immediate experience, he knew of slaves brought in the trading caravans. Did the Sultan fear the French would follow that same route?

'However,' continued Sidi Khalid, 'the British fleet had pursued them and there was a big naval battle in Abukir Bay, off the Nile delta.' Dob waited impatiently. 'The French were defeated: they lost many men and most of their ships.' Sidi Khalid frowned. 'It took a while to learn all the details since the French threatened to cut out the tongues of any Egyptians who discussed the battle. However, in due course the news was carried to Gibraltar by British ships heading back to England.'

'And that was how the Sultan received the news? From Gibraltar?' Dob drew the obvious conclusion.

Sidi Khalid's frown deepened. 'That is very much his dilemma, you see.'

Dob did not see. It was his turn to frown.

Sidi Khalid sighed. 'Perhaps because of being brought up by Amina I see the world outside Morocco, beyond the Dar al-Islam, with more interest, with less fear. The Sultan is intent, naturally, on securing his own kingdom and keeping his people safe from outside threats, both political and religious. He has only reluctantly realised that it is not enough to have strong borders and look only within those: the reality is that Morocco interacts with the wider world, in fact gains considerably from doing so. For the past century such interaction has been left largely to the traders, particularly those of the Gharb and even more particularly to its Jewish merchants.'

'The Gharb?' Dob queried.

'That corner of our country which faces north across to Jabal Tariq, what the British call the Rock of Gibraltar.' Sidi Khalid added wryly, 'The merchants of *Spain* cannot be depended on to supply the considerable needs of the British garrison there.'

Dob could see why that might be the case.

'Do you have any idea how many cattle a year are needed just to provide enough meat? Never mind vegetables, fruit, grain, oil and honey. And not to mention goods destined for onward portage – meat and mules to the West Indies; leather to the Baltic and Russia; leather, wool, copper, gold dust, ivory and ostrich feathers to France or to Italy and from there to the Ottoman lands.'

Dob's attention was caught by the mention of copper – and his mind astounded at the rest of the list. Bromby's lessons had taught history and geography in terms of military victories and political power, not merchandise and commerce. He doubted the majority of those who enjoyed the abundance of exotic goods available in London gave much, or even a single, thought to how they got there. He knew he had not.

He realised Sidi Khalid was continuing, 'And this trade route has served well enough as a diplomatic channel too. The merchants of Tangier have conducted their profitable businesses and alongside, as necessary, acted as agents for the Sultan in Gibraltar, in London or even further afield.

'Now the Sultan is of a mind,' Sidi Khalid smiled, 'to grasp the nettle, as Amina might say. Gibraltar has become ever more crucial to Britain in its present war; the needs of its garrison have become very substantial. As the numbers of Moorish merchants involved has increased, as well as Jewish, the Sultan has become ever more concerned about their spiritual welfare along with that of all other Muslims there: trading, resident or passing through on pilgrimage. He wishes, in short, to negotiate a treaty ensuring that they are not treated in any way contrary to Sharia law.'

Dob had little idea of what that involved.

'Of course,' Sidi Khalid said with the faintest lift of one dark eyebrow, 'direct involvement by the Sultan would at a stroke serve to remove diplomatic power from the Gharb merchants, bring them and that region more fully under his control; enable him to assume regulation of trade, and,' the eyebrow lifted further, 'of tariffs.'

Dob had no reason to doubt the Sultan's high religious motives but suddenly suspected that Sidi Khalid at least had a very clear vision of the political and fiscal benefits that would accrue.

It was all very interesting, but Dob knew Sidi Khalid must have a reason for explaining it in such detail. He asked.

'The Sultan has been pleased to appoint me as his personal envoy, to engage in talks with General Charles O'Hara, the British consul in Gibraltar; and if those talks go well, in due course to continue to London to see a satisfactory treaty signed.'

'Your fluency in English makes you an obvious choice for the post,' commented Dob, 'but I don't see where *I might* fit in.'

Sidi Khalid, for the first time, looked slightly embarrassed. 'I will, naturally, escort you to Gibraltar and see you onto a ship from there to wherever you wish. But,' he hesitated, 'I believe it would help my mission and the Sultan's cause to present you as a goodwill gift – if, of course, you were agreeable.'

Dob was silent for a moment, digesting this, then he laughed at the sheer absurdity.

It took Sidi Khalid some weeks to finalise arrangements.

Although impatient to be on his way, Dob enjoyed the interlude and felt distinct regret at the moment of departure: he'd luxuriated in Ali's care (comparing it sourly with Tomkin's); he'd appreciated every single mouthful of the food served to him; he'd been glad to have the chance of further conversations with Amina; he'd happily admitted total defeat to Slimane on the chess board.

And gravely accepted the boy's farewell gift.

'It is my favourite *shesh*,' Slimane confessed, offering the length of finest cotton muslin, 'it is very soft. For your neck,' he added.

65

The nearest harbour was Essaouira where the boat waiting ready for them was definitely no local trader. It sailed up the coast, passing various ports, including Rabat and Salé. At Tangier, Sidi Khalid had an appointment with the American consul James Simpson about the Treaty with the United States.

At dinner that evening he peered at Dob several times.

'Do you, perchance,' he said eventually, 'know the Earl of Pentridge?'

Dob's heart thumped. 'Why?'

'The American consul had a curious tale to tell. He received a visit from this English lord a little while ago; some weeks, in fact, after an American vessel, *The Katherine*, foundered off the coast. The Earl was convinced that his son had survived the wreck; at Salé he had heard of a young man matching the description, *very light-haired and with blue eyes*, being found on the beach by corsairs.' That bit was correct; the next was certainly not. 'And being brought to Tangier.'

'And what,' Dob swallowed, 'did Mr Simpson say?'

'He knew about *The Katherine* but only of three survivors, all American seamen, who had been picked up by an East Indiaman and taken to London. He knew of no Englishman and in any case, he only has responsibility for American citizens.'

'So?' Dob could not prevent himself asking.

'He could only suggest the Earl accompany him to Tétouan and search there; sometimes, the consul had warned him, those "lost" off ships ended up there, or in Oran or Algiers. The Earl had with him an Arab whom he had apparently engaged as a translator and guide and who enthusiastically agreed all suggestions should be followed up; although,' Sidi Khalid said ironically, 'Mr Simpson had the suspicion the fellow would have encouraged any action that would extend a plainly lucrative employment.'

'And Mr Simpson has not seen this English Earl since?'

'No, although he has heard of a substantial reward being offered in numerous places for information about the castaway.'

Dob almost laughed at the irony of it: he had decided not to ask his father to ransom him; his father had come, against all sense, seeking to do so. Dob frowned as he wondered at his father's motivation. He knew it was not paternal affection; although perhaps it demonstrated a certain belief in Dob's powers of survival.

Where was the Earl now? How far had he searched? Had he finally given up and gone home? Leaving the promise of a prize as a forlorn hope?

He might have guessed, Dob thought too late, that the Earl would have visited Gibraltar in his search.

'Well, well,' said General Charles O'Hara, 'now isn't this quite a gift you have brought me, Sidi Khalid. The Earl of Pentridge has promised a grand sum for news of this young man unless I am very much mistaken – which I shall have great pleasure in claiming in person.'

66

Dob paused by the gangplank of the ship bound for London.

The Gibraltar souk had furnished breeches, shirt and jacket; Dob's feet were very unwillingly encased in worn boots; a hat covered his stubbled head; around his neck was Slimane's *shesh*.

Sidi Khalid indicated this. 'You have something to remember my son by.'

Dob touched it.

'And I will have something to remember *you* by – every day that he lives.' He grasped both of Dob's battered hands in his.

A voice could be heard on deck loudly berating Forster for some perceived shortcoming.

Sidi Khalid indicated the Earl with a nod of his head. 'I know it is bad manners to be nosey, as Amine is always telling Slimane, but I should dearly love to know your story.'

'It's a long one,' Dob frowned. 'And is still not finished.'

Nearly all the old problems remained; the only thing Dob could be reasonably certain about was that Alicia would have passed her twenty-eighth birthday and gained control of her inheritance.

'Like One Thousand and One Nights,' suggested Sidi Khalid.

Dob smiled at the reference to Slimane's favourite tales.

'One day perhaps we shall meet in London and you will be in a position to tell it all,' said Sidi Khalid hopefully.'

'One day,' agreed Dob, with little conviction.

The voyage back to London passed without incident – and without any confrontation with his father. Dob did try to say, several times, that he would not be a pawn in his father's game – whatever it was.

However, the Earl dismissed any hint of resistance: he talked, almost incessantly, of how he would organise things when they landed, of what Dob would do, of how the ambitions of the family could be got back on track.

Since there was no way of escaping his company on the boat, Dob decided, for the time being, to let his father ramble on. Perhaps there would be hints of what it was all about.

But when they were back in England, things would be different, very different. Dob might still not have achieved his majority, but he had aged immeasurably in the past two years – in every way: he was worldly-wise, and physically strong, determined to be his own master, now and into the future.

The capital felt very strange – and it was not just the cold and the damp: he had never felt at home in the society circles into which his father had forced him and he would be even more of an outsider now, knowing what his purpose must be, even if he had little idea at this point of how it might be achieved.

His father was anxious to keep him away from the inevitable publicity, at least until Dob looked half-way presentable – and, Dob was certain, until the Earl had conceived some new scheme and thought of ways of coercing his son into it.

However, the suggestion of heading in the first instance to the Richmond villa fitted with Dob's own wish to see his mother, so there was no immediate cause for argument.

There was a warm reunion between mother and son which neither tried to curb or hide, in spite of the Earl's overt impatience and barely concealed contempt.

67

Next day, Dob announced that he was heading into the city.

The Earl declared that he would accompany him. Since, however, he was clearly keen to go about his own business, Dob suggested drily that he was certain Forster's escort would be quite sufficient.

The clothes and accessories left behind in Pentridge House would be long out of fashion and, in any case, would certainly never fit Dob's greatly altered physique. He would, he assured his father, be visiting the tailor and the hatter and the bootmaker and all manner of other tradesmen to make up the deficit in his wardrobe.

He made no mention of the other place he would be visiting.

While the various clothiers, delighted with the renewed Pentridge custom, promised to expedite the bespoke items, Dob donned several ready-made garments, including a warm coat and felt hat. Throughout all the measuring and pinning, he retained Slimane's *shesh*, loosely tied around his neck. There would be no cravats, even unstarched, for quite some time, if ever. The tradesmen were curious about this, as they were about his hands and his almost impossible feet, but their curiosity was greatly less than their appreciation of the financial rewards and none argued.

All that accomplished, he and Forster headed for Grosvenor Square. There was the central garden within its railings. There was Uppworth House with its six stone pillars. And there at the top of the shallow steps was the imposing front door – with its large brass knocker removed.

Dob's racing pulse missed a beat even though he had anticipated that Callie would no longer be there. But somebody would know where she was; there would be someone keeping house. 'Let's try the servants' entrance.'

There was indeed someone keeping house, several someones, all gathered at that moment in the kitchen. There was a neatly dressed woman with keys at her belt; an older woman with flour up to her dimpled elbows; a manservant of indeterminate age, in an apron. There was a young man who had manifestly just delivered a package of pig's trotters.

Recognition was mutual. 'It's the nob! Alive!' The spiky head swivelled to Forster, 'And that cove from the taproom in the Star.'

Forster was affronted. 'And who might you be?' he demanded.

'Peter Giblin,' came the reply, 'at your service; although that would depend on what service you requires.' His eyes narrowed. 'So, Pentridge's spawn has returned from the dead; resurrected from a watery grave.'

'As you can see,' said Dob evenly.

'Almost broke 'er 'eart, it did,' said Peter, unmistakeable hostility excising all aspirates. ''Earing that you'd drowned.'

It was quite obvious who he meant. Dob's own heart lurched. 'Where is she?'

'Never thought to send her word?' demanded Peter.

'It was not possible.'

'Mind you, would only have complicated things wouldn't it? Likely to complicate them now, your turning up again.'

The rest of the company were clearly mystified by the conversation.

'Where is she?' Dob repeated. 'What happened after she heard that … *The Katherine* had foundered?'

'They got married.'

Dob stared. Of course, he knew she would have found some way of living; she was resourceful and courageous. And it was certain such a remarkable young woman would catch the attention of some other man; it was even possible she would welcome it, believing that Dob was dead. Still, hearing it for certain, was painful. It was a moment before he picked up Peter's words. 'They?' he asked.

'Her and the Duke.'

'The Duke?' asked Dob stupidly.

'The Duke of Uppworth.'

Dob actually gasped.

'She's quite good enough to be a Duchess,' Peter bristled.

More than good enough, thought Dob but did not say so. He hardly knew what to say.

'They have a child now: a boy.'

Dob's reaction was more pain, although he had no entitlement.

'An Uppworth heir,' added the housekeeper with satisfaction.

Forster was more than willing to down several mugs of ale.

Dob, on the other hand, sat in the corner of the tavern nursing just one. A great part of him urged him to leave well alone. As long as Callie was happy and, wonderful to know, secure in a station befitting her then he had no right to disturb the situation. It was a huge blow: he could not deceive himself that his heart had still clung onto hope, however much his head had argued against it.

But there remained the promise to Amina: Dob had to fulfil that.

In a few days he would have regathered himself sufficiently to go and see the young Duchess of Uppworth.

Despite his own preoccupations, Dob observed his father carefully. There was undoubtedly A New Plan being hatched:

the Earl took himself off to the city but returned to Richmond for dinner – most likely, Dob thought sourly, to check *he* was still there.

One evening the Earl was clearly seething beneath the smooth civilities; next day there was a steely resolution; a few days later the Earl announced he was going away.

Dob was astonished: a date had been set for an appropriately grand function to reintroduce the Lost Son to Society and preparations for this were in train. Dob shuddered at the thought but recognised attendance at such affairs would be required for his own plans.

After all the tribulations of the past couple of years, the Earl explained, he needed some time to recuperate, doing what he loved to do – hunting. He had sent word to Mills to make all the necessary arrangements.

Mention of the Pentridge steward recalled Joey's fearful reference to the man and Dob's later suspicion that he had precipitated Callie's departure from Pentridge.

He peered at the Earl: there was something distinctly odd about his father's announcement, though Dob could not work out what.

However, his father's absence would make it easier for *him* to leave London, to do what he had to do.

The Earl of Pentridge smiled to himself. He had indeed sent word to Mills, but he would not be meeting the man at Pentridge Hall: the steward should already be at Pircombe Manor.

The Earl had no pleasant memories of a place he had not visited in decades: hopelessly out of date, cold and cramped. It was, however, perfectly located for his immediate purpose.

68

Dob viewed the White Horse in the village of Uppworth with some trepidation but mostly with relief. The murk had brought dusk at an early hour and he was glad to see the glow of lamps. Substantial sections of the Bath Road were well-maintained turnpike, but still it had been a tiring ride, particularly the last twenty miles when a cold, clammy fog had rolled in from the Bristol Channel and enveloped them.

Fortunately, the inn had rooms available. Happily, there was also still some of the day's stew to be had with bread made just that morning by the village baker. The plain fare suited Dob perfectly. He set to with gusto.

From a group of men seated near the fire came the burr of local voices. Dob, intent on his plate, scarcely bothered to try and understand the thick accent until a particular word struck his ear.

He slowed his eating and listened more closely.

Yes, the old man was definitely talking about Tentham. Lady Alicia had barely mentioned it and Dob had never bothered to wonder much about it, all his efforts being focussed on avoiding the place. Now he learned to his great surprise that it was close by; in fact, the Tentham and Uppworth estates adjoined.

The next words surprised him still further. 'Her Grace and Lady Alicia have become quite friends. They've both got good heads on their shoulders,' was the pronouncement.

Dob looked more carefully at the speaker. He looked no more or less than an ageing countryman, but he was evidently held in considerable respect. The company was listening attentively and no one disputed this unusual assessment of female acuity.

'And the ideas for cooperation between the estates make

a lot of sense.' The man went on to talk about various projects that were evidently well-known to his audience and there was a general nodding of heads.

'I'm off to my bed,' said the man, rising from his seat. 'Got to be up at the Park first thing in the morning, for the *board meeting,*' he chuckled, 'as his Grace calls it.'

'Should we be calling you *Mister* Walter Hibblett nowadays, Walt? Seeing as you'm like to be one of they estate managers,' ribbed one of his companions pulling his grizzled forelock in mock servility.

'Watch out, Will,' one of the other men warned the joker. 'Some of they estate managers kick out *peasants* like you and me, soon as look at 'em.'

'Wouldn't do that, would you Walt?' inquired Will.

'Not without her Grace wanting to know why!' said another man.

Shortly afterwards, another customer also left. He had come to the inn several times; he was civil but not forthcoming, saying simply that he was working nearby for a short while. He nursed his ale, seemingly content with his own company and his own thoughts.

However, he listened hard – to the locals. He did not attend much to the travellers who frequently passed through and that evening he had given no more than a glance at the pair hunched over their plates – although in broad daylight he would probably have noticed their sun-bronzed faces; he might even have recognised the features of one of them. But he was anxious to leave, to get back to his employer.

Despite his weariness, Dob lay awake for some time trying to make sense of what he had learned: somehow Miss Callie Smith (once companion and nurse to Lady Olivia) and Lady

Alicia Tentham had ended up not only neighbours but "quite friends"; somehow Callie (once a country girl on the Pentridge estate) had become involved in the running of Uppworth – with local Walter Hibblett advising on the management; somehow Callie, in spite of, or perhaps because of all these things, had become well-thought of.

Where, he wondered, did the Duke fit into this? He found it painful to think of the close relationship that must exist between Callie and the Duke – they had a child for goodness sake – but that was the reality. How ill was the man? Dob asked himself; then realised how that would sound spoken out loud. It was not that Dob wished his Grace into his grave, at least, he thought he didn't, but if Callie was holding the reins of the estate …

Finally, he fell into a fitful sleep.

Dob knew that Callie would not be available to receive a morning visitor: she would be at the board meeting with Walter Hibblett. He had penned a note with considerable difficulty on the poor excuse for paper which the landlord of the White Horse had dug out and despatched Forster through the swirling mist to deliver it. There would be a reply in due course, he supposed, suggesting when the Duchess might be free to receive him.

Meanwhile he just might find Lady Alicia at home.

He inquired how to reach Tentham Court and set off on foot. Suddenly impatient with boots and stockings, he pulled them off, set them aside with his jacket and hat and headed off for a run. The moisture filled his lungs and tried to catch at his elusive form. It hung thick in the air, obscuring sight and sound.

69

The Earl recognised that Mills had used his short time since arriving at Pircombe most profitably. The steward had learned, through a mix of discreet enquiry, bribery, eavesdropping and spying, how life proceeded at Uppworth Park. It was, he reported, a very orderly life with an almost unfailing routine – each morning during the week there was a meeting at the Park involving a young clerk called John Wilson and an ancient local called Walter Hibblett with either the Duke or the Duchess or both. Depending on the weather, after the meeting finished the Duchess usually drove out in a small trap – sometimes with old Hibblett on estate business, sometimes with her child on a more social excursion. Occasionally the Duke rode out with them too, in his specially adapted double-chair shay.

The Earl's view of the garden, through the mullion windows of the Pircombe manor house, was distorted – partly by the small panes of old glass but also by the mist that drifted on the still air, sometimes thicker, sometimes thinner.

Perhaps it would keep them all indoors – he scowled at the thought.

But if they did venture out, the obscuring dampness could be very helpful.

A little later he cursed that obscurity roundly – although silently. There was definitely a carriage coming along the track and the sound of high voices mixed with some bass, but he could not see their owners. He raised a staying hand to Mills who was himself hard to see, close up against a thick evergreen.

The clop of the horses' hoofs was muffled by the soft earth and the clinging mist. Then suddenly it was much louder and the vehicle came into sight.

It was the shay with a man driving; on the other seat was a woman with a small child on her knee.

The Earl's eyes gleamed. He dropped his hand. Mills hauled on the rope that he had laid across the roadway. It lifted out of its concealing cover of fallen leaves and tripped the horse.

The normally well-mannered dun mare was thrown into a panic. She shied; she reared; she pulled against the carriage to which she was tethered.

The figure who had been on the dickey at the rear was thrown off and lay unmoving.

The driver was fighting to regain control.

Next to him, the woman was clinging desperately with one hand to the edge of her seat and with the other to the wailing child.

The Earl's heart raced; then the swell of triumph ebbed as he saw that the driver, far from trying to stay the animal, was now intent on driving her into flight.

But Mills had also seen what was happening. Before the shay had barely started moving, he darted out and jammed an iron bar into the spokes. The crack of splintering wood was audible an instant before the louder sound of the vehicle crashing onto its side, spilling its occupants.

The driver lay pinned beneath the wreckage. The woman struggled to her feet hugging the howling infant to her. Making no attempt to disguise himself, the Earl stepped forward: no one would live to identify him.

He levelled his pistol; not that he wished to use the firearm, for it was all supposed to look like an accident – another accident – but he would use it if necessary; nothing must be allowed to prevent his success.

The Earl raised his voice. 'Shut that child up!'

The woman rocked the infant and murmured ragged words into its ear. The cries dropped to a fearful whimpering.

'Bring it here.'

The woman only hugged the child closer.

Earl stared at her contemptuously. 'They said the Duke had married one of his servants, but you certainly are a drab creature, aren't you? Though done very well for yourself – a husband with wealth and title, and not so crippled it seems that he could not get a child on you.'

The woman was gaping at him, speechless.

The Earl drew a ragged breath. 'But *my* son is the true heir.' The words came out with unconcealed malevolence. 'He is restored to me and I will not see him denied his rightful position. Pass me that boy.'

He moved forward and reached for the child.

Suddenly a figure emerged from the mist, launching itself at the Earl.

The gun in the Earl's hand discharged.

At almost the exact same moment another pistol fired.

Then another.

Callie had driven the trap as fast as she could, her heart pounding as she recognised Arthur's cries. Beside her Walter Hibblett hung on for dear life as the little vehicle plunged along the track. As they suddenly emerged from the mist, she hauled on the reins and surveyed in horror the scene that met her eyes.

Beside the ruins of the shay the Duke had hauled himself up against the shattered wheel and was pointing a still-smoking pistol at a man lying motionless on the ground.

Callie's eyes desperately sought her child.

Jumping down, she wrenched Arthur from the arms of the nurse and clasped the boy to her.

He wrapped his arms so tightly around her neck she could not, at first, move her head.

When she finally managed, she saw that Walter had descended with much less agility but no less urgency and hurried over to where his grandson, Hibbs, was trying to sit up, a shaking hand to his head.

She also saw, nearer by, that there were two other prostrate men, lying entangled. One gave a loud groan.

'Stand back!' came an agonised shout from the Duke. 'He may still have a shot.' He raised his own double-barrel flintlock and aimed it. 'Hibbs!' he called. 'Can you get the shotgun from the back of the shay?'

Callie, still clutching Arthur to her, was staring down at the pair of men and at the glistening pool of bodily fluids.

There was another groan and one figure turned his head. She had only ever seen him from a distance, usually mounted on a great hunter, but she knew who he was.

'Stand away,' repeated the Duke urgently.

However, Callie had already seen that the Earl of Pentridge's hands held no weapon: they were clamped to his belly in a futile attempt to contain its innards.

Her attention moved to the other, motionless, form and she stared in shock at someone she had known much more closely.

Beneath the heavier body of the Earl was a lean form, ridiculously underdressed for the season – no coat; his head uncovered, silver hair cropped short; his legs bare of stockings or boots.

She crouched and reached a hand beneath the soft muslin cravat. For a few moments her fingers were confused by the puckered skin, before they found the spot they sought – and a reassuring pulse.

She looked up at a still half-stunned Hibbs, the shotgun

shaking in his hands. 'For heaven's sake,' she said. 'Point that thing somewhere else.

'Walter,' she called the old man.

'Just checking this one,' came the reply. 'It's that bloke as's been in the White Horse several times recently. Called himself Miller.'

'Mills,' Callie corrected him shortly.

'Well the only use he'll have for any name now will be for his headstone,' pronounced Walter. He left the dead steward. 'And who is this one?'

'The Earl of Pentridge,' said Callie impatiently. 'Come on, Walter,' she said urgently. 'You and Hibbs need to move him.'

'Let him die,' pronounced Hibbs. 'Evil bastard.'

Callie did not have time to wonder at the vehemence of the comment. 'It's not him I care about,' she said. 'It's Dob.' She said the name without thought. 'He's still alive. But he'll die of cold if we don't get him out.'

'Hibbs!' came the Duke's voice. 'What the devil is happening over there? Have you disarmed the villains? Damn this useless body to hell!'

'Please,' begged Callie, 'move the Earl first.'

Arthur was still clinging to her. 'Could you let me go, sweetheart?' she asked him.

'Bad man,' Arthur pronounced as the Earl was moved, cursing in pain.

Callie could hardly disagree.

'Wanted to take me away from Nurse.'

Callie shuddered. She had no doubt her son had been in grave danger, although she had no idea why.

'Other man stopped him,' said Arthur, looking quite clearly at the still figure of Dob.

Another inexplicable thing to add to the long list – but to

be addressed later. 'He's hurt,' Callie said.' And I must help him. Could you let me do that?' she asked.

Arthur considered. 'Mm,' he said. 'If Nurse stands right next to you and holds my hand very tight,' he said.

70

It had not been easy or quick to get everyone back to Uppworth Park, but finally it was achieved.

The Duke had suffered nothing more than bruises – apart, as he put it bitterly to Hibbs, the bitter humiliation of helplessness. His batman offered the small comfort that his Grace's skill with a firearm was as good as ever: his shot had taken the Earl's accomplice plumb in the centre of his forehead.

Admitted to one of the guest rooms by a burly footman, Doctor Wells had frowned deeply over the wound in the Earl's belly but dressed it as best he could.

In another chamber the physician inspected the other patient. The ball had creased the temple, knocking him out and causing an impressive amount of blood loss but had hopefully done little real damage. Youth and obvious fitness would likely prevail. When the fellow roused, he should drink plenty of good ale and beef tea.

Callie nodded and bit her lip.

As she sat by Dob's bedside, she toyed with the letter that had been delivered that morning but which she had only seen on her return. She had recognised instantly the rather unformed hand on the packet, although she had only viewed it once before.

The Duke wheeled himself into the room. 'May I join you?'

'Of course,' she replied.

There were so many puzzles – from the past and going forward. The enormity of the tangle was only gradually revealing itself. But of one thing she was sure. She leaned over and took the Duke's hand. 'I know you have many questions and I will do my best to answer them. I too have much to learn and understand. But you should know immediately that I have only the greatest respect for you and gratitude for what you have given me and Arthur; that nothing will alter the commitment I have made to Uppworth, its Duke and its estate, now or into the future; nor lessen in any way the affection I have come to have for you.'

He squeezed her fingers. 'But your heart?' he asked softly, looking at the figure in the bed. 'You made no secret that it had once been given to another. Is that still the case?'

'I believe so,' she said, looking in the same direction. 'I thought Dob was dead. Now he has turned up again. In the meantime, my life has changed drastically – what of his? Where has he been all this time? What has he experienced?' She pointed at Dob's features beneath the white bandage. 'His face so deeply burned by the sun.' She lifted the edge of the cravat gently. 'And how did this happen?'

The Duke leaned forward and caught his breath. 'That looks like ….'

Brilliant blue eyes opened, vague at first then sharpened by memory and then recognition – of Callie at least. For some time, he studied her face before taking a deep breath and turning his gaze on the Duke. 'Your Grace of Uppworth, I presume,' he said.

The Duke nodded his head in acknowledgment.

'I also presume that was your son my father was intent on … seizing?' The words came out carefully. 'Is the boy all right?'

The Duke nodded again. 'Thanks to you.'

'It seems my life's task, like some medieval knight, is to restore little boys to their fathers,' Dob gave a faint smile. It faded. 'To fathers who love them dearly.' He hesitated. 'And my father? I remember that we struggled and his gun went off. There was a pain in my head and I realised he had shot me.' He gave a humourless laugh. 'That would have been the ultimate irony wouldn't it? To kill his own son and heir – particularly the heir! But it seems I am still alive.' He looked around. 'Where is he?'

'In another room,' replied the Duke. 'His henchman, Mills, fired wildly; the Earl took the ball in the stomach.'

'But is not yet dead?' Dob evidently understood the only possible outcome of a wound to the belly.

'Doctor Wells has done what he can. He will send for more laudanum to give what ease is possible.'

Dob was silent for a while, considering this.

'The doctor has also looked at your head,' put in Callie. 'He believes it will mend.'

Dob's lips twisted.

'But he says you must drink plenty of ale.' She poured out a liberal amount and lifted his head while he drank. 'And you are also to have beef broth.'

Dob gave another humourless smile. 'Couldn't you stretch it to mutton stew? Never mind,' he said. He looked at the Duke. 'Why?' he asked.

The Duke's eyes narrowed. 'You really don't know?' he responded.

71

'I have absolutely no idea why my father is not hunting at Pentridge as he said he intended but is here laying deadly traps with that toady steward, Mills; attempting, quite clearly, to take your son by force and … what?' Dob saw Callie shudder and turn equally questioning eyes on the Duke. 'I have long known,' continued Dob, 'that my father had no affection for me; that to him I was simply the carrier of the Pentridge bloodline. The arrangement of the marriage to Lady Alicia was clearly part of some hugely important ambition of his, but I still have no idea what.' He frowned. 'Nor how it could fit with what just happened. He said something about *me* being the true heir, that he would not see *me* denied my rightful position. What was he talking about?'

The Duke looked at him. 'How much do you know about your family?' he asked. 'Your father's relations.'

Dob frowned. 'There was my grandfather, but I hardly knew him and I know of no others.'

'Nevertheless, *he* had relations.'

'What do you mean?'

'Relations through whom he was entitled to claim the Earldom of Pentridge.'

'A virtually empty title: no stately home, no land. My mother told me that much.' Dob scowled at the conundrum she had not been able to answer. 'She did not know where the money had come from for the Pentridge estate, the villa in Richmond, the House in London. The Earl never talked about such things.'

'Who was your grandfather?'

'He had a small manor somewhere … in the west country.' Dob gaped.

'Pircombe Manor to be precise,' said the Duke, 'which lies,' he looked at Callie, 'adjacent to the Tentham estate.' He smiled at her. 'Do you know what *my* name is?'

'Arthur,' she said, 'Arthur Robert – it says so in the Uppworth bible.'

'Not quite, my dear. You read what I think you wished to see; for you think Dob,' he nodded towards the bed, 'is short for Robert.'

Callie was puzzled. 'Is it not?' she looked in the same direction.

'*Roberts*,' said his Grace dryly. 'My name is Arthur *Roberts*. This young man's registration of birth states Darius *Roberts*.'

'*We're* related?' Dob said dubiously.

'Distantly,' agreed the Duke, 'but closely enough for it to matter.'

'And there isn't anyone closer?'

'There was,' said the Duke succinctly. 'Baron Richleigh was much closer.'

Callie gasped. 'Who was killed by highway men.' She told of finding the newspaper cutting in the drawer in Mills' office at Pentridge. It made only too much sense now.

The Duke nodded. 'The Baron had a son, Nestor. I learned that he was not the sort of man I would really wish to be the heir to Uppworth, but that was what the law dictated. I also learned that he was serving in the army in Jamaica where sickness and disease kill many more men than enemy bullets. I therefore set out to discover who would be *next* in line.' He looked straight at Dob. 'And found it was someone I had heard of only in a quite different context: your father, the Earl of Pentridge. Where had I heard of him?' He answered his own question. 'In the course of my investigations into the abominable practice of slavery and its associated trade in unspeakable death and human misery.'

Dob tried to sit up, grimaced and subsided again. 'That is where the Pentridge family money comes from?' He began to laugh and only stopped when his sore head reminded him.

'You find slavery a subject of mirth?' demanded the Duke.

'Oh yes,' Dob said, his voice heavy with irony. 'A veritable *divertissement*.'

Understanding dawned. 'Your neck,' the Duke said. 'I saw scars in the southern states of America like that – and on other parts of the body.'

Dob obligingly displayed one scarred ankle and damaged foot. 'Perhaps we could leave the other parts,' he said sardonically.

'Oh,' Callie gasped, holding back with difficulty tears of outrage and shared pain.

'But I was lucky,' said Dob, now completely serious. 'I escaped. Many never had the chance; more never will.

'Nestor?' he asked abruptly.

The Duke's mouth set into a grim line. 'I did not like what I heard of the fellow, but all in all he seemed preferable to what I *knew* of your father. Not that the law offered me any choice in the matter. Then I learned Nestor had vanished. His disappearance could easily have had a natural explanation – desertion or disease or an accident – the army was hardly bothered, but I needed to know. I sent someone to investigate. He found proof of the man's death and that quite clearly from natural causes: some tropical fever. *But* people had been bribed, with substantial sums, to keep the death secret. Further research uncovered the source of the bribes – a shipping agent in Georgetown, who regularly handled "cargo" for the Earl's ventures.

'The only logical explanation to my mind was that the Earl wanted *me* to believe that my heir, Nestor, was still alive, to maintain some kind of false *quietus*, while he put the final touches to his plan.

'I had already worked out what that was, of course – from the moment he and Stackling tried to force through the marriage between his schoolboy son,' Dob winced, 'and

Stackling's then-ward, Lady Alicia Tentham; a marriage which would have brought Pentridge the Tentham lands and fortune. On my death, which could be at any time,' Callie bit off a protest, 'the Earl would be "discovered" to be my sole heir and thus inherit the adjoining Uppworth, both title and estate. On *his* death, *his* heir, you, Dob, would become a leading peer of the realm, with property and wealth to match.'

Dob's oath was incomprehensible but its meaning quite clear.

'I have to apologise at this point for assuming that the Earl's son was made of the same stuff as his father, as ruthless and scheming, and never taking the trouble to discover anything different. I only began to realise my error on that point when you and Lady Alicia quite evidently cooperated to upset the applecart.

'By then I had contrived a scheme of my own. For years the Earl thought his plan was watertight: there was nothing, he believed, that *I* could do about it,' continued the Duke. 'And that was what I thought too: fate having taken from me my children, my wife and my potency.'

Dob looked at him sharply, then at Callie.

'Incidentally, after discovering the extent of your father's perfidy I thought very hard about the circumstances of those terrible events and had to conclude that they were not his work: they really were the work of a malevolent providence. However, I believe they planted the seed of his gross scheme.

'But to continue with *my* scheme. Confirmation of Nestor's death concentrated my mind in a singular fashion and I realised there *could* be a quite simple solution; it required some deception but nothing illegal and the ethical price was well worth paying. Although I could not actually produce an heir of my own, any child born to my lawful wife, acknowledged by me, would be held to be my legal issue.'

Dob stared at Callie and opened his mouth.

The Duke raised a hand. 'Let me finish. Of course, the simple solution proved complicated to put into practice. First, I had to find a woman willing to cooperate with my unusual demands; next I had to hope that any child would be a boy. Although, I already knew the joy a daughter could bring, so would welcome a girl if things turned out that way.

'However even my wealth and title proved to be insufficient bait. And in truth, in spite of my desperation, I found it difficult to stomach the marriage mart and the females paraded there.' He pulled a rueful face. 'I never got to propose to any of them. But,' he nodded at Callie, 'then the perfect answer presented itself, right under my nose: a young woman for whom I already had the highest regard and liking, also a victim of ill-fate.'

Dob closed his eyes. He wanted to sleep, not to hear the next part. But he could not close his ears.

'Shall I tell the rest?' the Duke was speaking to Callie. 'I have guessed it now, of course; although I cannot imagine how it came about. But it belongs to you. Do you wish it said?'

Dob did not understand the words, but there was silence for so long that, against all inclination, he opened his eyes again.

Callie was looking from him to the Duke and back again, in an anguish of indecision.

'For what it is worth,' said the Duke gently, 'it will make no difference to my feelings, to any arrangements. And should not the man fit to be the father of my child know the whole?'

Dob gaped at the last words, grasped at the most unlikely of straws. 'When,' he swallowed, 'when was Arthur born?'

He laughed weakly as he did the arithmetic.

72

The next morning the Earl was still alive. As promised, Doctor Wells had sent for more laudanum and stayed to administer it at intervals during the night.

Dob seriously thought of leaving his father to it – to dying alone, to dying believing that he had killed the son on whom he had foisted his terrible ambitions.

Dob himself had slept for several hours before being woken by his sore head; he ignored the laudanum left for *his* use: it would not ease the tangle in his brain which had nothing to do with the injury.

He carefully went over everything he had learned the day before and fitted it into what he had already known or suspected. It was rather like slotting together the pieces in one of John Spilsbury's puzzles, he thought.

Finally, he felt reasonably confident he had the whole picture – of what was and how it had come about.

The big question now was a picture of the future. What could that look like?

The biggest piece in the puzzle was Callie; his dearest Callie – married to another man.

And there was now a piece depicting Arthur. Twenty-four hours ago, Dob had not known who he was; now the diminutive person figured large.

But Arthur was legally the Duke's son: one day he would be the next Duke of Uppworth. Dob had no right to claim him; and why should he anyway?

Although, now he knew of the child, he could feel the beginnings of a strange primeval tug.

How could he be part of his son's life? How could he bear not to be?

The questions and half-answers lobbed backwards and

forwards like a game of battledore and shuttlecock.

Then the full irony of how events had played out struck Dob: one of the Earl's terrible ambitions would be realised, after all – through the *grandson* he had tried to eliminate.

Dob made his decision. He stood up carefully and waited until the stars faded from his vision.

He had discarded his coat, boots and stockings for his run; while he was unconscious someone had removed most of his other clothes – leaving him clad in just a less than presentable shirt and Slimane's *shesh* around his neck.

Trying not to bend his head, he pulled the cover off the bed and wrapped it around him. Catching sight of himself in the glass he realised he had created something very like an Arab robe and a hysterical urge almost had him reaching for a towel to fashion a head cloth.

But all levity left him as he opened the door and trod cautiously along the passage.

The burly footman roused from his doze and stared, his eyes coming to rest on Dob's bare feet.

In the chamber, Doctor Wells also woke with a start. 'I do not think you should be up,' he remonstrated.

'I needed to come and see him,' Dob jerked a finger towards the bed, 'before I lost even the slightest will to do so.'

Doctor Wells nodded, having gathered a little of the situation.

'How long does he have?'

'A few hours, a day at the most, I should say,' came the equally frank answer. 'He is still lucid some of the time. He refused the laudanum at first but not now.'

The Earl clearly recognised Dob; the moment was followed,

almost inevitably, by a look of disappointment.

There was nothing like a conversation and never in the intermittent and disjointed phrases that emerged from time to time was there the faintest suggestion of remorse.

Later in the day, as he slipped ever more frequently out of consciousness, he made one last intelligible remark. 'Not the Pentridge curse,' he said. 'No such thing.'

And the Earl would never know the absolute proof of that, thought Dob with dark satisfaction.

He could not quite decide to leave. He accepted the doctor's orders to rest on the day bed. He drank the ale and supped the beef broth.

He watched without emotion as his father breathed his last.

He was now, he realised, the new Earl of Pentridge. He shuddered at the thought and the associations the title would always have for him.

Could one give up a title? He wondered.

73

The local magistrate listened to the account of events given to him by the Duke and recorded that the Earl of Pentridge had been shot and grievously wounded during an attempted hold-up by one Jonas Mills. In defence of his family, the Duke had shot dead the same Jonas Mills. The Earl had died the following day from his injuries. A brief summary of events, not too far from the truth.

Dob was happy not to be mentioned or involved and content enough with the ruling. It cleared the way for other matters in which, however, he had most certainly to be involved.

He sent a packet to his mother. A note to her gave the same abridged account of her husband's demise and Dob's belief that Pentridge Hall would be the appropriate place for the Earl to be interred. He asked her to pass on a letter to the Earl's solicitor and a notice of the death to the leading newspapers.

His mother replied immediately expressing no false sorrow. She would travel direct to Pentridge for what she sincerely wished to be the very last time. Thereafter she hoped to live out her days peacefully at Richmond.

Dob hoped that for her too but was aware that the Earl's will might yet hold unwelcome surprises.

There was every reason to set out as soon as possible for Pentridge and in most ways Dob simply wanted to get the whole thing over. Still he hated the thought of leaving Callie whom he had just found again; and Arthur whom he had just discovered.

Not that he had any idea how he could be part of their lives. He had discovered in himself both respect and liking for the Duke; he felt fairly sure the feelings were reciprocated. But beyond that? The Duke had acknowledged Arthur as *his* son; as, of course, had suited his purpose. However, to accept that Callie had loved another man previously was one thing, to have that man reappear was quite another. Theirs was a white marriage, but it was a very real marriage in every other sense. How could there be any place for Dob?

The three of them had an early dinner together. Dob declined several of the dishes offered him.

'Your head is bothering you?' the Duke inquired.

'No,' Dob replied. 'It is doing well enough. Oh,' he realised the Duke's inference. 'I cannot stomach much rich food.' He smiled wryly. 'Ali said it was possible I never would. But it is a social inconvenience I am quite happy to live with.'

The Duke nodded.

'Ali?' Callie queried.

'The Arab who tended me after I escaped,' said Dob a little tersely, realising where his careless reference might lead. This really was not the moment to explain about Amina; but then, when would be?

'That is part of a painful story I imagine,' suggested the Duke, 'but one I hope you might share with us – when you return.'

Dob stared at him.

'I believe we could forego the brandy and retire immediately to the sitting room?' The Duke nodded to the servant. 'Please ask for tea to be provided for the Duchess and myself and,' he raised an inquiring eyebrow at Dob, 'ale for the Ea …'

'Lord Roberts,' interrupted Dob.

The Duke adjusted the position of his chair, near the fire but not too close. 'I feel the cold,' he commented, 'not being able to exercise the lower part of my body. I suppose you might also feel the chill, being only shortly returned from warmer climes.'

Dob nodded.

'Which I really do wish to hear about,' the Duke picked up his earlier point, 'as I'm sure does my wife.'

Dob tensed at the words and lifted his mug of ale to cover his confused emotions.

The Duke watched him. 'Our situation, that of myself, my wife and my child,' he continued steadily, 'was already *unusual*, but your arrival and the circumstances of it has definitely made matters even stranger.'

'I know,' Dob said wretchedly. 'And I don't see how they

are to be resolved.' He did not dare look at Callie.

'No more do I,' said the Duke, 'but I believe for the sake of all of us, we have to try. It will take some while for you to attend to the consequences of your father's death and that will give us all time to ponder. However,' he grimaced, 'time is not on my side. I must ask you to return to Uppworth as soon as you may.'

Dob swallowed. Pain and difficulty were obvious whichever way one looked, but they had to be faced.

The next morning Callie joined him outside the coach house where the Earl's coffin was being loaded into an Uppworth carriage, serviceable if distinctly dated.

Both were well aware that they were in plain view of the house.

'May I take your hand?' Dob asked.

'I believe my husband would not mind,' she said. 'And I believe, on balance, that I would like it.'

'On balance?' he inquired softly.

'The pleasure against the risk that it will shake my resolve. And I *do not wish* to lose my resolve. You do understand that, don't you?'

He sighed. 'Yes,' he said. 'I'm afraid I do.'

The spark was instant as he moved his deeply-scored fingers across her less than aristocratic hand; a painful mix of love and loss.

She evidently felt the same. 'Love can never be wrong, can it? Is it not the most precious quality of being human? Although there are, I have learned in my short life,' she gave a self-deprecatory chuckle, 'different sorts of love: the Duke says the ancient Greeks had words for at least six.'

Dob regretted how little he had made of the education Bromby had offered.

'In a way,' she continued, 'I see love as a divine gift, a blessing to be enjoyed but also to be treasured, to be honoured. We cannot will it into existence, but we can will how we use it. That is the great freedom and burden all men and women have carried since Adam and Eve.'

Dob squeezed her hand. 'I don't have your way with words,' he said huskily, 'but I know you are right.'

He bowed his head and kissed her palm, lightly and briefly; that much he could manage.

74

Finally, Pentridge Hall came into sight. It looked very much the same as on the previous occasion; it was even the same time of year. But the reception was different: Dob was now the Earl and the staff all stood in line to welcome him, bobbing curtseys, bowing. It felt very odd, but it did have the advantage that he could order the accommodation for himself and his mother exactly as they would both like – well away from the rooms with bad memories.

It also meant that he could command the services of Joey Hunt. The lad had grown considerably in stature but changed in little else as far as Dob could tell as he listened to an exuberant telling of the doings of numerous hounds and puppies, and numerous members of the Hunt family. He handed over the lengthy letter which Callie had given him to deliver.

'You can read, can't you?' he quizzed Joey.

'Of course,' said the youth indignantly. 'All the boys have to learn their letters with the parson.'

'Boys? Not the girls?'

'Naagh.'

That scornful dismissal brought Dob up short. There

were unjust assumptions and practices much closer than Africa or Jamaica that also needed to be tackled. He suddenly had a glimpse of what lay ahead of him.

The funeral was conducted with all correctness. The parson, happily unaware of what the new Earl would demand of him before the short day was out, declaimed the words of the service; the local gentry attended, sombre and with quite correct reasons not to linger; the estate tenants stood in suitable pose at a suitable distance and dispersed without undue haste. Nobody displayed dislike or hostility, but then nobody showed any regret either.

Joy at Mills' permanent departure was less muted.

Dobs interviewed the man left as acting-steward. He did not much like what he found, but Longstaff was better than nothing. He recalled the arrangement at Uppworth and with considerable pleasure presented his ultimatum: Longstaff could continue in post, provided he acted only after consultation on all matters with Barney Hunt, the kennelman. Furthermore, he was to take Joey Hunt as his apprentice. Each week Joey was to write a report (the lad's face dropped) and present it to Longstaff – for literary correction only – before it was posted to Dob.

It was a fortunate irony, not in the least lost on Dob, that his twenty-first birthday passed on the eve of the icy January day in London on which his father's will was read.

He was surprised, and relieved, to discover that the Earl had set out no restrictions: no establishment of any trust; no decree that Dob should have to wait to inherit beyond the simple age of majority.

Of course, the will had been made when the Earl had no doubts about the success of his plans: he had expected everything to be settled before Dob reached that age. And when Dob had confounded those plans, the Earl had taken no time to change the terms.

There was unequivocal provision for his mother to live for the rest of her life at the villa in Richmond. There was no mention of any change to this even in the event of her remarrying – Dob suspected that possibility had never entered the Earl's head.

The grand function to reintroduce Dob to the *haut monde* had, of course, been cancelled in view of his father's death; although Dob knew he would have to force himself into arranging another at some point, in order to join the ranks of the rich and powerful who might be persuaded to help change attitudes towards slavery and the other grave social injustices he had become painfully aware of.

He attended a meeting of the Society for Effecting the Abolition of the Slave Trade and left with unexpectedly equivocal feelings: his experience as a non-African of being traded and enslaved seemed strangely irrelevant to some members and made him the object of salacious curiosity to others; his prime value to the Society, he gathered, would be the fact that he was now a peer: he could represent the Society's aims in Parliament – an opportunity which the non-conformists and Catholics would eagerly have seized but one which Dob found daunting if not positively alarming.

He also wondered about the wider implications of slavery: of course, trade in human beings must be ended as soon as possible, but what of goods produced by slaves? His previous experience of the London Season had given him a glimpse of the unthinking liking and demand for chocolate and sugar. For himself, he would never again look at copperware without wondering under what conditions the ore had been quarried, broken up and smelted.

He was quite clear there must be an immediate end to any Pentridge involvement in the terrible trade built up by his grandfather and father. What was much less clear to him was what other ventures might be undertaken instead – for he knew, from the figures once quoted to him by Callie and confirmed more recently by Longstaff, that the Pentridge Hall estate generated only a modest income. And (yet another irony), Dob could not actually share the aristocratic contempt for trade *per se*. A landowner was respected for providing a livelihood to his tenants, for encouraging good husbandry, for making profits from agricultural produce; why then should a tradesman be looked down on for doing much the same thing in a commercial setting? There was, Dob realised, the crucial ethical question of *what* trade, but otherwise respect or criticism should be on the grounds of how well those with means used their position for the general benefit, not on how ancient their bloodline was.

Pentridge House on Pall Mall was of no more interest to him than to his mother. It might be sold in time but meanwhile could be rented out.

On the other hand, Pircombe Manor was of great interest. Dob had never seen the place but knew it was small and old. He would not mind that in the slightest: its supreme appeal was the fact that it lay only a few miles, as a crow might fly, or a young man might run, to Uppworth Park.

Given the chance.

Affairs in London all took far longer than Dob wished, then February brought bad weather – although not as bad as much delayed newspapers reported from Scotland, where eight days of continuous heavy snowfall had been piled by gales into huge drifts. Nevertheless, the roads of southern England were frozen solid, the ruts iron-hard beneath their own icy covering.

He and Forster were numb with cold by the time their steaming mounts wound their way up the last slope and slithered to a stop beside the small building of golden stone, sheltering beneath its thick snow-laden roof-tiles. Dob had sent notice of their arrival and candles gleamed a welcome behind the leaded panes within the stone mullions. The heavy oak door was dragged open and while Forster took the weary horses to the stables, Dob was ushered into a flagged hall with a roaring log fire in its smoke-darkened hearth.

At last his fingers, clasped tightly around a pewter mug of mulled ale, were unfrozen enough to open the missive awaiting him.

The Duke and Duchess of Uppworth were happy to hear of his imminent return to the district and invited him, on any afternoon, at his very earliest convenience, to Uppworth Park – for tea with little Lord Arthur then dinner with their Graces.

75

Dob was not sure the boy remembered him and perhaps it was as well the child had forgotten the ambush and its violence. However that might be, in the familiar surroundings of the Park and in the company of his mother and father, he greeted the visitor without shyness and an offer to show Dob his farm.

There were numerous sheep with rather chipped coats balanced precariously on the hillsides of a lifted hearth rug; there were red and white cows on sections of green pile, the diminutive figure of a milk-maid crouched on a three-legged stool beside one of them, milking into what was almost certainly a thimble; there was a horse (on wheels) pulling a wooden plough, along lines combed into the Turkey carpet with an unsteady hand; there were pigs, white with black spots, rooting beneath bits of kindling.

Dob crouched beside him and listened as Arthur moved the figures around, describing what was happening. The boy's imagination sometimes outran his tongue, but mostly, Dob realised, the words were quite understandable, the speech well formed.

A lump formed in his throat as the reality truly struck: this person was his son.

He glanced up to see that the Duke and Callie were watching.

What did they see? Was the boy like him? He knew the answer immediately: the same blue eyes had looked back at him from the mirror just that morning.

'Sometimes we make the farm in the dining room.' The words caught Dob's attention. 'On the table, so Papa can reach.'

The word "Papa" brought Dob back to earth.

Arthur's Papa was the Duke. Dob admitted that there could scarcely be a more educated, more principled parent; nor one more fond, he realised. And felt as if he had been hit in the gut.

Evidently his feelings had shown. 'Later,' the Duke said in a low voice.

Dob took a resolute breath and caught up with the adventures of the escaped pigs.

The farm had been packed away, as had the rugs so that the Duke's wheeled chair was unimpeded.

Dob accepted a cup of tea this time; his thickened hands and scarred fingers making an odd match with the delicate porcelain. He had reported the essentials over dinner: news of Pentridge and the Hunt family, what he had managed to achieve in London.

'And how do you find Pircombe?' The Duke edged the conversation nearer to Uppworth.

Dob said he liked it very well.

'Well enough to live there – for a while?'

Dob nodded.

'I have no time to beat about any bushes,' said the Duke. 'My body reminds me often enough of that and Doctor Wells is good enough to be honest on the subject.

'You know the situation and my reasons for contriving it. My primary aim was to save Uppworth from falling into the hands of your father – and I did not at that point know even the half of his villainy! After years of malevolence, fate smiled on my endeavours: I was given my heir.

'I also discovered I had been given so much more than I had even suspected: a woman with remarkable fortitude and ability, eminently capable of running Uppworth for the years that would be necessary after my death, until the boy came of age.

'Now I believe fate has brought yet another blessing: you.'

Dob stared.

'I am aware, that with your father's death, you are now Uppworth's heir-in-remainder.'

Dob shuddered to think of how his parent had anticipated that fact and tried to make evil use of it.

Callie clasped her hands more tightly in her lap.

The Duke lifted his cup, found the tea gone cold and put it back in its saucer. 'In view of all this, I have a proposal to make,' he said. 'You did not know of Arthur's existence until recently; now you have met him and evidently been as charmed as the rest of us. You have equally clearly discovered the mysterious and powerful feelings of fatherhood.'

Dob nodded.

'In addition to being patently in love with his mother.'

Dob was not going to make any false denials.

'One day, in the not too distant future, she will be free to marry again,' said the Duke baldly, putting out a hand to Callie to soften his words. 'And I can tell you with absolute honesty that I would wish nothing else, for either of you.

'But until then I would like you to know your son and he to know you. The wider world will not think it strange that I should nominate you as the child's guardian; nor, therefore, that you should come here to see him; nor indeed that his mother should bring him to visit you at Pircombe from time to time.'

Dob stared.

The Duke added drily, 'I hope that would not cause problems of a different kind? My body may be crippled now, but my mind remembers very well the powerful pull of love.'

Dob glanced at Callie. 'Love was described to me not long ago as a gift to be treasured but also to be honoured. I would hate to sully that; to bring any dishonour to Uppworth's present or future duke.'

76

Not that it was always easy and they had to set themselves boundaries; but by and large the presence of Arthur was both a joy and a protection.

A late spring was followed by an indifferent summer, depressing even the most fatalistic land-worker. Well maintained drains and ditches made cultivation possible on land that would previously have been merely bog; but no man, nor woman, could stop the cold rain that fell so incessantly and discouraged the crops.

A fine day was to be greeted with a flurry of urgent activity, but the latest visit to Pircombe Manor had been announced to Arthur before the weather had made up its fickle mind and he was adamant that Mama should *not* go out with Mr Hibblett. The boy particularly wished to see the young dogs of the man he called Lord Dob, or sometimes just Dob.

The pups, two of them, had mysteriously turned up in the stables of the Manor. Forster swore that he knew nothing about them and the fact that they had appeared the same night he had returned from the White Horse in the early hours, blind drunk, was pure coincidence.

They were of largely unidentifiable parentage but looked set to grow into something hound-like: bright and inquisitive, keen of nose and eye, and built to run. Dob could almost certainly have joined the Berkeley Hunt had he wished – apart from anything else, his mother was distantly related to the family – but the association of hunting with his father was too strong and, in any case, Dob quite simply preferred running. Mindful of what he had learned once upon a time in the company of Joey Hunt, he was careful of overtaxing Castor and Pollux before they were full-grown, but he enjoyed their company over increasing distances as he jogged around the neighbouring countryside, climbing the steep slopes through Pircombe's woods and out onto the rolling uplands of Tentham, with the amused permission of Lady Alicia.

He also taught the dogs to do tricks – mainly for Arthur's enjoyment. They would fetch sticks however often he threw them, or wherever. They would wriggle under or jump over whatever obstacle he could invent. They would roll over in ecstatic anticipation of being tickled. Less enthusiastically they would lie still on command, although in general Arthur's patience for such an uninteresting state of affairs ran out before theirs.

Today Dob and Callie sat in the very informal garden of the Manor while a short distance away Arthur put the animals through their paces. Callie dug into her pocket and produced the note that Forster had delivered the morning of the Earl's attack.

Dob had not forgotten about it – he had simply not found the right moment.

'What did you mean,' Callie asked, 'about needing to talk about the past? *My* past?' She studied him. 'What *part* of my past? And why should you *need* to talk about it? I am the by-blow of an unimportant nobleman – the Duke knows this, as do you. What does it have to do with anything?'

'Not your father,' said Dob. 'Your mother.'

'My mother?' she frowned. 'She was a housemaid he took advantage of and who died after I was born.'

'Who told you your mother died?'

She frowned harder. 'Lady said so. Everyone said so.'

'Did they?'

'Why on earth are you asking this?'

'Perhaps they did say so, to give you the simplest answer. But that was not the truth,' he said quietly. 'The truth is that your mother was sunk in shame.'

Callie gasped.

'I think you did not suffer any depression after Arthur was born?' She shook her head. 'But I understand some women do – particularly if their circumstances are difficult. After you were born, *your* mother was in a black despair, ill in spirit, her malaise made all the worse by the local priest castigating her sinfulness.'

'And what of my father?' she said angrily. 'What of his sinfulness?' She paused. 'Are you telling me my mother killed herself? How can you possibly know!'

'No, she did not kill herself, but she ran away. And I know because she told me so.'

He recounted Amina's tale.

The long silence was broken only by the sound of Arthur's piping voice and the panting of the young dogs.

Dob said softly, 'I promised your mother I would let her know how life has turned out for you. What should I tell her?'

She looked at him. 'Need you ask?' She allowed herself to touch his hand briefly. 'May I write to her myself?'

'I believe she would like that above all things.'

77

The Duke of Uppworth survived another brush with death, the Grim Reaper driven back yet again by the ferocious efforts of Callie and Hibbs.

By the end of the year, however, he was once more confined to bed, too weak to do more than smile as Arthur laid out his farm on the coverlet and manoeuvred the pieces, playing out some new rural drama.

As he started to pack away, the child whispered something to each animal.

'My faith in God has frequently been shaken,' the Duke said softly to Callie. 'More often I have seen the hand of a random and malign Providence in both life and death.' The words had tired him and he was silent for some moments. 'I wish many things had been different,' he managed, 'but now, at the end, I find I am content.' His eyes rested on Arthur before turning back to her. 'Is that not a miracle?'

'Goodnight, Papa,' said Arthur planting a kiss on one emaciated cheek then the other before indicating the box of toys on the top of a nearby chest. 'I have told the animals that I can sleep without them tonight; they must stay here; to keep watch over you.'

Carefully ranged small wooden heads peered out. There were a few more ears broken, more noses worn and chipped, but otherwise they were very much the same creatures that had kept the Duke company in his own boyhood years in the Nursery.

78

Some eighteen months after the death of the ninth Duke of Uppworth, the London Season was to culminate in a wedding that attracted the interest of the *haut monde* in exact reverse to the inclinations of its chief participants.

However reluctant, Dob and Callie knew it had to be: to establish the position of the young tenth Duke. It was also an inevitable adjunct to Dob's high-profile – the result of his speaking in the House of Lords to end the slave trade and, just as fascinating to the popular press, of his close association with the outlandish Khalid ibn Abd al-Salam. The Moroccan special envoy had come to London to finalise the details of the Treaty of Commerce and Friendship between King George and Sultan Suleiman.

The Duke of Branksdown, deputed to greet the delegation, had been put off his stride by the envoy's inquiry. 'The Earl of Pentridge's son? Oh, you mean young Dob – at school with my Willoughby, before he went off … oh, ah, um. I see: met in Morocco, of course. He's the new Earl now and the Lords is in session; he's presently at Uppworth House, on Grosvenor Square – although he'll move out before ...' Branksdown ground to a halt, unsure where to start in explaining the relevant etiquette to this exotic visitor. 'I could get my man to deliver your card there, if you like,' he had offered.

The Sultan's envoy had politely declined: he would go in person, having already learned that any hackney would be sure to know the direction.

'Peace be unto you,' he mischievously greeted the young man who answered the knock at the door.

'Good grief!' The *major domo* abandoned the hauteur he had carefully cultivated as appropriate to his elevated station and the fine outfit that went with it. 'It's a blooming Saracen, like on the sign over Snow Hill tavern.'

'A different sort of Saracen, Peter,' Dob put in, hurrying across the chequered black and white flags. 'Salam alaikum!'

'Wa-alaikum salam,' replied Sidi Khalid.

'Come in,' Dob urged him. 'I am expecting you to stay here for as long as you are in London.'

There was the distinct sound of a snort.

'Peter, please see that the hackney is paid off.'

There was a muttered comment.

'Are all English servants so unruly?' Sidi Khalid inquired in Arabic.

'Peter is a special case,' Dob replied in the same tongue. 'A very special case.'

The person in question, hearing his name, glowered even more fiercely.

'Be so very good, Peter,' said Dob with exaggerated mildness, 'as to advise Mrs Ballance to air the rooms for our guest and his entourage. And request Cook to send refreshments to the sitting room in half an hour.'

During that time Dob showed Sidi Khalid around the house, pointing out the notable artistic and architectural features.

'Very pleasing,' commented the Moroccan. 'Different from my abode and yet not so different,' he echoed thoughts Dob had once had.

'There is one thing very much in common, newly finished,' said Dob with a grin, leading the way down to the basement. He opened the door and gestured triumphantly to a bath sunk into the floor. 'I tried to recall the motifs in your house, but I fear I do not have the eye for that; then I thought English tiles could have English flowers like on the carpet upstairs.'

Sidi Khalid identified the roses and tulips immediately; the daffodils, crown imperials and morning glories were new to him.

'There is also a similar bath at Uppworth Park,' said Dob. '*And* another pool being built behind the orangery, big enough to swim in.'

'Ah,' murmured Sidi Khalid. 'You are still a keen swimmer, then?'

'I often swim in the river or the lake, but the indoor pool will be nice in the winter and a good place for children to learn. The tiling of that one is to have scenes in blue and white of the animals and birds which live in the countryside.'

The Treaty was officially signed on the fourteenth of June. It granted no special privileges, but it did give mutual assurances about the treatment of British and Moroccan subjects abiding or trading in each other's lands. Nobody was in any doubt that the main trade centred on victualling Gibraltar – a source of considerable income to the Sultan's treasury and a matter of the utmost strategic importance to a beleaguered Britain.

The work of the Moroccan delegation was at an end and the envoy was free to depart with the Sultan's copy of the agreement.

Moreover, Sidi Khalid had heard over several evenings Dob's own version of the One Thousand and One Nights.

However, there was one tale still not complete and Sidi Khalid had absolutely no intention of leaving before the wedding that would make a fitting end to the saga; nor indeed its celebration, to be held a fortnight later.

There would be the official ceremony in the capital for Peter's "nobs", a very public and legal stamp on the couple's present status and Arthur's future standing; then a gathering at Uppworth where people might actually enjoy themselves.

Except for the very highest echelons of society, an actual wedding ceremony was generally only attended by those close to the couple. On this occasion, however, St George's was positively crowded. Many a duchess, marchioness or countess had eagerly persuaded her husband to accept the invitation, and their brightly-clad personages packed the front of the church; while at the rear were pressed a substantial number of the more plainly dressed spouses of well-born baronets and gentry.

Of course, curiosity was at the back of it – the whole affair was singularly captivating, starting with the fact that someone born the wrong side of the blanket had ended up as Duchess of Uppworth; although the aristocratic part of her blood must *obviously* have something to do with it. But which aristocrat in particular had provided that blue blood? Speculation was rife – although not one *on dit*, as it happened, suggested any title beyond the bounds of England.

And how did the Dowager Countess of Pentridge, the groom's mother, feel about it? For she was surely the epitome of ancient breeding: graceful of body and bearing, of flawless face and shining silver hair.

And everyone knew now, of course, that the old Earl of Pentridge had actually made his money from trade, the trade in slaves. For most of the *ton*, the first factor was the weightier since *any* commerce was regarded as downright vulgar (although few did not recognise the usefulness of wealth, even though it must never be mentioned). There was, nevertheless, also disapproval of the slave trade in particular, since support for its abolition was becoming quite *à la mode* – and nobody wanted to fall behind the fashion.

And the story of the erstwhile Viscount Kelton was *so* romantic: the impossibly fair young hero taken captive by heathen pirates before being rescued by a minister of the Sultan himself, the self-same exotic Arab presently seen on the streets of London.

Of course, since inheriting, the young man had put an end to his father's trade. His new ventures were wilfully ignored, with all attention focussed on the fact that he was heir-in-remainder to Uppworth, proof absolute of a nobility beyond just that of his mother. The old Duke had very clearly recognised this, naming him as guardian to the new young Duke and appointing him joint administrator with the widowed Duchess of the estate's considerable assets, until the child came of age.

At the very front, on the bride's side, stood one witness, the Honourable James Millburn while next to him a chair had been provided for Sophie, heavy with their third child.

On the groom's side was the other witness, the Lord Willoughby Landston. Willo was simply amazed at what his school-mate had endured and achieved, and was generally very happy for him – although he did shudder at the thought of taking on a wife and step-son (not to mention the responsibility for a dukedom) at barely twenty-three years of age; Willo planned to steer well-clear of any such burden, not least because he had just purchased a commission in the army, eager to help avert the stalemate into which the war against Revolutionary France seemed to be heading.

Mind you, Willo reflected, glancing at his friend, most people would take Dob for considerably older.

The broad back and shoulders were clad in an impeccably tailored cut-away coat of Stroud broadcloth, the strong neck emerged from the soft cloth of snowy-white muslin, the lean, muscled legs were outlined by the close-fitting breeches and silk stockings above carefully lasted shoes; but it was much more than physical maturity: it was the way he carried himself; the lines sculpted by a harsh sun into his fine features; the resolution that intensified the blue of his eyes; the stern mouth.

Although, even as Willo watched, his friend's face lifted as his bride joined them. And, Willo suddenly realised, unknown parentage or not, she was a quiet beauty: her body shapely but not thickened by motherhood, shown off by the simple but beautifully fitted gown trimmed with antique lace; a flush to her face, a shine to her grey eyes that betokened simple good health and – Willo could see it quite clearly – the deep glow of requited love.

Maybe not such a burden, Willo suddenly realised.

79

The occasion at Uppworth could not have been more different. Although the date had been set months beforehand, the English weather could not be so tidily managed. As time and tide waited for no man, nor did hay harvest – quite simply when the meadows were ready and the weather was right, then hay had to be made. And it involved all available hands of whatever size or age.

That being an essential fact of country life, Dob and Callie adapted their arrangements: they would join everyone else in the fields. The safe gathering of what promised to be a good harvest would be all the more reason to make merry afterwards.

The few invitees from beyond Uppworth's boundaries could take part too – *if* they wished.

Lady Alicia Tentham sent a note on behalf of herself and Miss Berriston of polite demurral and offering an alternative for anyone else similarly disinclined to rustic labour: a viewing of her very fine string of horses.

The two guests from further afield took up her offer. Of course, Sidi Khalid and Lady Horatia had talked at some length on the subject that formed the primary link between them: the girl born Roísín Mac an Ghabhain, known to Lady Horatia as the housemaid Rose Smith and to Sidi Khalid as his beloved foster-mother Amine.

As he listened now to the talk of horses, Sidi Khalid wondered if there might be something else to be made from the connection. The patently knowledgeable Lady Alicia was making a large offer for one of Lady Horatia's animals. When and how did Lady Horatia plan to return to Ireland? he inquired. Might it be possible for him to accompany her? He did not need to journey back to his country *quite* immediately and, after all, he was sure Amine would appreciate a first-hand description of her old homeland …

Lady Horatia looked at him shrewdly. 'And the Sultan Sulieman might just appreciate some good Irish horseflesh, if you *happened* to find some?'

Sidi Khalid smiled. 'If you *happened* to have something suitable.'

Lady Horatia laughed. 'Virtually two sales in one day, and from such prestigious customers – how my dear sister-in-law will hate that! First, she had to swallow her husband's by-blow becoming a Duchess, a rank above a mere Marchioness; then, the Acts of Union curbed the power of the Irish aristocracy to suppress rebellious Irish Catholics and peasants in the ways that the Marchioness favoured, like house-burning and pitch-capping; now, she will not even be able to keep *me* in my "proper place", with the stud providing me with an independence, in all senses of the word!'

Lady Alicia had been listening to this with very close attention; at the last part she cried, 'Bravo!' And Miss Berriston gave a delighted clap.

The work was hard but nothing like breaking rocks. Dob had not done anything *that* demanding since his return to England, but he was still strong enough to pitch the hay into the wagons as easily and for as long as any other man on the estate.

It was strange that dreams of that time in captivity still woke him sometimes to a state of helpless despair and yet today's labour, aching limbs and muscles and all, provoked no unwelcome memories.

He paused, with the others, to down copious amounts of the weak ale brought out to them by the women.

His eyes sought out his son.

Callie pointed to the fair head in the midst of a group of estate children. Even as they watched, Hibbs moved towards the boy and clamped the lost hat back in its place.

Hibbs had been much more than just an employee of the old Duke: he had been childhood friend, confederate and personal attendant. And it was entirely self-evident to Hibbs that he should simply do the same for the old Duke's young heir. Another mortal attack was unlikely, but childhood was beset with myriad other dangers, including too much hot sun.

80

Although they had been legally married since the ceremony at St George's, Dob had not officially moved out of Pircombe Manor: the union needed the blessing of Uppworth first.

And the festivities following hay harvest provided that.

The long warm day was filled with games and dancing, feasting and drinking, music and laughter; adult voices raised in conversation and song, children's in glee and squabble, babies' in chortle and wail.

By mid-afternoon Lady Alicia and Miss Berriston felt they had had enough of the bucolic scene and drove home to Tentham Court, Lady Alicia's expert hands on the reins.

Lady Horatia and Sidi Khalid invited Walter Hibblett to join them in the shade of a large oak tree and proceeded to interrogate him – storing away every fact and anecdote about the ex-Duchess of Uppworth: Lady Horatia quite simply for her own happy contemplation; Sidi Khalid so he could add more tales to the Thousand and One Nights for Slimane and Amine.

As the sun began its long descent of the clear skies, people began to search out children, to gather up drowsy toddlers; to head home to the cows and pigs and hens which needed tending, whatever the day of the year.

Swifts screamed high above; swallows swooped low through air still perfumed by the scent of newly made hay.

Dob and Callie made their way up to the mansion, swinging Arthur between them.

The presence of the old Duke was tangible in the rooms that overlooked the gardens, but it was infused with the blessing he had given their marriage. There had been no question but that Dob would join Callie in the suite on the first floor; nor that the distant Nursery would continue in its role of store-room.

Arthur, in spite of the hour, lay with his eyes, their blue scarcely muted by the candlelight, fixed on Dob. 'Do I have to call you Papa, now you are married to Mama?' he asked.

Dob swallowed. 'No,' he said. 'You do not have to call me Papa – unless you want to.'

The boy considered. 'I know we talk about my old Papa and I never ever want to forget him, but,' he added, 'perhaps Mama will have other children.' Dob managed not to smile at the thought – or the prospect of helping it become reality. 'Then they will call you Papa and it would be confusing if I talked about Papa, meaning old Papa, wouldn't it?' Dob did not comment. 'Do you think he would mind?'

'I think,' said Dob, 'that he would be happy with whatever *you* think is best.' He laid a finger on the boy's lips. 'Sleep on it,' he said. 'You do not have to decide tonight.'

'Yes,' said Arthur. 'You'll be living here now, won't you? I can tell you in the morning.'

Dob hoped it would not be too early.

81

There had been the one, all too brief, break in hostilities with France: little more than a year had passed between the signing of the Peace of Amiens and Britain declaring war once more, as it observed the French Consul Napoleon pursuing control of all that part of Europe just across the few salty miles of the Channel.

By the end of the next year, Napoleon had crowned himself Emperor and built up a large and highly effective army, including a hundred and eighty thousand troops massed at Boulogne. However, before he could invade

Britain, he needed control of that narrow waterway, and even in alliance with the Spanish could not achieve the necessary dominance at sea, the Royal Navy, under Lord Nelson, delivering the *coup de grâce* in the waters off Cape Trafalgar.

Napoleon turned his attention back to building up power in Europe. In spring, he became King of Italy. In the autumn, using the hundred and eighty thousand troops from Boulogne, he trapped the whole Austrian army near Ulm and took over Bavaria. Within weeks he seized Moravia after doing battle at Austerlitz. The day after Christmas he signed a treaty at Pressburg which took Austria out of the Coalition, leaving only Britain and Russia opposing France. At that point, they too might have been inclined to make peace, but Napoleon would make no concessions.

Before the first month of the new year was out, Britain's prime minister, William Pitt, plagued all his life by ill-health, died suddenly. His cousin, Baron Grenville, assumed the leadership of what was called a Ministry of All the Talents as it included members of different political persuasions. It was to last only one hundred and thirty-eight days. Grenville's position was not strong enough to oppose the will of the King and the Baron was forced to surrender the seals of office to a monarch resolutely set against any concessions to Roman Catholics. His successor, the Duke of Portland, and the fractious group he headed, were outraged by what they regarded as an abuse of the royal prerogative and demanded new elections to restore the power of Parliament.

The elections would last for over a month and the new assembly would then only have a few weeks to sit before the start of the annual recess in mid-August. Dob had been happy to leave London with the prospect of spending the rest of the year at home. A warm spring had made the turnpikes dusty, but as he (and the remarkably durable Forster) covered the last miles, the countryside was still in its glory of new green leaf and white blossom.

Those at Uppworth Park afforded him their normal joyous welcome. Arthur, conscious of his approaching tenth birthday, managed a dignified face and bow before throwing himself into the usual bearhug. He nudged his head against Dob, his fair hair a little darkened but his triumphant eyes as blue as ever. 'See, I am nearly up to your chest!' The boy was like to grow at least as tall as Dob; he shared the litheness too but with the sturdiness of his mother. Legally, of course, Arthur was Dob's step-son and nobody said otherwise, although some knew the truth and more guessed. Arthur himself never raised the matter: he talked happily of Old Papa and, at the same time, acted entirely as if he recognised his natural father. Perhaps, sometime in the future his bright mind might put the question, or perhaps it would be appropriate to explain the matter, but for the moment it really was of no importance – to anyone.

The boy had no time for any further comment; all other news would have to wait, as "the twins" thrust him aside and seized a leg each. They were not, in fact, twins having been born exactly a year apart, but the girls acted as if they were. Both Livy (Olivia Rose) and Ratia (Horatia) had their mother's dark hair; both had inherited the grey eyes of their fabulous grandmother, of whom they had heard stories ever since they were little, and they chose to share everything else: a bed; washing in the tiled basement bath; swimming in the orangery pool; a desk in the library where Mama taught them to read, write and factor – and to explore the wealth of the books around them; a corner of the great scrubbed table in the kitchen where cook imparted her culinary skills. They shared all their clothes too but strangely did not demand matching items.

Last to arrive, his legs being somewhat shorter, was Will (named for Willoughby, who had seen something of the world – Hanover, Naples and the Cape of Good Hope – but not much action). The toddler thrust his golden head with determination between his sisters and shouted, very loudly, for his share of attention.

Dob hoisted his youngest above the fray, swinging him up onto his shoulders where Will's cries of frustration turned instantly to crows of delight.

It was evening before Dob and Callie were at last alone: Arthur was propped up in his bed with Pope's translation of the Iliad and instructions to put it away when the clock in the hall chimed the hour; the younger ones were, hopefully, already asleep.

Dob and Callie sat companionably side by side discussing the latest news from London.

'How good that the slave trade has finally been abolished,' commented Callie. 'The old Duke would be very pleased.'

The ever-tireless Wilberforce had persuaded Grenville to introduce the necessary legislation and this time it had been passed with little amendment by both Houses of Parliament. King George had given it his royal assent on the very same day he demanded Grenville's resignation.

She lifted Dob's hand, scarred and blemished as it would forever remain, and kissed it in tribute. 'And to know that the United States have also forbidden the importation of any new slaves,' she added.

'But slavery itself remains,' said Dob with a shake of his head. 'How long before *that* will be ended? There are still so many enslaved in the British territories and in America; not to mention all those in the various countries of Africa!' he added with particular feeling. 'Its continuation is justified by all sorts of trumpery, nonsense about the inferiority of those enslaved, but quite simply it provides dirt-cheap labour. How else can the plantation owners continue to reap the huge rewards of white gold or tobacco? If people stopped buying the goods, of course, that would soon put an end to cultivation and production, but I can't see that happening: even among those who know the misery and degradation involved, I have heard a reluctance to give up sugar for their tea, coffee or chocolate, sugar for their cakes, biscuits and puddings, sugar for their syllabubs, ice-creams and comfits.' He pulled a wry face. 'The taste for its sweetness is strongly-held.'

'Is there any news of the efforts in Silesia to produce sugar from root vegetables?' asked Callie.

Dob made a noise of frustration. He had heard of the work, encouraged by the King of Prussia no less, to breed a beet with enough sugar to make it a rival to sugar cane. Dob would have loved to go and see how it was grown and refined, perhaps bring back seed and experiment himself. 'The war in Europe obstructs many things,' he said shortly.

'And yet it is an ill wind that blows nobody any good,' Callie said. 'The cloth mills in Stroud and the valleys take every one of the fleeces we and Tentham can produce for uniforms. The victuallers in Plymouth and Portsmouth take every pig to salt; every sack of flour for hardtack; every cheese and barrel of butter.' She grimaced. 'Uppworth is like to make a fortune out of misfortune!'

'And no sign of an end to hostilities,' Dob nodded at the broadsheets he had brought with him.

'But they must end one day,' Callie said, 'and Uppworth must be prepared for whatever comes; all the money it is earning now from the war must be ploughed into other ventures for the future.'

'Do I gather that you have some new idea?' he teased her. 'What must poor John Wilson get his head around now?'

They smiled at each other, well aware that John Wilson needed no pity, having more than grown into his post since old Walter Hibblett had died peacefully in the inglenook of the White Horse.

Brick tanks on a nearby hill, filled from local springs with the help of a windmill already supplied plentiful clean water through a growing network of fired clay pipes. As well as water for drinking and washing, there was now water enough for the water closets which had been installed in all parts of the mansion and in many other dwellings. For single cottages, the waste was simply drained away to a distant spot where it could be eaten up by plants and trees. For the Park and the village another network of pipes had been installed. Callie did not want the sewage just to end up in the local river, carried in sluggish fashion across the flatlands to the sea. Moreover, it was well known that human waste could be an excellent fertiliser, not to be squandered: there were ongoing experiments involving, among other things, fields of onions and osier beds, both of great interest to the Admiralty procuring agents.

Another construction nearing completion was the new school. There would be no boarding for Arthur or his siblings: the Uppworth Academy would provide education, free to both boys and girls, up to a level at least as good as the Crypt School in Gloucester.

Within the expanding village were other opportunities for practical training as the blacksmith, the candle maker, the saddler, the cooper, the carpenter were all encouraged to learn about the latest developments in their trade and to take on extra apprentices. During the quieter winter months, the farmers and other land-workers were invited to talks on improving animal and crop husbandry; these being held in a room converted for the purpose – which just happened to be adjacent to the White Horse.

'Tomorrow,' said Dob, 'I very much look forward to hearing about your latest hare-brained schemes as well as seeing the progress of those in hand.

'But that is for tomorrow,' Dob repeated. 'Right now, I wish to catch up on quite other matters.'